Strew on her Roses, Roses

Peggy

Strew on her Roses, Roses

Ken James

A SQUARE ONE PUBLICATION

First published in 2000 by
Square One Publications
The Tudor House, Church Street
Upton upon Severn, Worcs WR8 0NU

British Library Cataloguing in Publication Data
is available for this book

1 899955 43 7

Typeset in 11pt Times New Roman by
Avon DataSet Ltd, The Studio, Bidford on Avon B50 4JH

Printed by RED Design and Print, East Sussex UK

LIST OF ILLUSTRATIONS

Sketches by Ken James

This book is dedicated to the memory of Peggy.

She illuminated the world around her. . .

CHAPTER ONE

Awareness shattered a dream – a voice . . .

Again . . . "We must hurry, dear, they'll be here soon."

"Who?" I forced from my night-tasting throat.

"Don't know. PLC said they'd come."

I dragged open my eyes; Peggy had switched on the light and the mirror showed her lolling on the side of the bed, Velázquez' Rokeby Venus – she had stripped off her nightdress. It was five-thirty; the heat didn't come on until six. Hazy with sleep, I recalled Peggy asking long ago when we were looking at the actual picture: "The mirror reverses the world side to side; how does it know not to turn it upside down?"

I took her hand. "You've been dreaming, Peg, dear," I said. "Get back into bed in the warm."

As we snuggled down in animal warmth, she said, "Sorry about that, Ken. Funny way to dream; I was awake. PLC of all people."

A quaint enough incident for a note in my diary for 6 April 1991, although at the time I attached no particular significance to it. Strange that Peggy had dredged up a memory of PLC deep from our past, Peter Lonsdale-Coombes CMG, dead ten years or so. He was Peggy's boss when we first met over half a century ago. Oddly, he was responsible for our getting together – he and Norman Colquhoun.

A DOZEN rationed shopping days to Christmas 1940, I was chatting to Norman Colquhoun when Lonsdale-Coombes, Head of the Division, came in to talk to Miss Pratt at the desk opposite. I didn't know much about Lonsdale-Coombes, and had always found him difficult to approach; he seemed knowledgeable, highbrow and I feared his scorn. Gossip dubbed him a snob and said he and his wife dressed for dinner and left the curtains open for the neighbours to see. Miss Pratt was not overawed by her boss: business complete, they were chatting like neighbours over a garden wall.

Norman gestured with his Sherlock-Holmes-style pipe for me to listen to the conversation. PLC was expanding on the virtues of wines he had savoured on a tour down the Rhine before the war, a fluent lecture. Miss Pratt, eyes sparkling interest, injected a few apt comments before taking an enthusiastic lead herself, seeming at least equally well informed.

PLC left, resetting his face aloof as he went.

"Seemed almost human talking to her," I said to Norman.

"I told him I thought JDP was her uncle."

"Is he?"

"Shouldn't think so."

The civil-service cult of referring to people by their initials followed naturally enough from their use on papers circulated around the office. The practice suited well the clipped environment of war-time civil service – letters on half foolscap, re-used for the reply; small brown envelopes repeatedly re-addressed with a label until they fell apart; shorter words and sentences. Even speech was snappier. JDP was James Davidson Pratt; a tall, handsome Scot with a Clark Gable moustache, our Director, remote and God-like.

In the clattering canteen at teatime, I manoeuvred to be next in line to Miss Pratt – I had been fascinated by her easy way with PLC and, looking at her with new eyes, I found her alluring in other ways too. We shared amusement watching the woman behind the counter – she was pouring tea at speed into a double line of cups from a huge teapot with two spouts.

I tried to match Miss Pratt's composure as we sat at table:

"You're quite an expert on wine," I said.

"I know almost nothing about it."

"But with PLC . . ."

"He knows even less."

She went on to say that most of his apparent erudition was sham. He had a photographic memory: he could read a page of text and reproduce it verbatim the next day to air his knowledge. You could always tell you were in for it from his struggles to get around to the subject. Her impish smile was infectious and I reflected it, enjoying in retrospect her baiting of PLC.

"Impressed you could answer in kind."

"I just made it up. If you're just slightly off his text he's lost."

A couple of weeks later, Friday, 27 December, my twenty-fourth birthday, Norman Colquhoun and I were lunching in a pub in Chandos Street, across the Strand from the Adelphi building where we worked – we were part of the skeleton staff on duty for the week after Christmas. Norman and I had once shared a flat in Swiss Cottage where he had taught me the rudiments of boiling an egg. "No point in having anything else for breakfast," he would say. He had also taught me with his portable wind-up gramophone that there was a world of music beyond jazz. My tastes had been drilled in my late teens playing guitar and trumpet in a 'semi-pro' band I had formed with a school friend, Cliff Townshend – we had both needed to earn money to keep ourselves at school. Cliff made jazz his career[1]. Norman might say, "Now, I think you'll like this: Solomon playing Chopin's Military Polonaise." Over our beer, he said:

"Doing anything Tuesday evening?" He tried to make it sound an off-hand remark which, according to my diary, clearly it wasn't – I can't think now why it was clear.

"New Year's Eve?"

"Miss Hands and I are going out to dinner and wondered if you would makeup a foursome with Miss Pratt."

I'd thought often of her attractive smile since our tea-break together. Norman misunderstood my delay in answering. He said:

"It's over a year now, Ken. It's time you had a look at the world again."

I fingered the long scar on my forehead; less puckered now but still livid. In recent weeks I'd continued to feel lifeless and un-

[1] Cliff played saxophone and clarinet and, during the war, was with 'The Squadronaires', the Royal Air Force band – their best selling disc was "Zambezi", featuring Cliff's saxophone solo. Pete Townshend of 'The Who' is Cliff's son.

enthused, as I had since the car crash that killed my wife, but it had become my way of life, a habit. True, I still had the recurrent nightmare of her sprawled in the road in a growing pool of blood from her severed jugular vein. I dreamed too of what might have been, of the other life she had carried within herself to the grave. Awake, I had pushed below some sort of barrier in my mind the horror of all that, the later sorrow and the guilt.

Tuesday morning, Norman telephoned to say that Miss Hands had cried off – she had acquired a family commitment for the evening. The table was booked at l'Ecu de France in Jermyn Street and he'd cancelled two places, assuming I would still like to take Miss Pratt. I find it difficult now to recall my real feelings while I was trying to decide: I know I struggled to free myself from the net of despond that had ensnared me since the accident, to convince myself that I must drive forward into a new life. Now, reading my diary is like reading about someone in a novel – it isn't me as I now see myself and as I thought I had always been . . .

It was very dark in the street walking to the restaurant, but the night sky showed over great piles of rubble in gaps that had once been fine buildings. The few passing cars with their shrouded headlights were a nuisance rather than a help in the 'black-out', causing us temporary loss of dark adaptation. Pedestrians, like fireflies seeking lovers, were using small flashlights to avoid walking into lampposts or each other. I used mine, and it was natural enough to offer Miss Pratt my arm for guidance. I thrilled to the familiarity.

We pushed through the black curtains at the door of the restaurant into the warmth and the buzz of many conversations. Soft, pink-shaded light disguised the walls and ceiling, long past their time for redecoration. A white-haired waiter, stooping at a table, looked up and came to greet us. The stoop remained. He led us through the dining room, past tables occupied mostly by uniformed couples intent on each other – tomorrow she'd be off to an AA site in Scotland, he'd embark for North Africa, or on a corvette to the Arctic, or take off with loaded guns in a Spitfire. We had the last vacant seats.

Talk was exploratory at first, and Fate soon presented an omen: Miss Pratt was Margaret-called-Peggy Pratt; my wife of just a year had been Margaret-called-Peggy Partridge.

Peggy-Two seemed conversant with menu language and I asked her to do the ordering, which she did in fine-sounding French. I must have been signalling my admiration; she said:

"Madame Lacrois at Brondesbury and Kilburn High School: she used to say you have to change the shape of your mouth on the inside."

The ancient waiter turned out to be Spanish.

I studied her face while she was concentrated on her first course: little make-up; high cheek bones; satiny skin, faintly pink; straight nose, not over large but a feature; pencilled eyebrows in the fashion; long fair eyelashes . . .

She looked up – her eyes were opal-blue – again that smile:

"Get on with your meal, Ken. My turn to look at you." She tossed her short honey-coloured hair (softly blonde might be less of a cliché but has brassy overtones) as though used to it longer.

The meal was a masterpiece derived from rationed food, taking full advantage of allowable extras but kept otherwise within the legal price restriction of five shillings each – food rationing was only a problem for those who, despite price control, couldn't afford to eat out. We exchanged life stories in brief. She didn't ask about my scarred face – the result of a wheel coming off my Wolseley Hornet, which then turned over on the long hill down into High Wycombe – the story of the accident was well known in the office. She told me her father had wanted her to follow in his footsteps as a pharmacist and, when she was sixteen, entered her into pupilage with him. After 'Matric.' at school, she started on a degree course at University College, London, but decided pharmacy was not for her.

"I'd lived with it for nearly twenty years and it seemed dull," she said. "What's more, I didn't believe in half the things we rolled into pills. The snag was I didn't know what to do instead, although I did fancy being a high-paid super-secretary to a captain of industry."

Such uncertainty was, surely, out of character – she seemed to me incisive, pragmatic, with a mind more collected than most. Later, I recognised that, like most of us, she was searching.

She went to a secretarial college for a while, but at the outbreak of war an advertisement in the Daily Telegraph persuaded her to join the Ministry of Supply as a Technical Assistant, a wartime grade. She was paid the grand sum of £154 a year; but that was in the days when male chauvinism was an accepted ploy in courting display, and a girl's ultimate dream was still said to be a husband with a thousand a year. We were on the same salary band, but my pay was higher by two tiny increments for my service so far – I had joined the Department before the war as an Assistant III when the organisation was under the War Office.

My spine tingled as the insistent wail of the air-raid warning silenced conversations for a moment in the dining room. The waiter raised his voice a little to tell us about the puddings as anti-aircraft guns in Hyde Park barked *staccato fortissimo* at droning intruders in the night sky. There were a few banshee shrieks of falling bombs, and split seconds of tension awaiting the crumps – one, not far away, flickered the lights and brought down a few flakes from the ceiling – but nobody left the dining room for a shelter. The Blitz of September, when London and suburbs had taken a battering from over five-thousand tons of high-explosive bombs, had hardened – or should that be softened – most of us to a sort of fatalism.

As we left the restaurant, pulses were soothed to normal by the long friendly note of the 'all-clear'. Peggy took my arm and, again, I felt the warm glow of companionship – and something more.

In the bar of the Captain's Cabin we sat telling each other little secrets of our past while sipping a cognac apiece. My own stories seemed to me flat and ordinary, but Peggy's face glowed with interest as she listened, soft lips slightly parted like those of a child enthralled with a fairy tale. As for me, I was a stranded mariner thirsting for the fresh water of her history.

A quarter-of-an-hour or so from midnight we left the pub and walked to the Embankment to 'see in' the New Year. The Westminster tower, thrust high, a monument to our righteous belligerence, was outlined against the sky but, since Big Ben was blacked out like the rest of the country, we couldn't see the time. I lit a cigarette for Peggy and my own straight-grained briar while we waited for the clock to strike midnight.

As the familiar, slightly-out-of-tune chimes rang out, I took Peggy in my arms and kissed her, gently, a friendly New-Year's-Eve kiss, which warmed as we responded to each other. We outlasted the bells by minutes.

"Happy New Year, Peggy," I said, breathless; exultant.

"Happy New Year, Ken. It's started well."

We collected my old Austin 10 from behind the Adelphi and I drove Peggy home up the Edgware Road to Brondesbury Park where her father, Arthur Pratt, had a chemist's shop. Our goodnight kiss in the car left me quivering – you didn't go any further in those days.

I drove home to Hounslow West where I was lodging temporarily with my late wife's parents, the Partridges, and Henry, my black Labrador with corns on his elbows – the previous owner had kept him in a barrel. I recalled my feelings when, as a teenager, I first kissed a girl good night: I had danced down the road elated, triumphant even. I felt like it again, still thrilling to the soft warmth of Peggy's body, vibrant and yielding. I sang all the way to the Great West Road.

My stride was significantly longer than usual the next morning, walking down the Strand to the office. The makeshift shop windows staring unwashed and bleary from their boarded frames failed to depress me. I twirled my rolled umbrella as I turned into Adam Street, and amazed a couple of gossiping women I recognized, Air-raid Wardens in black tin hats, when I raised my trilby to them with old-fashioned exaggeration. I turned into the sandbagged entrance to the Adelphi building, occupied mostly by the wartime Ministry of Supply. The stony-faced guard nearly returned my smile while checking my pass as though he had never seen one before.

Farmer, the messenger, was startled when I greeted him with a bright "Good morning". With a flush almost of enthusiasm I got down to the business of the day, so-called Chemical Defence. My concern was with weapons for disseminating chemical warfare agents – it was said that to devise effective defence it was necessary to study offence. Peggy Pratt and I had similar jobs, but she dealt with what went into the weapons rather than the ironmongery.

Our department in the Ministry of Supply was the headquarters for the Chemical Defence Experimental Station in Wiltshire, called Porton for short, although that was the name of the nearby village. Our organisation was, effectively, little more than a post office between Porton, the Military Staffs and the outside world. We had agreed at dinner that our jobs were not only boring, but also valueless. Peggy labelled us junior bumph pushers – at our peril would we inject any original thought into our dealings. The department was also a technical secretariat for the Chemical Defence Advisory Board and its various sub-committees. Peggy did the Chemistry Sub-Committee while I had the one for Air Weapons.

Farmer brought in my morning post. On top of the pile was a small brown envelope sealed with an economy label, hand-addressed to EKJ. He glanced at it and winked at me. It was a note from Peggy:

'Ken. Thanks for a lovely evening. My treat next time. Peggy.'

So, there was to be a next time.

I was still smiling when Norman came in:

"How was dinner?" he said, with a grin, or perhaps a leer, twisted around the stem of his pipe.

"All right, I think. Everything else was splendid, you cunning bastard."

CHAPTER TWO

In May 1991, the day Rajiv Gandhi was assassinated, Peggy and I subjected ourselves to a medical check-up. The doctor was very thorough. His verdict, "The healthiest couple I've seen today", sounded like a death sentence.

I went to London the next day – I was 'researching' a book, a biography of Auguste Escoffier, the French chef who at the turn of the century introduced us and the world to French cooking. Pierre Escoffier, a grandson, was visiting England and I had, pretentiously, invited him to lunch at my club, the Athenæum. When I got back to Salisbury late afternoon, I found Peggy with her feet up, one leg swathed in blood-stained bandage. She had fallen over the low stone wall of a raised bed in the garden.

I cleaned up her leg and dressed it again. There was a closed cut and some abrasion, but no obvious need for medical attention. What worried me was that Peggy wasn't clear what had happened. One moment she was walking along the garden path intent on doing some weeding, and the next she was face down in a patch of white-flowering arabis. Had she had a stroke? I asked her whether she had fainted.

"No, nothing like that. When I tripped, it was as though I didn't know what to do to balance myself."

She was in good spirits the next day and her leg was comfortable.

We drove to Addlestone, Surrey, to see my 92-year-old mother, Jessie, in Fermoyle House Nursing Home. She was weepy at first and went through the routine of wanting to get out and, in particular, to live with us. Jessie – she had objected to being called Mother or Mum since her second marriage to the much younger man she had outlived – had previously been nagging my sister, Georgina, to take her in.

"Georgie's a bitch," she said. "Years I looked after her on my own."

That was the first time, she had spoken to me, even by inference, of taking six-year-old Georgina with her when she left Dad, leaving me behind. I pointed out that neither Georgie nor I could handle her – it took four people to lift her – and give her the full-time attention she needed day and night. She insisted she could look after herself.

I felt guilty, not because she was my mother – I scarcely knew her as such – more because she was a human being trapped in the hollow nothingness of old age and there was little I could do about it. Georgie, seven years younger than me, had assumed the job of overseeing Jessie's care. She did a great deal for her, visiting frequently, nagging the nursing-home staff, shopping for her and walking her out in her wheelchair. She clearly had a filial affection I lacked; nevertheless, I had more than a twinge of conscience leaving her to it.

Jessie went on to detail as usual her view of the family history, dripping venom from her loose dentures. That cheered her up and she then carefully inspected the wrapped box of chocolates we had brought her as if deciding how best to defuse it – we had chosen the present carefully since she was inclined to examine all orifices of a gift horse.

As we left, Peggy was disinclined to talk; she seemed upset. As we approached the Motorway Services on the M3 she suggested we stop for coffee. We sat down with our tray, and she took my hand:

"It was awful, Ken."

"Jessie?"

"No, all those poor old people."

We had been in what was called the Day Room, waiting while Jessie was being attended to in her bedroom. There they all were, sitting silently chewing their tongues, staring through the walls at their short bleak futures. It was, indeed, awful. I said something inane, like:

"Perhaps they don't mind just sitting, Peggy dear. Wouldn't they bleat otherwise, like Jessie does?"

"Don't you feel compassion?"

"I feel something. I don't know what it is." What I actually felt was the horror that I might one day see Peggy like that or, since as a woman the expectancy was she'd outlive me, she'd finish up like that without my being around to keep her out of a home. That was an unbearable thought, and I closed my mind.

"You might be right, Ken: perhaps when it happens you don't care. But I think it's more likely you know why your family has thrown you out, and you live in a state of frustration because you can't express yourself. You bleat like Jessie until it's clear nobody cares, then you just sit back and die."

In July we took a working holiday: we drove to the South of France for more research on Escoffier. In Villeneuve-Loubet near Nice, we spent a couple of weeks in the museum that had been Escoffier's family home. Peggy did a great job; she was much better at dealing with old French letters – well, that's what they were – than I was. We also went to lunch in Monte Carlo with Timothy and Maryse Shaw. Timothy was writing about the life and times of Escoffier. Maryse it appeared was what she called *une espèce de cousine* of the great man and had been brought up by parents who had used him as a bogeyman. Then, we stopped work and drove to Kandersteg in Switzerland where we had spent many holidays walking or cross-country skiing in the mountains. One minor glitch: the morning we were to leave, someone had bent our car door in the hotel car park. They had left a note in German that said, essentially, 'Sorry. Mine's worse than yours, but your insurance won't have to pay for that,' and that was all. Peg said, "Heil Hitler". We drove home with the door tied shut with an old shirt trapped in the closed window.

The year went on, getting mistier as my left eye hid more and more behind its cataract – the other one wasn't very good – but I couldn't overcome the inertia, or perhaps my cowardice, to get treatment. I was almost shocked into it by the optician who told me my 'good' eye was getting very close to the limit for driving. Peggy delivered the coup de grâce with typical pragmatism: "Better get it done while you can still see something with the other one." She almost spoilt the prompt with: "Well, you never know, the op might go bad."

I walked into the operating theatre at New Hall accompanied by two young maidens. It was like going for afternoon tea in someone's living room, except for my surgical gown and slippered feet and the odd paraphernalia scattered around – the hospital was a converted country house, previously owned by John Creasey, the novelist. The second movement of Chopin's first Piano Concerto emerging softly from hidden speakers enhanced the social atmosphere. I thought of the novelist in his heyday sitting in this noble room in his chintz covered armchair, writing-pad on knee, constructing sentences for villainy. I was helped by the nubility on to the high, well-padded operating table. With soft, comforting words they covered me with a sheet and manoeuvred it for me to see the ornate ceiling through a hole – until some highly technical stuff was lowered completely blocking my view. Butterflies were copulating in my belly. My right eye was blacked out and some sort of restraint was applied so that I couldn't move my head.

'Hallo, Mr James, are you comfortable?' A new voice, the surgeon's – the butterflies on a gang-bang climaxed together. The music stopped. The real business was about to start. Inevitable now, and I was calm.

"Just a few drops in your eye; then a few injections . . ."

The injections were distinctly uncomfortable rather than painful, but not for long. The side of my face, it seemed, had dropped off. There were mumbled words between nurses and surgeon and my imagination got to work: I remembered a shock opening to an *avant-garde* film of the forties where an eye, filling the whole screen, gushed as it was slashed by a razor.

"Going very well, Mr James . . ."

I wasn't even aware he'd started. My steel-hard rigidity jellied as I relaxed and tried to make sense of the shufflings and muttered instructions.

A grunt.

Silence.

Nothing for several minutes, then:

"Try the top drawer."

God, hadn't they got things ready? I must have spoken without realizing it:

"No, it's all right, Mr James, I have decided to put in a different kind of implant." Whatever that meant.

Then, came the mumbled words again. I think I dozed off until:

". . .all tidy now." The romping third movement of the Chopin faded in; brilliant light as the cover was removed from my right eye, and there was the ceiling again.

"Careful when you stand up; the nurses will help you. Sit for a while with a cup of tea before you go home. They'll give you some painkillers in case you need them overnight. Come and see me in the morning and we'll take off the dressing." Or that was the gist of it, mixed with kindly and reassuring words.

I didn't need the painkillers overnight. The surgeon removed the dressing next morning and the beautiful world I had forgotten was revealed: the bookshelf in front of me was a brilliantly illuminated garden with reds and greens, yellows and blues. I closed my left eye and the drab grey world returned.

"Good?" he asked.

"Wonderful, thank you."

"A bit fuzzy, I expect, but that will improve as the scar settles down. Then, we'll see whether you'll need spectacles."

I asked him why he had changed the type of lens implant during the operation. He explained that the capsule that had retained my cloudy lens had split and the type of prosthesis now used would have fallen through into the eyeball. Catastrophic. He'd used the older type with external retainers. He went on to warn me not to do any lifting for a month and to wear an eye shield in bed to avoid putting any pressure on the eye.

I spent the rest of the day in Heaven, delighting in my plastic eye.

The next morning was not good. I awoke with an immense black spider crawling around in my eye. In a panic I rang the surgeon.

"Often happens," he said. "Just an air bubble. It will gradually absorb."

It did.

Having taken the plunge with my eye, I arranged a few weeks later to have a large lump on my forehead excavated – it had been embarrassing people. I was surprised when the GP rang me later with the news from the lab. that the lump had been benign – to think, I'd gone around with it for years without worrying. Then, Peggy fell against a cupboard door and cut her head: I worried. The next morning I fell down the spiral staircase rushing from bed to open the door to the postman who was unable to get a package through the letter box – a package, it turned out, addressed to next door. No serious damage from the fall except to my self-esteem, and a cascade of i.o.u's in the heavenly swear-box – perhaps Peggy worried about *me*. I hoped it was long enough after my cataract operation that the shock had not caused any damage.

November came, and we went to dinner at the Three Lions, Stuckton. I remember the meal particularly for its superb main course, a seafood dish in a curry-flavoured sauce – we accompanied it with a gewürztraminer by Hugo which cut through nicely. I also remember it because we'd had a lunch party at home on the previous Saturday with Peggy's sister, Barbara, the middle one of the three Pratt girls, and some friends, a celebration four days early – Wednesday at the Three Lions was the occasion of our actual Golden Wedding Anniversary.

Afterwards, we sat close in the car in the car park chatting. After a gentle kiss I felt idly for the pulse in Peggy's neck:

"I love it when you touch me gently like that, darling," she said. "What are you doing?"

"Counting the beats."

"The bleeding to death of time in slow heart beats," she said, quoting Robert Graves.

Our kissing became more intense as the windows steamed up. Peggy said:

"This is how it all started, Ken dear, during the war, smooching in our Riley Kestrel . . ."

THE WAR was more than a year old, and I was in a 'protected' job – I wouldn't be called up for the armed forces, and I felt uncomfortable about it. I had volunteered for a short-service commission in the RAF in 1938 – I went for a fitting at Uxbridge to check that a

Spitfire wouldn't be too tight under the crotch. It was a seller's market before the war and, having no degree, I was offered non-commissioned rank. I accepted instead a job offered by the War Office – I was keen to do chemistry, which they said I would be able to do at the Experimental Station at Porton. They allowed me to stay in the London office to finish my degree course at evening classes. I married then. When war was declared in 1939, I was sent to Porton with the rest of the London office, and that seemed to end my chance of graduating. Peggy-One left her job, and we lived cosily in a caravan conveniently parked outside my office window in the administrative building – perhaps aptly named The Main Block. Peggy-One and I used to chat through the window over coffee, but that convenience was soon lost: Baron Victor Rothschild, nominally a consultant, took over my office. He was not aware of my displacement, of course, and it was to be many years before he again cast his shadow my way.

At Porton I had more contact with the sharp end of the 'Chemical Defence' business and, in particular, the research laboratories. I was fascinated. The atmosphere of the place was that of a university. There were scientists, it seemed, of every discipline – there was even an archaeologist who had dug around Stonehenge. There was an expert to be found on almost anything from the feeding antics of aardvarks to Zyrian syntax.

There were also some distinct characters. One, Arthur Ford-Moore, a brilliant organic chemist, who invented compounds Nature hadn't thought of, could, it seemed, synthesize any of them from a scuttle of coal. He was nothing if not eccentric: he once said to weekend guests at breakfast, "We have no inhibitions here. If we want to throw our porridge on the ceiling, we do." And to 'Moggs' his wife and their daughter Peggy, "Don't we?" They all did, and formed stalactites that dripped on stalagmitic guests during the rest of the meal.

I joined discussions with these brilliant scientists in star-struck humility, but I was left forlorn when they went back to their research, a closed shop to those without an honours degree.

We stayed only a couple of months at Porton before being shovelled back to London. The new Ministry of Supply, which had taken us over from the War Office, doubtless felt it more important to make policy judgements than to receive information on which such judgements could be based.

A few weeks later, I was in hospital in High Wycombe being patched up, a widower.

The world was an uninteresting place for me when, after a couple of months, I got back to work. It was a colleague, Edgar Neale, who spurred me into activity again. I thought of him as a genius. He was a few years older than me and had achieved a first class honours degree in chemistry from evening school – very few did. We talked chemistry, and gradually he restored my enthusiasm. I started again at evening school on a course, now somewhat abridged by air raids, for an internal London University degree. Then came Peggy-Two.

Peggy Pratt and I, after our first outing on New Year's Eve, spent every moment together we could find. We found all too few, but we managed lunch together most days, and at tea breaks we learned a lot of the family history of the lady in the canteen with the two-spouted teapot. Evenings were difficult. Peggy was in the ARP, the Air-Raid Precautions organisation set up with unusual foresight by the Home Office in 1924. Most nights she sat in a sandbagged shelter in Kilburn ready to put on her tin hat and help drag out broken bodies from smoking wreckage. That was very much in earnest, a real job and a dangerous one.

I was in the Home Guard and I had only the vaguest idea what we were supposed to be guarding. I was particularly puzzled in the early days, mid-1940, when the force was still called the LDV, Local Defence Volunteers, and I was detailed to stand guard on the roof of the Adelphi building with a pike – a bayonet stuck in the end of a length of gas pipe, the only weapon provided. Newspaper pictures showed us lined up, in the present-arms position with our pikes, being inspected with one eye by Herbert Morrison, the Minister of Supply.

Later, we became the Home Guard and I exchanged my LDV armband for full, if ill-fitting, khaki battle dress and a blackened-brass shoulder flash of the King's Royal Rifles. We were issued American .300 caliber carbines of the Great War. Still, the idea of home guarding conjured the image of my standing foursquare in Trafalgar Square pointing my ancient rifle resolutely at German tanks thundering down The Strand. However, despite this ludicrous picture, we took the whole thing seriously: invasion seemed imminent and I think we all felt defiant. In our own company in the Adelphi, we certainly got aggressively steamed up for action when a colleague was killed, blown off Hungerford Bridge the night Charing Cross railway station was bombed. And, in general, the spirit of the men in the Home Guard, soon to amount to a force of half a million, was such that I felt sure any Nazi invaders would be given a very rough time.

I had no difficulty swapping weekday duties with those anxious to avoid night parades at weekends, and so I didn't have to miss evening classes on that account. Evenings with Peggy, however, were largely frustrated, and I skipped a number of classes to be with her.

I was very mixed up, elated, in a sense, but with a nebulous underlying unease. I still thought a lot about Peggy-One: not just the scene of her death, which persisted as a nightmare, but about our short time together. We'd been very happy, and I suppose I was feeling guilty, as though keeping company with Peggy Pratt was a desertion. It was, however, the new Peggy who straightened me out.

We had taken a day's leave on a Monday. It was a cold day, but fine, and we drove with a picnic to Cookham on the Thames. On the way back, I coasted down a long hill to save petrol. Getting back into gear, there was an ominous clonk and the engine revved with no power to the back wheels. There was a garage at the bottom of the hill and I pulled in. With the thought that I probably hadn't enough money in my pocket to pay our train fare home, I said to the attendant, "How much for the Austin with its broken half-shaft?" He fetched the boss who walked round the car kicking the tyres. He came to the window:

"Ten pounds."

I'd paid twenty for it a year earlier. I accepted the offer provided he drove us to the station.

The next day Peggy and I went in the lunch hour to Jimmy James's in Euston Road to have a look at second-hand cars – they specialized in Rileys, which I had always fancied. The central showpiece was a beautiful Riley Kestrel – cream with red leather upholstery, twin SU carburettors and only two thousand miles on the clock. It had a silver kestrel in flight on the bonnet. The snag was the price tag, £195. We drooled over it for a while and then walked around the older machines at a quarter the price. When the salesman came up to us, Peggy told him to come back later, we would like to browse for a while. He went off and Peggy said:

"Make him an offer for the Kestrel."

"It'll be a year's salary. I can't afford that."

"I'll pay for it."

"I knew you must be rich, you smoke Churchman Number Ones. It'll take years for me to pay you back."

"We'll talk about that later. I'm not rich – an aunt died and left me a little."

We got the car for £185 on the road, taxed for a year and, illegally, its tank full of petrol.

The first trip in our dream car was for a picnic near Tring in Oxfordshire. On the way we almost reached an amazing eighty miles an hour – I slowed to sensible speeds as an unwelcome image flashed into my mind. We sat in the car on top of a hill, steaming up the windows drinking our coffee. Our conversation was po-faced – the war had done that to us; we shrouded our deepest emotions in small talk and allusion. But our talk then was to shape our lives. I recalled it for my diary in some detail, recognizing I'd reached a turning point in the course of my life.

Peggy said, as though about to make a cup of tea:

"I'm going to make a great sacrifice."

"You just did. You bought the Kestrel."

"Seriously, Ken, I want you to concentrate on your classes and not take evenings off for me. You have to get a good degree. I ducked out, and I'm already regretting it. It's much more important for you."

"You could make it important, Peggy," I said. "I'll get down to it if you'll marry me."

"You're just saying that so you don't have to pay for the Kestrel."

"Of course. But will you? You go so well with the car. And I love you."

"Do you still think about your wife?"

Was it a condition that I didn't? "Yes I do, Peggy, a lot," I said, fearful.

"I want you to talk to me about her, Ken, don't bottle it up."

Suddenly the world was a brighter place. Just those few words brought me freedom. "I'd like to do that, Peggy," I said. "Will you marry me?"

"Of course. That's why I paid for the car. I love you too."

"The windows steamed up even more, and the coffee went cold.

CHAPTER THREE

The year of our Golden Wedding anniversary, 1991, was dying but still had fight left in it. December saw John Major's claim to a Maastricht triumph, and my mother die of pneumonia.

My mother's funeral was on Christmas Eve at Woking Crematorium. An articulate vicar took the service and did a good job, but to me it was all very unreal, like people play-acting a funeral – I didn't even weep when we sang 'Abide with me', where normally I'd get dewy eyed if someone mentioned the title. I tried saying in my mind, "That's my mother in the box", but I registered only what fine wood the coffin was made of, too good to burn. I supposed the handles were plated plastic . . .

On my birthday I was bad tempered. It wasn't because I'd lived three quarters of a century, and it wasn't because nobody remembered it was my birthday until after morning coffee. It might have been because, again, I had a black spidery floater in my new eye; also, I saw flashes when I looked rapidly left.

New Year's Eve we went to Mary Lovell's party in Lyndhurst. Mary had become a friend, a dear friend, starting the day her partner died in her arms. Mary was forty-ish, wrote best sellers, flew aeroplanes, rode horses, loved life and infected everyone with her joyful spirit. She had a new man, Geoffrey Watts, a successful businessman of intellect. In his late sixties, he was a dedicated skier, a qualified pilot at airline standard and was learning to fly a helicopter. He was a very nice man, and Mary was threatening to accept his invitation to marriage. Mary also liked champagne – vintage, of course. It was a good party.

My diary started the new year with its usual enthusiasm – full pages which shrank as the year went on, to become cryptic notes such as, "What happened to Sunday?" In January, it said, we listened to a reading from John Cheever's journal on Radio 4. I was impressed with the intensity of his thought processes and his writing from deep inside himself with an insight and honesty I could never match. Peggy, discerning as usual, said, "He tears himself apart. What's the point of dragging out all that misery when at the end he doesn't understand himself."

There followed a programme about genes and it was my turn. The reader said that Natural Selection was not Panglossian. I said, "One-upmanship. He'd have reached a wider audience if he'd said that it didn't produce the best of all possible worlds – or does he think we all have Voltaire as bedside reading?" Peggy said, "Now who's Pottering?" – I always lost on these exchanges. She went on:

"Are you any good at lumps?"

"One of my strong points, Poomphie," I said. "Lumps?"

"I've got one in my left breast."

I had a sudden empty feeling. "May I look?"

She undid her blouse.

I was in fact no good at lumps, but I was good at panics and I was in one. Peggy never panicked, but she was looking tense. The lump, which was just visible, was only too obvious to the touch. It had to be taken seriously, but I didn't know what to say that would not increase her worry. I said, "You're lucky to have only one, Peggy. I've got dozens." Which was true. "How long have you had it?"

"Don't know. I only noticed it this morning: it's a little bit painful."

"They tell us we should get all bumps checked. We'll pop in and see the quack in the morning on the way to Tesco's."

"What do you mean, you've got dozens?"

"Had them for years."

"Why haven't I noticed them?"

"Too busy with my more interesting protuberances, I guess."

I kissed her and we warmed to the theme. A sofa saw action it hadn't seen in years.

The doctor prodded around looking serious. I felt sick. Peggy said to him, "Doctor, your hands are cold."

He looked up and smiled: "Nothing to worry about, it's a cyst. We'll dig it out in no time." He went on prodding.

He looked up again. "On second thoughts, it's a little deep, and doing no harm, we'll leave it. Keep an eye on it and if there are any changes come and see me again."

There were changes. Peggy was increasingly uncomfortable and the matter came to a head on a Sunday, literally – it was a boil.

"All right, Pharmacist," I said, "How do you treat boils?"

"Daddy had a whole shop full of remedies for anything you could think of, but for a boil he'd always use a steaming-hot bread poultice – perhaps he had something special for boils on boobs."

PEGGY PRATT and I had been engaged about three months when Pratt's the Chemist suffered a close encounter with a very large bomb – an 'aerial mine', fused to explode in the air. The building stayed up, but the inside was wrecked. Mr and Mrs Pratt escaped injury – Mrs Pratt complained only of the indignity of having her voluminous knickers blown out of the window and not being able to find any more in the wreckage. Scampy, the Manchester terrier, was never quite sane afterwards. The shop, a poem in mahogany, Arthur Pratt's pride and joy for quarter of a century, had become a multi-coloured, smelly, rubbish dump. The floor was a heterogeneous morass of syrups and toothbrushes, linctus, lozenges, ceiling plaster and daggers of glass, a microcosmic sample of a rundown universe, chaos that could never be re-ordered. Peggy prodded around in the mess picking up little things she recognized, like a little girl collecting the pieces of her broken doll, sadness for her father shown in the droop of her body and her screwed-up face near to tears.

The bomb did knock down several houses nearby, and our Kestrel was flattened under one of them.

We married, 6 November 1941, in Willesden Registry Office, in a somewhat extended lunch hour. Peggy sported a little blue pillbox hat with an eye-veil for the occasion – hats were not normally her scene. Witnesses were Peggy's youngest sister Evelyn, her mother, and someone dragged in from an office next door. Middle sister, Barbara, was in Cairo doing whatever the Foreign Office does in such places. Peggy's father's absence was, I think, an expression of his disapproval of a marriage not sanctified in church – I'd tried it once and didn't like it. Nor did Peggy go much on the church – it was years later when she said she could get more spiritual on skis in virgin snow. Her father had made a Victorian formality of my request for his daughter's hand, and even asked about my financial prospects; but he had readily agreed to the union. As for my own family, my sister, Georgina, was in the ATS on an AA gun site somewhere. I hadn't seen my father for many years – he was heavy on the bottle, the reason my mother had walked out on us, and that I had left him a little later. My mother was driving Army lorries somewhere in the Midlands. We went back to work in the afternoon.

Peggy's father took us to dinner that evening at the Coq d'Or in the West End. We went home by Tube to a furnished flat, upstairs in a 'semi' in Pope's Lane, Gunnersbury. It was a wonderful feeling arriving home together and going unguiltily to our bedroom.

It took us a few days to realize that all was not well, that our landlady was a fussy old biddy – she even fussed about the bed creaking. We moved to another flat in Kew Road, opposite the Pagoda in Kew Gardens. We were on the top floor; the kitchen comprised a cold-water tap over a stone sink on the landing and a tiny Belling cooker; but we were snug and private.

1941 was drawing to a close with the Americans suffering their Pearl Harbor and entering the war, and the Japs sinking HMS Prince of Wales and HMS Repulse. I was still in my job in the Ministry of Supply, but Peggy had gone to the BBC as a recording engineer – married, we were not allowed to work in the same department in the Civil Service. The snag was that Peggy was on shift work and some days we only met *en passant* on Richmond Station, me going to work, Peggy going home, or vice versa. We would sit and smooch for a few minutes until the Waterloo train came in. Peggy might say, endearingly, "We recorded 'The Brains Trust' last night. I can't stand that Professor Joad and his 'all depends what you mean by . . .' "

"We're not all Humpty Dumpties," I might say, with reciprocal passion, and add, "I've left you a sausage, and the last egg."

When Peggy was working weekends, I swotted with a sandwich, a thermos flask, and a bag full of books, under an exotic tree in Kew Gardens – those days, it was only one duodecimal penny to get in.

It is difficult now to realize that we had any time together to be happy in, but we had. Somehow, we managed to go to the cinema, we went to dances – we danced to Joe Loss at the Astoria. We went to plays, mostly at the Richmond Theatre, and lunchtime concerts at the National Gallery. We talked, we laughed, we made love. So precious was our time together we had none for friends.

At last, came finals – examinations at Imperial College. You couldn't go in without your gas mask. I forgot mine one morning. Peggy saw it hanging on a door handle at home and raced up to Kensington with it, arriving while I was trying, with little hope of success, to talk my way into the examination room.

There were many questions on the honours papers I hadn't covered at all in my abridged course; although, I had one or two bits of luck. Nevertheless, I got to the end of a gruelling week with a heavy heart.

The results: Peggy and I went to Imperial College to study the notice board. We started at the bottom. The long pass list had a couple of James's, but no EK. The Second Class Honours? No. Second Class Honours, Special Chemistry? Not very many, but there it was, James, Edwin Kenneth. It was a great moment, but a strange one. There was reasonable success; there was the release from the bondage of organised study; I could get into the research labs; but there was also a flatness, like the relapse following the shot of adrenaline you get in excitement. Could it be that I would miss having to kick myself into activity? Would I miss the perverse satisfaction of having driven myself with determination from the soft easy life? Nonsense, of course not. Euphoria set in.

I lost no time telling the Department, and a few weeks later they promoted me to Junior Scientific Officer with a posting to the Experimental Establishment at Porton. Peggy resigned from the Beeb and we went to live in the Officers' Married Quarters on the Camp, as it was called. We were one up from mud huts, spacious and waterproof, if primitive. Electric power was sufficient only for lighting, there was no gas, and we cooked on Primus stoves using a biscuit tin as an oven. The one tiny coal fire in the living room fought a losing battle with drafts, which lifted the linoleum off the leaking floorboards. Peggy said:

"A bit crude. You'd think we could do better by now; modern science is three hundred years old this year." She quoted the mnemonic:

"In 1642 – I'll be your guide –
Newton was born and Galileo died."

But, we didn't mind going to bed early. We revelled, too, in the vast amount of time we had together, began to cultivate friends, and learned to play Mah Jong. Peggy enjoyed cooking and did wonders in the biscuit tin. With my slightly enhanced pay and the much-reduced rental, Peggy had no need to seek another job – just as well since she was pregnant.

CHAPTER FOUR

It was a cloudy, cold, January day of 1992. Peggy and I were on our way back from New Hall hospital having had my forehead inspected by the surgeon who had dealt with my bump. I was signed off. We had been talking about my mother's funeral and the various people who had turned up, but Peggy had gone quiet. I took a quick glance. She was frowning and looked thoroughly miserable.

"Cheer up, Poomphie," I said, vacuously. I'd first used my pet name for Peggy many years ago, when she misquoted from Tommy Handley's wartime radio programme, "Itma". She announced herself on the telephone to me mimicking one of the characters:

"Diss iss Poomph spicking."

"It's Fünf," I said.

"Dat's punny, I thought that's what I said."

That was a long time ago. Now, she said, still looking sad, "I'm all right, Ken, dear."

"Thought perhaps talking about Jessie's funeral depressed you."

"Good heavens, no. We all have them, you know, and she was almost ninety-four." She still looked despondent.

I volunteered to do dinner that evening, and, painstakingly following Escoffier's instructions line by line, cooked a couple of lobsters *à l'Américaine*, with all the trimmings and a suitable wine. Normally that would have revived Peggy's spirits, but it didn't – perhaps I should have started with live lobsters thrust into a hot oven, as the Master recommended.

She continued introspective and unresponsive for the next two days. When I asked, she said she was all right but might be sickening for a cold or something. We then had another appointment at New

Hall, this time with the eye specialist who was to give Peggy laser treatment on her left eye. She had been on eye-drops – Timoptol and Pilocarpine – since glaucoma in both eyes had been diagnosed a couple of years previously.

I settled down for a long wait at the hospital, but not to my book. What was it that had upset Peg? The thought of blindness, perhaps? I knew the feeling. I'd had it myself when my cataracts promoted themselves from incipient to frank. Like me, Peggy would remember in our childhood the prevalence of tapping white sticks, inevitable then from cataract or glaucoma, which were now both treatable.

I had not finished with the thought when Peggy appeared. The operation had taken no more than ten minutes and she came out positively bouncing. Uncharacteristic, but presumably she had indeed feared the possible failure of the treatment. When I asked, she said her imagination had been working overtime.

There was a call from Jonathan Meades on my answerphone when we got home. I rang him. He said he'd had a telephone call from his aunt in Cyprus where she and his mother, Bunty Meades, were on holiday. The aunt had said Bunty was "difficult, thoroughly gaga", and Jonty wanted to know whether I'd noticed anything wrong with her recently.

We had known Jonty since his childhood – his parents, John and Bunty were our friendly neighbours in Salisbury and we had spent many holidays with them touring France. John had been dead ten years. Jonty, author, journalist and TV celebrity, now lived in London. He had always had a fine eye for a phrase, picturesque – 'prepare to face the lime-green posing pouch of reality' – if Braque-ish. The last time he had visited his mother he came to see us with his twin daughters, Holly and Rose. They were perhaps ten years old. At the door, one of them, Holly I think, said: "This is my sister, and that's my daddy, and there's an old lady in there called Bunty Grandma who doesn't understand much. Now I'm afraid I shall have to go." She seemed to be studying my face as though about to sketch it. She said, "You haven't got much hair, Ken, have you? Goodbye now. Perhaps I'll find time to come back." It was Holly's childish observation that brought us to realizing Bunty was indeed getting rather vague.

On the telephone, I told Jonty we had noticed that Bunty was a little confused, but after all, she was eighty years old. But, gaga? We certainly would not have put it so strongly.

That afternoon Peggy was sad again. I took her in my arms:

"Something's really troubling you, Poomphie. Tell me."

She started to cry – a rare phenomenon. Then she managed a half-smile and said, "Sorry, Ken, I'm being stupid. It's just that I've realized I'm falling to pieces, rotting away."

"Poomphie, you've had a nasty boil under your arm, and you've got glaucoma, which is well under control. That's not rotting away."

She said she agreed, but that there was more to it. "I have a funny dull feeling, Ken. I fall about, and I sometimes don't know how I got where I am. This morning I couldn't remember how to open the 'fridge."

I didn't know what to say. She did fall about a bit but she had always had this tendency – except on skis when she was remarkably stable. She had of late been noticeably depressed and miserable. The phase seemed to have started with her last bout of cystitis and the consequent treatment with antibiotics; but this was the first time she had mentioned having a dull feeling.

I said, "Let's have a chat, Poomphie." I made some coffee and we sat close and talked seriously for an hour or so. I said the usual trite things about being well past our three-score years and ten, and that we couldn't expect to be leaping around beaming intelligence. Eventually we got down to brass tacks. It had started with Jessie:

"It was those poor old ladies in the nursing home, Ken, Hogarthian women with bent faces, effigies of human beings that nobody wanted to know. I felt you wouldn't want to be with me when I got like that. Since then, I've noticed every little quirk that suggested the decline had started. And now poor Bunty . . ."

I got quite worked up assuring her that we would stay together come what may, while the picture in my mind was of me drooling vacantly while my behind was washed by some muscle-bound Amazon in white. With mutual reassurances that made us both weep a little, we took to the kitchen and shared the cooking.

Peggy seemed all right after that, but the gods hadn't finished with us. The telephone rang. Lene, a much loved, adopted aunt of Peggy's, had suffered a stroke and was in intensive care. Then, a call from Bunty next door: just back from Cyprus, she couldn't get her

TV to work. We both went in to welcome her home. Her TV was easy, the remote control needed new batteries; *she* was not going to be so easily repaired. I was appalled at her deterioration: she had suddenly become a wizened old lady, confused, disorientated and scarcely able to put a sentence together. I wondered if she even recognized us. She was very upset.

I regretted bringing Peggy but, unexpectedly, she was not only taking the new shocks in her stride, but was wonderful with Bunty. She soon had her calmed and even smiling.

I was not so sanguine. I hadn't registered seeing any real signs of Peggy going downhill to Bunty's state, although I could visualize myself doing so. From what Peggy had said, she could also see herself slipping. That was what exercised me, the thought of her becoming like Bunty was now.

The next day started the Chinese New Year and Mary Lovell, our writer friend, visited us – she had succumbed to Geoffrey's ardent wooing and they were getting married in July.

It was past time to snap out of our despondency: we all went to the Jade in Salisbury, our favourite Chinese restaurant, and had a New-Year's feast. I didn't record the meal we had – it was complicated – but Peggy was back on form, and I did note the essence of some of the discussions we got into. Mary seemed uptight about Maastricht: "What's wrong with everyone, of course we have to get into Europe." This was strange since I knew she was anti.

"Why join the gang that hates us," said Peggy. She had on her impish smile and I realized she was joining the game and just prodding Mary.

"The Germans?" said Mary.

"The French."

"Thought you liked the French, Peg."

"That's personal. We're national enemies."

"What about the Germans?"

"They hate the French, not us."

"But they're in cahoots with the French now."

"They've tried war. This is easier and the Americans don't get in the way."

"So, what would you do?"

"Get into bed with the Americans."

"What!" Mary exploded, "and get screwed?"

"Nice," said Peggy. "We're already kissing cousins. They love us. The Canadians sleep happily in a twin bed. They'd drool – they love us too."

We talked of many things and went home happy.

But the Gods were still at it – the answerphone said that Lene, Peggy's adopted aunt, had died 'peacefully in her bed'.

Peggy said, "Peacefully? Perhaps she just couldn't scream."

Our daughter Carolyn came to stay over Easter with her partner, shall we call him Derek. They'd been together for nine years, but there was trouble. Peggy and I were not fond of Derek. His neatly trimmed black beard, grown to cover a receding chin, and his six-foot status gained with platform shoes, described his character. We had kept our feelings under wraps – mine anyway since Peggy had somewhat kindlier thoughts. I rationalized that Carolyn seemed fond of him and, anyway, he was an improvement on the husband she had divorced. Derek seemed fond of her – unless it was an act for our benefit – although his treatment of her took full advantage of her tolerant and forgiving nature to boost his own feeling of masterful control. She was his slave to be called to the bedroom as required. But that's the view of a father. We both resented his attitude of supercilious scorn for old people, including us. For him, we had lived far beyond our 'best before' date.

Within minutes of arriving on this occasion, Carolyn said she'd had a problem on her computer. Could I help? It was an excuse to get me alone in the library.

"Daddy, I'm going to leave Derek."

That put me in a quandary. My immediate thought was that it couldn't be soon enough. I said something like:

"You must have thought this out very carefully, dear. I rather thought you'd found a partner to grow old with. Its no fun being alone in your dotage."

"I'm fifty next year, Daddy, as Derek delights in telling me. Already he buys me hair dye so my grey hairs don't show. He's only forty-two and so vain he'll be off like a shot to flaunt some fancy young thing as soon as my wrinkles start to show."

"But that's not why you want to leave, is it?"

"No, it's because he is so domineering and strict. Life has to be his way. It doesn't matter what I think. He makes me miserable and life shouldn't be like that."

She cried on my shoulder and I patted her, feeling totally inadequate. I told her that only she could judge the wisdom of leaving and that she could always live with us if she wanted to. "But remember," I said, "we are not immortal."

She dried her eyes and said, "Thanks, Dad. I would like to come home, I was born and grew up down here and it is home to me, but I'd better stay in London and keep my job. Anyway, not much fun being old without a pension." She gave me a hug and then said, looking worried, "Is Mummy all right?"

I temporized. "I think so. Why, dear?"

"She seems so remote and vague."

I told her of our recent chat and of Peggy's concern about old folk abandoned to a nursing home.

"Does she think you'd abandon her?"

"She did."

"But you wouldn't"

"Of course not, not voluntarily, that is."

"If it came to it, Daddy, and you couldn't look after her, I certainly would – both of you if necessary."

It was my turn to have salty eyes.

1942 WAS ENDING and Peggy was getting agitated – her hormones were saying that being in draughty quarters with a biscuit-tin oven was no environment in which to welcome our child. We rented Greenacres, a modern house on its own near the top of the hill above Ford, a mile from Salisbury; and I bought an old Ariel motor cycle to get to work. The house was well appointed and newly furnished, and I could shoot rabbits from the bathroom window to eke out the minuscule meat ration. Electricity came from a generator with a Diesel engine in the otherwise unoccupied pigsties at the end of the garden. We shared the house with Jessie and Edgar Neale and Peter, their two-year-old son – Edgar, my genius friend, had also been posted to Porton from the London office. We settled in well together, with only one snag from our point of view: Edgar had smelly feet, which he toasted in front of the fire.

Carolyn was born in March, a Wiltshire Moonraker, in Spero's Nursing Home in Salisbury. I didn't think of asking to be present – one didn't in those days. When I went in, everything was clean, neat and tidy, and Peggy was happily counting fingers and toes.

"She's all complete," she said, and wept with a smile on her face.

You couldn't take a new born baby around on a motor cycle so I bought a Morris Eight saloon from Walter Busbridge, Head of Photographic Section at Porton – his main claim to fame was to have taken photographs of every nubile young lady at Porton, as nudes in his back garden. He was an attractive fellow.

Carolyn was eighteen months old when I was posted abroad to an odd sort of job in Australia. I hadn't got to know Carolyn very well by then – well, you know, at that age she wasn't much on communication – but I felt we had established a bond quite early on. She would break into a grin when I leaned over her, give a little chuckle – or whatever you call the croak they make when they're a few weeks old – reach up, touch my bristly moustache and chuckle again.

To say I was posted abroad might give a false impression: I was asked if I would like to go by a charming Colonel Owen Wansbrough-Jones, an academic, a chemist, who had what was known as an emergency commission in the army. He had busied himself setting up and staffing mobile anti-gas laboratories in France and the Middle East. He told me he had heard there was a possibility of my being promoted to Scientific Officer, and would I care to do this important job. I didn't have the courage or the gall to ask whether the promotion depended on my answer. When I asked Peggy's opinion she said it was better for her than my driving a tank or flying a Hurricane. I wanted to go, not only because it seemed an adventure not to be missed, but also because it might relieve to some extent the uncomfortable feeling that persisted of my being in a safe job when others were being shot at. I said I'd be pleased to do the job. I wasn't aware at the time that this was not the last time Owen Wansbrough-Jones would figure in changing the direction of my life.

Edgar Neale was also to be one of the team. We gave up Greenacres since Peggy and Jessie wanted to live with their respective parents in London while we were away. They were both firm about it, while

Edgar and I worried about air raids. However, the German onslaught with flying bombs, the V1s, was dying out, and we didn't know about the V2 rocket bombs to come; we gave in.

I wasn't going off to risk being a hero or anything like that. It was just that the Japs might use chemical warfare methods working their way down through insular jungles towards Australia – some of their CW munitions had already been discovered in Papua New Guinea. We didn't know much about the use of nasties like mustard gas under jungle conditions, or whether our protective clothing would work soaked in sweat, and so on. A few people had gone out previously to Queensland to do some experiments in rain forests, but it was reckoned a larger team would be necessary to do any good. I was to replace the man already there looking after the weapon side of things.

At Porton, far from doing the chemistry I'd been looking forward to, I'd been directed to what was euphemistically called the Technical Chemistry Section. I'd worked on the design of chemical warfare munitions – the idea was to ensure we were not caught out, as we were in the World War 1, without the means for retaliation should the Nazis use gas on us. With less than two years experience and labelled a weapons expert, I was to head a new Munitions Section at the Australian Field Experimental Station which had been set up by the Australians to be manned by a mixed Allied team. I didn't know why the man from Porton was being sent back; I thought perhaps his accent was too fruity for the Aussies, although I learned years later that he had boobed rather dangerously in an experiment with 3-inch mortars.

A dozen of us went off from Liverpool in the *s.s. New Zealand Star* in convoy across the Atlantic to New York. Next to us in the fleet was a trim little Norwegian fruiter, which would sometimes come close for the crews to banter through megaphones. There were often explosions during the crossing, but I think we only lost a couple of ships; the Norwegian fruiter was one of them.

We holed up in New York for a couple of weeks while the ship was being loaded with night-fighter aircraft – Northrop P61s, known as Black Widows – for that conflict quaintly referred to as the Pacific War. We then cruised solo to Australia through the Panama Canal.

Awaiting me in Sydney was a stack of air letters from Peggy – she had written almost every day. It turned out that while her parents were kindly and welcoming, Peggy had soon found the confined quarters above the shop depressing. She wondered how her mother and father had managed to bring up three girls under such conditions. The kitchen, used as a living room, was almost filled by the kitchen table. In there, the cooking, the eating, the washing up, the ironing and so on, went on, and it was the only place to sit. It was all very clean and tidy and Peggy's mother did wonders with the wartime food rations, but Peggy found that restraining Carolyn's exuberance under such close confines was too wearing. She moved to a flat in nearby Radnor Road, which did a great deal to ensure continued good relations among the three generations. Her letters were, of course, stilted with an eye to censorship, and were like correspondence from someone on holiday. She had in fact been to Cliftonville with Ella, a friend from school days, and on the beach Carolyn had stamped on little Anthony's sandcastle. Peggy's love-talk, however, was poetic, and my homesickness became almost a physical pain.

The Sydney papers carried news of V2 rocket attacks on London – the rockets arrived at three times the speed of sound each carrying a ton of explosive – Edgar and I worried again.

The next eighteen months we spent hacking pathways through virgin jungle for our sampling apparatus, emptying the sweat from our boots, and drinking Cascade beer, nectar from Tasmania, to put back the fluid.

A favourite pastime in off moments was to throw a machete to slice through a Black Snake, venomous and plentiful in Queensland. Stan Crawford, our meteorologist, a great friend, who bore some resemblance to 'Groucho' one of the Marx Brothers, would often act out the similarity. Once, bending over a recent snake victim, tapping the ash from an imaginary cigar, he said:

"Look at the creepy, crawly, sneaky, slimy brute. No wonder they call 'em snakes".

Life was hectic. We all felt a sense of urgency – which was enhanced when the Japs bombed Darwin. We bombed rain forest on uninhabited islands in the Whitsunday Passage with mustard gas, we sprayed Queensland beaches with the stuff, and confirmed results in New Guinea where it was possible the Japs might use it. We got minor burns from mustard gas going into contaminated areas or gas chambers with Army volunteers to test protective clothing. We accompanied the troops to demonstrate there was no danger – which we couldn't have known to be true, or why were we testing the clothing. However, we had no serious casualties.

In all the time I spent away, Peggy and I kept up our correspondence of three or four air letters a week each. Like Peggy, I had difficulty keeping mine newsy as most of my activity was on matters the censors would blot out.

I changed my mind about sending one piece of news and tore up the air letter. A little river flowed through our camp and the locals told stories of voracious crocodiles in it when it became a torrent in the wet season. We saw none and took the tales with a pinch of salt until one ate a two-year-old girl. Remains were found slung into a tree on the bank. We went on a croc hunt but found none.

Peggy's letters sometimes had erasures, presumably about the progress of the European war, until one letter early in May 1945 said, "It's over this end, darling. Carolyn and I long for you to come home so we can live again. We need you so much."

Three months later, war with the Japanese beginning to go our way, I was dealing with an unexploded mustard-gas bomb on an Australian island – one of our own bombs – in case the Aussies wanted to use the place for holidays after the war. This was no big deal: we just had to tape a slab of gun cotton and a detonator on the side of the bomb and push a plunger at a safe distance. I had my hands on the handle, poised to fire, when somebody rushed up and said, "The Yanks have dropped an atom bomb on Japan and blown up the whole country."

The plunger went home. "What?" I said, when my ears stopped ringing.

CHAPTER FIVE

Mid-February 1992: Carolyn and Derek were still hanging on together. I was getting itchy feet watching the ladies cross-country skiing relay in the Winter Olympics on the box.

Our idea of skiing was to come out of the back door of our hotel, clip on our long, thin cross-country skis and take off into the mountains. No derring-do, but we did like to be away from ski lifts and the crowds of young people queuing for them, and make our own tracks around the contours. We had cancelled skiing this year mostly because of my cowardice – Ian and Mary Pearce, so often our skiing companions, had not been able to get away to come with us, and I'd conjured up an image of Peggy or me with a broken leg, stranded in snowy wastes. Put another way, it didn't seem wise for a couple of old dodderers to go off skiing on their own.

A few days later we were shopping in Salisbury when Peggy drew me into the ski-shop:

"I must get some warm clothes; I'll probably not be able to ski very far."

"You mean . . ."

"As long as it's Kandersteg where we know our way around."

She was doing this for me. Had my hankering been that obvious?

But we didn't go. Peggy had another bout of her urinary infection, which discouraged me, if not her. The doctor didn't seem unduly concerned about the recurrence: "Probably a resistant bug; we'll see what the lab. says, but meanwhile we'll try another antibiotic."

Spring arrived one afternoon in April, or perhaps we hadn't noticed it before through the mists of election campaigning we had endured until then – two days later the Conservatives were back in with a majority of twenty-one. Then came Easter.

Carolyn and Derek came to stay over the holiday. Derek now had a white Savile-Row dinner jacket, he happened to mention.

I was still worried about Peggy – her waterworks seemed to have recovered, but she looked peaky and said she didn't feel quite herself. I just hoped we'd done all we should. Carolyn was the next worry. She'd been getting back pains and was awaiting results of X-rays.

Peggy prepared a splendid dinner on Easter Monday with a menu worthy of the Savoy. Even Derek was impressed with the meal and suggested Carolyn take lessons, but added that he supposed it didn't matter now. He and Carolyn then discussed calmly with us their probable parting. He was very much on his best behaviour, scarcely rude at all. He clearly wanted us to side with him in persuading Carolyn not to leave. He could on such occasions be charming, even entertaining – qualities difficult to link with his usual boorish insensitivity and rank self-centredness. My diary, no respecter of persons, says, 'nobody could be such a sod all through'. Carolyn surely must have seen something less unattractive under that disagreeable exterior.

When they had departed in the morning, Peggy had a call from Eleanor, a neighbour, inviting her to coffee. She was a charming lady several years older than we were. She wanted to talk to Peggy about euthanasia.

Peggy got back all right and reported that Eleanor wouldn't be doing anything drastic – not immediately anyway.

"Was she intending to?"

"I'm not sure. She was pretty depressed."

"Anyhow, you've talked her out of it?"

"Not really. We just talked about the war. She said how flat it had seemed when it ended, but then, with her children growing up, how wonderful life had been. And that was it. She was cheerful again."

It was the end of June before Carolyn finally left Derek. The X-rays had not shown up anything nasty, but she still had pains in her lower back, which had been cleverly diagnosed as 'Lower Back Pain Syndrome'. She had found herself a flat, and Derek had spoken to

me about dividing the proceeds of the sale of their existing house:
"Since you paid Carolyn's half I thought you might be interested."

THE WAR was over and fifty-five million people had been killed, about equivalent to the total population of the UK. There was a bit of a delay in my getting home to England. Wansbrough-Jones again, now Brigadier: would I mind just staying on a while to dispose of the stocks of mustard gas. Oh, and the Americans had left quite large quantities up country, in 1-ton containers and in thin-walled bombs. Oh, and some of the bombs were leaking.

"Sorry to impose on you, Ken, but it's quite a problem, and you are the only one here with the expertise to handle it." It was like Peggy once saying after dinner to some friends, in the days before washing machines, "Nobody washes up like Ken."

I reached home in February 1946; Carolyn was almost three years old and I was given the 'Who's-that-man?' treatment. It might just have been that I looked different – I was no longer the tall, bony streak that had left England. I had gained twenty pounds on a steady diet of Australian steak and eggs. It was three months before she would brush her fingers over my bristly moustache. The chuckle had been replaced by an impish grin, like her mother's.

I went back to Porton to work on weapons. Not happily at first – it seemed pointless effort since, with atom bombs a reality, who'd be bothering with our stuff. The hydrogen bomb was yet to come, and there was no thought of large nations balanced in powerful impotence, unable, for fear of precipitating World War 3, to restrain small fry wielding affordable chemical or biological weapons.

In the event, I found a lot to interest me. I had my own small research team and we dug into some fairly fundamental work on the break-up of fluids – physics rather than chemistry, but better than assessing bomb performance in the jungle. One tool we used in the lab was a magnetron, ex Radar, to produce microwaves to set Bakelite resin. It didn't occur to me even to reheat my coffee that way, and I missed out to Mr Spencer in the States who patented the microwave oven the following year.

We had found a delightful old stone-built house, Warren Farmhouse, which we rented, furnished. It was in Wilbury Park, near Newton Tony, Lady St. Just's Estate – a new farmhouse and dairy had been built near the main house.

War Damage Insurance paid out on our bombed Kestrel – £175, which was just enough to buy a fifteen-year-old two-seater Morris Minor open tourer. When we drove up to our new home we had the car and its dicky seat crammed with the three of us and some of our junk. As we got out, a large boomerang I'd made in Australia fell out too. I'd been shown how to make it by an aborigine – splitting a slice from a bent log cut from a tree elbowing out of the bank of a creek, followed by a long job shaping its twin aerofoils with a pocket knife (my tutor had given up chipping flints). I had to show off my prowess with it, telling Peggy to stand with Carolyn to watch out carefully for its return. I threw it, and congratulated myself on not losing my touch as it spun away in a climbing turn. It would come back nicely and fall just short of us. But it didn't. Still climbing, it hit the trunk of a huge beech tree and split asunder.

It was a lovely place to live. Apart from three farm cottages and a barn nearby, it was a mile from anywhere. Peggy would cycle down the rough track to the new farmhouse for the milk, often with Carolyn on the carrier.

Early on, we had an invitation from our landlady, Lady St. Just, to visit for a glass of sherry. We drove up to the imposing entrance to her house in our old Morris. The butler came out and opened the car door for Peggy with a flourish. It came away in his hands. Impassively, he clutched it to his chest to allow Peggy out, put it carefully on the seat and escorted us into the house.

Lady St. Just was a delightful conversationalist and we stayed at her insistence through several sherries, lounging back on chintz-covered sofas. When we left, the car door was back on its hinges. The ruts in our little lane guided us home.

At the farmhouse, Peggy looked around the living room – not unlike the one we had just left, if on a smaller scale and without the ancestral portraits. We then had a discussion, which in my diary I called seminal. Peggy said:

"I don't like chintz now."

Nor did I. It took me back to early days I didn't want to remember. Peggy hadn't such antecedents as far as I knew.

“Why, Poomphie?

“Florence has spoiled it for me. The poor old thing lives in a chintzy past.”

“She’s not old, and I didn’t get to calling her Florence.”

“You didn’t get to go to the lav. with her. She’s over fifty and has a baron for a son. But I agree that’s not old. She just acts old. The war is over and there’s a new world out there, Ken. Let’s have some.”

That was a view of Peggy I hadn’t had before. It was exciting. She was reflecting my inner thoughts. Since returning from Australia I’d been vaguely uneasy. Settling into a humdrum routine of a life was attractive after the restlessness of the war years – too attractive. I also realized, belatedly, that Peggy’s war had not been restless. She must have had a dull time – even the constant threat of air raids gets dull. She had written often of the enjoyment she got from Carolyn’s company, but never of the tedium of lacklustre days, the grim bomb sites, the sandbags, the meagre rations, the hour-long queues for the rare luxury, the dark of night in blacked-out London streets, news of friends killed or maimed. Hers had been a monotonous existence, waiting for the war to end so that life could begin again. She was looking to me to get it started.

I wanted to. But how, and to what end? I knew Peggy wasn’t being trivial: she didn’t think that grasping at the new world was just ‘having a good time’; also, I knew she was too pragmatic to want to join the popular international sport of putting the world to rights. After the Great War, British survivors from the trenches had returned to be inspired by Lloyd George to make the country fit for heroes to live in – there were differing views in other countries on what would suit their heroes, and the arguments culminated in, but were not resolved by, World War 2. After that conflict, even hereditary Tories came home to Britain and voted Labour – officers had found that their men, companions in danger, were real people. But there was more to it. The landslide swing to Labour that ousted Churchill, the erstwhile war hero, spoke of a massive change of heart: we must get away from the old ways. It was not just starry-eyed altruism, the war had opened our eyes to our basic weaknesses – there should be more to life than mindless greed. Peggy and I, in our long-distance air-letter discussions had written of greed and its Darwinian survival value, which, on its own, led ultimately to the extinction of species.

Survival would best be served by a brain able to forecast greed's effects and to pre-empt them. Essentially, one creature's greed was another's death. The family tie helped, but families feuded. Tribalism? Tribes went to war. For humanity, religions offered unification in aims, but became excuses for wars. Tribes became nations. Bigger wars. World unity? Peggy said that wouldn't happen before Christmas, in fact, not at all until other worlds to war with had been discovered. Meanwhile, what were we to do with our lives?

"Anything in particular you'd like to do, Poomphie?" I felt I was amongst the starry eyed and needed Peggy's pragmatism.

"No, dear, and nothing in haste."

She seemed embarrassed. She probably didn't want me to think she was trying to direct our lives.

"What then?"

"A lot of things will happen to us we can't avoid: we have to make a living, Carolyn has to be educated. Life is dictated to some extent. All I would like to avoid is settling into a suburban type of existence – tea with the neighbours, coffee mornings, cocktail parties, bridge evenings, exchanging dinners, all with the same circle of people. What I long for is a sense of advancing, and variety."

"Right, we'll make it that way." I meant it, and we entered a new era.

CHAPTER SIX

We were almost half way through 1992. Carolyn and Derek had not yet sold their house, but Carolyn was looking for a flat near her job in Teddington. In a fortnight, Mary Lovell and Geoffrey Watts were to be married in Lydney, Gloucestershire – I was to give away the bride. We had rehearsed Peggy in her new outfit and she looked splendid. Moss Bros. had provided me with the usual uniform, and Mary had faxed me a comprehensive brief.

Well ahead of time we were ready to go, but Peggy was worried. For some time, her trips to the loo had needed to be increasingly frequent – little difficulty at home, but likely to be embarrassing elsewhere. The doctor told her she had a prolapse. He put her on flavoxate, which certainly helped the waterworks, but her worried state changed to one of depression – I wondered whether this was a side effect from the drug due to its mild anticholinergic action. The doctor halved the dose of the drug without affecting the drug's main job. She did then, perhaps coincidentally, seem a little happier.

The month of July was born in a rainstorm, which cleared enough to allow some tennis at Wimbledon. That night I had a nightmare: I went through my 1940 car crash in all its detail, except it was the second Peggy lying in the road dying. In the morning, there was one of those coincidences that give rise to myths. I heard a shriek in the garden. Outside, the air seemed heavy under a leaden sky. Silence. No twittering of birds or rustling of leaves.

Peggy was lying on the pavement face down, quite still. I rushed to her.. She looked up and smiled. "I'm okay," she managed, "just winded."

She had walked off the edge of the patio a couple of feet above. I broke down completely, and it was some minutes before I could control myself and check her over.

The next day was Peggy's seventy-fifth birthday. She seemed quite unaffected by her fall and even, perhaps, more sprightly than of late. She was in good form, too, when we went for dinner at our favourite place then for spoiling ourselves, The Three Lions at Stuckton with its eminent owner-chef – previously at the famous Chewton Glen, New Milton. After that, the depression returned but, wishful thinking perhaps, she seemed not so bad as she had been.

Then, the wedding: a symphony Mary and Geoffrey had scored and arranged to perfection even to the last phrase, their eventual escape on honeymoon by helicopter. Peggy wore a pad as a precaution but, in the event, had no difficulty. We thoroughly enjoyed the whole affair and, far from depression, Peggy was vivacious. But, on the way home, she was miserable to the point of tears, as though the effort to be bright had been too much for her.

Later that week, I noticed something new in her behaviour, a certain confusion in the placing of things. Even laying the table was a matter of some thought. Things new to her gave particular trouble. I'd made a simple rack for the ampoules of eye-drops for her glaucoma – she had a fairly complicated routine to follow. The rack laid out the day's procedure so that she merely moved each ampoule on one space when she had taken her dose. It didn't seem to worry her that she always messed up the process and got her dosages wrong.

I found it most distressing, not just that a highly intelligent woman was unable to follow the simple system, but that it was Peggy – I lost my temper and broke the thing apart.

Contrite, I undertook to look after the routine for her. She said, "Thank you, dear. I don't know what I'd do without you. I'm not dead keen on this business of getting old."

What is surprising now, reading my diary entries is that I recorded no concern about Peggy's oddities beyond that occasioned by each event. My attitude, Peggy's too, seems to have been that we were experiencing the normal, inevitable ravages of advancing age. Our

GP took the same line. But then Peggy seemed always to behave so well with him or with other people around, and nobody, with the exception of Carolyn who, like me, knew her well and could detect the slightest deviation, seemed to have noticed anything amiss.

The last day of July was a beautiful summer day and Peggy had taken herself off flavoxate. She said: “It’s better to pee your pants than fall down the stairs”. She was much brighter and, to further illuminate the day; the stock market was doing well and a publisher accepted my book. I said to Peggy, “There’ll be an earthquake tomorrow.”

Tomorrow came. On the breakfast news was a report of an earthquake in Wales, Force 3 on the Richter scale. Mid-morning, Peggy fell down some steps in a neighbour’s garden. She broke her jaw and her collarbone.

The history of Peggy’s falls went back to when we bought our first house in Salisbury, when she broke her ankle . . .

THE NEW life we had promised ourselves started mildly for us on Tuesday 2nd July 1946. While Peggy took Carolyn to watch the auction sale of livestock in Salisbury Market Place, I went off to find a house in Salisbury for us to buy. The first house agent I tried had a likely place at the right price – unbelievable now: £1100, with four bedrooms.

I met Peggy and Carolyn, as arranged, at the Cadena Café for coffee and we went to view the place. At the house, 18 Hillview Road, we met Mr Searle, who was standing in for a younger brother, the owner. Our meeting had an unexpected outcome.

The house was no mansion. It was the end one of a row in which each inhabitant had impinged his personality in paint, and in care, or lack of it, in his minuscule front garden. The view from upper windows over the hoardings opposite was across the city to the cathedral, surely the most elegant one ever built. The house was ideally placed for us: five minutes walk from the city centre and on the Silver Star bus route to Porton[2]. Peggy was flushed with excitement and I had no feeling that there was anything momentous in buying our first house, and so we agreed without hesitation, and without haggling, to buy. The agent went off to find us a mortgage.

Mr Searle, who lived next door, invited us in for a glass of sherry and to meet his wife. When we were settled, Peggy said:

"I knew some Searles from Salisbury when I was little. We used to meet them on holiday in Devonshire."

"At Paignton?"

"Good heavens, yes," said Peggy. "Were you ever there?"

"Sometimes, yes. My eldest brother, Aubrey, and his family were regulars. I remember they had some friends they met there, Arthur Pratt and his family." He jumped out of his chair, excited. "My word, you're little Peggy Pratt, Arthur's daughter."

"And you must be Uncle Ted." She looked at Mrs Searle. "And . . . and Auntie Kit."

"That's right. You came to stay with Dorothy and Aubrey once when they lived across the road on the corner of Milford . . ."

They chatted on, reminiscing, while I was delighting in the coincidence and in the fact that the sherry seemed so much better than the St. Just's.

Carolyn had made herself at home – she was on Kit's lap, happily munching jelly babies. Kit, it emerged, had no children of her own but several nephews and nieces. Ted, was a carpenter on the railway, intelligent, quick-witted and fun. Good neighbours to have.

We asked to have another look around next door and Ted took us in. The paper was hanging off an outside wall in the living room.

"We'll have to do some decorating before we move in," I said. I pulled at the paper to strip it off. We all jumped back as the plaster cascaded from the whole wall.

"Whoops," said Ted.

It was a month before the purchase was completed, and we went along to the house to see again what we would have to do before moving in. It was a pleasant sensation opening the front door to our own house. Inside, the place was manifestly clean and fresh smelling – no fallen plaster and the whole of the ground floor had been redecorated. Ted, in blue overalls and carrying a stepladder, came

[2] During the war, troops returning to camp from an evening out in Salisbury would insert among the bawdy songs: Twinkle, twinkle Silver Star – How I wonder what you are – Driving blindly through the night – Thanks to Shergold and to White. The latter had started the service with an old Chrysler car after WW1.

down the stairs to greet us. He said he and his brother had thought they ought to clean up a bit before they handed over. There was a small table in the middle of the living room supporting a huge vase of roses. Peggy gasped with pleasure and went over to smell them. She looked up, her eyes glistening tears:

"Uncle Ted, you're wonderful. You remembered how I love roses." She turned to me: "Please, darling, make sure I have plenty of roses at my funeral."

I shivered.

Our first few months in the house we spent sprucing it up as best we could. I took over one of the bedrooms on the top floor for a workshop and Ted taught me some real carpentry. I made several pieces of furniture, a help financially, and it meant we could have what we wanted rather than the standardised, although well made, 'Utility' furniture introduced during the war, which was still all one could buy new. Such essentials as we bought had been on hire purchase. We bought a non-essential that way, too, a Humber Snipe, to replace our old Morris that was falling to bits.

I began to get cold feet at this stage about overspending. Peggy certainly wasn't happy about being in debt – unlike me, she hadn't been brought up on the edge of a precipice. We could just get by on our money, but we had to budget carefully. Peggy said it was as well we enjoyed what we were doing since we couldn't afford to do much else. She added:

". . . that's how one gets to be suburban minded, rationalising the inevitable. Why does one beggar oneself to build a home, Ken?"

"Tribal instinct, perhaps?"

"Tribal fiddlesticks. It's just to keep up with the Jones's."

"All right then, we don't know any Jones's. Let's stop."

And we did. We sold the car on the rising market for as much as we'd paid for it – we saved also the rent on a garage owned by a friend of Ted's. We had bicycles, and I fixed a seat for Carolyn on the back of mine. With petrol rationing still with us, the roads were a cyclists' paradise. We picnicked in every beauty spot we could find in Wiltshire and Hampshire. We could even afford to do a little hacking, and Carolyn was soon riding as though born in the saddle.

Our gadding around was temporarily interrupted when Peggy fell up the step from the kitchen. She was carrying a box of cereal she had just opened and which projected its contents at high velocity into the dining room. That was when Peggy broke her ankle. She shed her plaster cast just the day we prised the last rice crispy from its cranny.

When Carolyn started school, Peggy went to work in the Pathology Lab. of Salisbury Infirmary where she analysed blood samples from patients. A colleague, Nora Lane, needed digs and came to us as a 'paying guest' – the 'in' term at the time – and I was promoted to Senior Scientific Officer. With these improvements, we could afford a live-in housekeeper-nanny, although we didn't keep that up for long. We tried several without finding the 'treasure' we had visualised. We gave in when I came home one afternoon to pick up some papers and found the nanny in bed, our bed, with her boy friend. There were empty tumblers on the bedside cabinets and a half-empty bottle of whisky, our whisky. After that, Carolyn went home from school with a friend whose widowed mother was glad of some pin money. Peg collected her on her way home from work.

With our enhanced income, life style, as we would now say, had appreciably improved and we no longer felt suburban – not that we weren't; it was just an attitude of mind, and we had plans.

Plans were put in disarray in 1949. I'd said we didn't know any Jones's to keep up with, but I'd forgotten Wansbrough-Jones. He was a civilian again, Scientific Advisor to the Army Council. He came to see me, a flattery in itself.

He told me that in England during the war a process of scientific assessment had grown up, particularly relating to Radar – Radio-location, as it was then called – and the bombing of Germany. The process had acquired a name, Operational Research. He said it was the sort of thing I'd been doing in Australia. He went on to say that there was now an Army Operational Research Group based at Byfleet in Surrey, which had a strong team in Germany with the British Army of Occupation of the Rhine. They wanted somebody from Porton to go out and do some special studies.

"What about it, Ken? You've done this sort of thing before. Just a couple of months or so . . . Family? Can't do that on a short term appointment . . ."

Peggy said, "Of course you must go. It's what we've been talking about: variety. You never know where it might lead."

And so, clothes rationing having just ended, I bought a new suit, and went.

In the event, I was away for six months, but we got together several times during the period, and we travelled around Germany in a Volkswagen Beetle I had on loan from the Army. The best part of the deal was that we had a two-week summer holiday together at the Army's Rest Centre at Ehrwald in Austria. After austerity England it was a dream. The holiday was embarrassingly cheap since the Army subsidized accommodation. As for the rest, I'm not proud of myself . . .

I lived in the Officers' Mess with 2-Division in Hilden, near Düsseldorf, where the Mess Steward, a German, had volunteered to get me some Austrian schillings for our holiday. I asked him how I should pay for them – we used a special currency in the Army of Occupation called British Armed Forces Special Vouchers, BAFSV, which we called Baffs, and I didn't think it would be legal to use those. He told me he would ask at the bank. Later he handed me a wad of Austrian notes and asked whether he could take over my gin ration while I was away – gin was not available on the open market. I agreed, and signed a mess chit for a very small sum. When I raised the question of paying for the schillings he said, "Sir, haf no vorry," and walked off smiling.

We both cherished a vivid memory of our first sight from our Gasthof the next morning of an Austrian alpine valley, softly green with dewdrops glinting, cuckoo-clock houses here and there with long shadows, sheep and goats tinkling fairy bells on the sloping meadows, a backdrop of high peaks with snowy tops painted pink.

We took a cable car up the Zugspitze – we hadn't yet learned the joys of footslogging up mountains. Near the summit was a tunnel leading through to the German side of the mountain above Garmisch-Partenkirchen. It was an uphill, icy walk and there was a notice warning people to go slowly because of the rarefied air at that altitude. The admonition appealed to Peggy and she quoted it many times in later years when we were about to embark upon some new venture: *Lieb Wanderer, langsam gehen, die Luft ist dünn*. Meanwhile, we had started our love affair with mountains, not just conquering them as peaks – although there is magic at a summit where everything is down – but just to be amongst them. It is not only their timeless grandeur, which is awesome, but also the perspective one gains from recognition of one's own ephemerality.

Back at Porton, they had a new job for me with the grand title of Head, Planning and Reporting Section where, again, I was to do Operational Research. Also grand, was that I was promoted to Principle Scientific Officer.

Peggy was still enjoying her haematology in Salisbury Infirmary and had made many friends. Nora Lane was still with us at Hillview Road. Carolyn was at Leadenhall School in the Cathedral Close.

Our finances had improved a lot and I wondered about getting a car again – I'd got used to having one in Germany. The trouble would be finding somewhere to keep it since Ted's friend's garage was no longer available – parking in the street was not an option since in those days side and rear lights had to be left on overnight.

Across the road from us was Jung's Garage – Mr Jung had graduated from manufacturing sausages to repairing cars. Peggy went in hoping to get some information on private garages nearby. Mr Jung said that garages to rent were "as rare as ant's teeth" but he would be able to do something for us. Peggy said he had a fantastic car in there that he probably wanted to sell us. She said I must go and see it but, ". . . for heaven sake don't buy it".

The car was a Rolls Royce that had belonged to King Zog of Albania. It was impressive – it even still had a half-full bottle of Johnny Walker Black Label in the cocktail cabinet . . . but, four miles to the gallon of rationed petrol? He offered it to me for two hundred pounds with free garaging; however, what had caught my eye was the Humber shooting brake next to it in pristine condition. Big mistake: I bought it and free garaging for the same price. The mistake was that the Humber – it was the model with a wooden body and huge tyres similar to that used by Montgomery in the Western Desert – had a thirst almost as demanding as the Rolls'.

Compounding the error, we heard a few years later that the Rolls, part of the estate of Mr Jung deceased, had been sold at auction for a fortune.

We drove carefully to Lynmouth in Devonshire on holiday and got back without running out of petrol coupons. Jung welcomed us with the information that he had a customer for the car and would give us four hundred pounds for it – I knew prices of cars were rocketing but this was remarkable. I was glad of the opportunity to get rid of the Humber and I couldn't resist a hundred percent return for a few weeks' investment. I said four-hundred-and-fifty pounds and he agreed. He then sold me a Vauxhall drophead coupé with a body by Martin Walter – who also built bodies for Rolls Royce – for two-hundred-and-fifty. It had probably been two hundred before the deal, but I wasn't grumbling, particularly as that day petrol rationing ended.

As she settled back in the comfortable leather seat on our first trip in the car, Peggy said, "From bicycles to this in three years. Not bad." She was looking at me strangely, and went on, "But we mustn't measure progress by the luxury level of our cars, d'you think, Ken?"

I wrote quite a bit in my diary that night about her remark, which had troubled me. At the time I said I didn't think of cars that way: I just liked cars. She said she did too and nestled into her seat. "I like this one," she said, stroking the padded dashboard. She leaned over and kissed me. "And this one."

We were not allowed more than a few months to settle; the Scientific Advisor to the Army Council, Dr Owen Wansbrough-Jones, saw to that. He rang: could I drop in to see him next time I was in Town. No urgency, he would just like a chat. I went the next day.

It turned out the Americans wanted to set up an *Operations* Research Group – they seemed to regard our adjective as a bit toffee-nosed – in their Army Chemical Corps headquarters at Edgewood Arsenal, near Baltimore, Maryland. They wondered if we had someone with experience in this field who could advise. All expenses paid, of course.

It would be no great change of job for me since Edgewood was the American Porton and I would be concerned with setting up a group like my own. Unlike Porton, the biological warfare side was not on the same site as the chemical, but some eighty miles away at Fort Detrick, in Frederick, Maryland. The new group would be concerned also with the work there. A friend of mine, Ken Calder, a mathematician from Porton, was stationed at Detrick – how great a friend I was to find out later.

I suppose I had the choice whether to go or not, but ambition drove me to the affirmative: in my experience, it wasn't those that sat on their butts in laboratories that got anywhere in the Civil Service. Peggy agreed. She said that when I went away it was like hitting her head with a hammer, it was so nice when it stopped.

I had an extraordinary trip to USA. I flew out – leaving Peggy and Carolyn to food rationing – in a Douglas DC-4 of the US Military Airlift Command, my first flight across the Atlantic. Fuelling stops were at Prestwick in Scotland, Reykjavik in Iceland, Goose Bay in Labrador, and we landed in Washington, DC after eighteen hours flying time – six years later the Comet 4 did the trip non-stop in a little over six hours.

I was travelling under American orders, of which I had fifty copies. I was to hand one out to anyone who doubted I was at two-star General level and entitled to VIP treatment – I gathered later that such temporary elevation was a standard form of flattery for visiting firemen. I did my best to look old enough and dignified enough to deserve such respect. The snag was I was credited with the most senior rank aboard and, at each stop, everybody had to remain seated while I was escorted off to take the salute of a welcoming party.

In Washington, DC, I learned that a recruiting team, led by Professor Albert Noyes – scientific advisor to the General commanding the Chemical Corps – was touring Universities in the States and Canada collecting staff for the new group. I caught up with them at Stanford University in Palo Alto, California. The journey from there included a stretch on the Canadian Pacific Railway through the Rocky Mountains. Superb. I determined Peggy must experience it.

The Canadians had an Experimental Station for field trials with Chemical warfare agents at Suffield, near Medicine Hat in Alberta. We stayed there a couple of days and then went east to visit more colleges. Back in the United States again, the last university we visited was Columbia in New York, where Albert Noyes had his chair. I thought New York City incredibly dirty. People seemed to have no civic pride. They would just throw their rubbish on the sidewalk, be it a hamburger wrapping, a cigarette package, a newspaper or a dead cat . . . I didn't suspect that, come the sixties, London would get to be the same way. As usual, we were ten years or so behind the States in acquiring things or habits, good or bad. However, I enjoyed New York, and again determined Peggy and I must visit it together. While I was there, I visited The Embers and other centres of excellence for jazz and, in the Museum of Modern Art, I put my name down in a large book as a bid to be a crew member for a space shot to the moon. I thought it a joke, an Americanism. I didn't know that the first space shot was already in preparation at White Sands, New Mexico, using a V2 rocket with four monkeys aboard. It was kept quiet for fear of reaction from animal lovers. It was secretly launched a year later, at the end of 1951. The passengers were landed safely having been up eighty-five miles.

The OR Group was successfully launched at Edgewood, and I was persuaded to stay with it a few months before returning to England.

Back home, Peggy and I decided it was time, with our continuing interest in a life of variety, to go up-market a little in our housing. But we didn't get far:

"Look, Ken, we are putting on you a bit, I know, but the Americans want you to go out again as civilian head of the group you started." Wansbrough-Jones, of course: I felt sure I was to be sent merely as a diplomatic pawn, although I couldn't imagine to what strategic end. We were lunching at Wansbrough's club in Pall Mall, the Oxford and Cambridge. I was about to say that under no circumstances was I going to desert Peggy again, when he forestalled me:

"You'd be going under our banner, for two years, with your family." He added – unnecessarily, since on his first words I'd already visualized taking Peggy and Carolyn to New York and to the Rockies – "I can assure you, Ken, it won't do you any harm."

CHAPTER SEVEN

August 1992 came in on the crest of a heat wave soon to break. Barbara, Peggy's sister, who lived near Wood Green in the New Forest, came to tea in the garden and helped us clear the lawn of eviscerated walnut shells the squirrels had discarded. It was three years since Douglas, her husband, had died and she had coped well living alone in her bungalow set in five acres of groomed woodland. She stayed to dinner and, with the cheese, we tried for the first time a Tokay Pinot Gris from Alsace – it went very well with the Jarlsberg, Barbara's favourite cheese.

Peggy tried a little of the wine, although she had given up alcohol saying she was confused enough without it. She had a discerning palate for wine and enjoyed her few sips of the Alsace. Her appetite had not suffered since her fall in the garden: her cracked jawbone made chewing a little difficult, but had otherwise given her surprisingly little trouble. A week or so later, when her bruised face and black eye had paled to a sickly greenish-yellow, she declared herself repaired.

I worried a lot about Peggy considering herself confused; she seemed sharp enough to me. True, she had some difficulty handling and arranging things, with locking and unlocking doors, and she didn't react quickly enough to save herself falling when she slipped or tripped, but it seemed to me that most people of our age had such problems. Bunty, next door, had been that way for years; now she was confused, and obviously so. Peggy wasn't at all like that.

Our GP pulled and twisted Peggy's arm, and got her to walk across the room looking for signs of Parkinsonism I imagined – and took a lot of trouble testing her short-term memory. He said there was nothing to worry about. He did add, "Drop in and see me again in three months, or before if there's any change – but not with a broken bone, eh, Mrs James?"

Within three weeks there was a change: Peggy had nightmares. She woke up several times a night shouting, and obviously very frightened, although she couldn't remember the reason.

To catch up on our sleep, we took to having a nap after lunch when Peggy slept peacefully; but the nightly dreams got worse – perhaps due to her having less need for deep sleep. We gave up napping in the daytime, but the lack of sleep soon affected us – Peggy became morose and I got bad tempered and liable to fly off the handle at her moodiness. The doctor gave her diazepam, which even in a small dose had a startling effect – her shouting out of the dream state became screaming, and she remained no more than semi-conscious for most of the next day. We didn't repeat the experiment, and over the next few weeks the nightmares, of their own accord, became milder and less frequent – or perhaps Peggy just got used to them.

Apart from the dreams, which were now less trouble, and the slight handling and arranging difficulties, which weren't, Peggy seemed in good health. On days we didn't get a reasonable walk, we would usually 'do the steps' . . .

Leading from the Old Blandford Road, nearby, to Bouverie Avenue on Harnham Hill, was a short cut, a flight of one hundred and seventeen steps. We used these for exercise, more particularly in the autumn when we felt we should get ourselves into shape for skiing. Peggy could go up and down the steps a couple of times non-stop at a cracking pace with no sign of respiratory distress – and leave me gasping.

She hadn't mentioned mental confusion again and certainly she showed no evidence of it. I did a little test when we had friends staying, Ian and Mary Pearce, we had known since we first learned to ski cross-country on a Ramblers holiday in Switzerland.

Ian and I were liable at any time to break out from ordinary conversation into the realms of pop philosophy. We were discussing free will and I drew Peggy in. She was always reluctant to join in such talk; essentially practical, she regarded as a waste of time discussion from which there could be no useful result – but she had always had input if pressed. I remember once the question of free will came into a discussion with her clerical brother-in-law, Peter. She asked him how you could have a God who knew all that would happen, when we have free will to alter it. Peter nearly fell into the trap, but choked on his first word and smiled beatifically.

On this occasion, Ian said something like, "It's easy to believe in free will if you're a dualist."

"Descartes style," I said, " 'Self' watching 'Mind' at work?"

Peggy said, "Like watching TV? What is this 'Self', a sort of soul? And where does it sit to watch?"

"You'd have to ask Descartes. I'm not a dualist."

To Ian, she said, "Do you think 'Self' is a brain function?"

Ian looked at me, "I suppose we do."

"So, we do what the brain – which is 'Self' – decides. All mechanical; no free will," she said, already looking bored with the discussion as though this were all childishly obvious and not worth discussing. I couldn't let her get away with that pat decision. I said, ponderously:

"Being mechanical doesn't make your will unfree if you are the machine. To have free will is to do what you decide you want to do. Your composite 'Brain-Self' having gone through its mechanistic processes acts on the outcome, doing what it then 'wants' to do. And so, in that sense, it has free will and, since it is you, so do you."

But she had the last word:

"That's not a general argument, you've just given one definition of free will. Whether or not we actually have free will, whatever that is, it feels free and that's what matters."

Ian, tactful as usual, changed the subject:

"Perhaps we've evolved with too much brain. Great thoughts don't make for happiness. We tear ourselves to pieces searching the unknown for meaning."

I agreed: "Plenty of geniuses go mad in the search – Schopenhaur, Göedel . . ."

"Idiots go mad too," Peggy said. "In any case, less brain power would merely lower the level of the unknown and we'd still worry about it.

She walked to the kitchen and came back with a glass, "My great free thought is that I'd like to try a little of the wine."

I thought perhaps she less confused than we were.

WE CROSSED the Atlantic on Cunard's *Parthia.* It was good to escape food rationing still with us in 1951 – Peggy said the shipboard food was even better than we'd enjoyed in Germany. Our two major accomplishments on board were: I beat the captain at deck tennis; and Peggy won twenty pounds on the ship's lottery, guessing the daily mileage.

Washington DC was a sultry, Southern, overgrown village in those days: it was still self-conscious and hadn't yet decided it was the central keeper of the world's ethics – it was still some years from recognising that growth of a world power needed world soil well fertilised with its own brand of ethics. But then, as now, it was a steam bath, and we were glad, after checking in with the Embassy, to escape to Edgewood, Maryland – hot, but with less steam.

We had been allocated a flat in Edgewood – known as a Wherry apartment, but we lived in the Officers Mess on the Post for a few days while we got the place ready for habitation. Furniture turned out to be no problem. Two members of the OR team, Drs. Bert Reynolds and Wendell Weber, friends from my earlier days with the group, produced almost all we needed – they had both recently married and four sets of generous parents had overstocked them with furniture.

The natives were friendly and helpful and we soon felt very much part of the community – mostly army families – and, since my pay was made up to American standards, we could live well. Peggy soon had many friends and quite obviously enjoyed the life. Carolyn, now nine years old, went to school on the Post and in a few days had a marked American accent. She, too, enjoyed the new environment and was particularly intrigued by the variety of cultures around her. She came home one day still wide eyed from an encounter:

"Mummy," she said, "is it true that if you jump over people you stunt their growth?"

In the gym, she had jumped over a girl lying on the floor who had immediately gone into a screaming frenzy calling for Carolyn to jump back over her. Carolyn had done that and the girl smiled happily and explained. Her mother was Turkish and had passed on to her the ancient belief.

Getting back to work with the OR team was exciting – it comprised mostly young PhDs, all bubbling with intelligence.

A car was essential, public transport being almost non-existent. Wendell Weber took us to a local dealer and we bought what seemed to us an enormous car, a three-and-a-half 'liter' Mercury sedan – new, it cost less than a Hillman Minx at home. It gave a feather-bed ride.

We lived an American life: we would drive out to the local diner for breakfast on Sunday mornings and eat a stack of waffles with maple syrup and probably an egg fried 'sunny-side-up'; we would go with friends in the evening to Gabler's Shore on Chesapeake Bay and feast on crabs and ice-cold Schlitz Blue Ribbon beer – later we bought an outboard motor, went crabbing in a hired boat, and cooked our own catch. Weekends, we would travel around the country, into Pennsylvania, to the Atlantic coast, as well as around Maryland. We often spent weekends with Ken and Rene Calder in Frederick, our friends from Porton who had made up their minds to make US their home. Ken was a brilliant mathematician – why does that adjective seem so naturally to attach itself to mathematicians? Is it that they seem like stars to ordinary planetary folk? Anyhow, Ken shone through his modesty but said that as an 'ex-pat.' there was no hope of advance in his career in the US service and so they were preparing to become American citizens.

Carolyn was still keen on riding, and she would go off at weekends with friends who had ponies. It was her riding that introduced us to TV. In England, we had resisted the call of the box, but when Carolyn fell off her mount and her friend's parents carried her into the apartment, she looked up at me, eyes starry with tears, and said:

"Wouldn't a television set be nice for a little girl with a broken arm, Daddy."

Well, what can you say?

Hindsight, that crystal ball in reverse, is a fraud. You can look back and recognize that some trivial occurrence led to a momentous event; but it's a fraud, because, obviously, everything leads to something else and, in the extreme, our very existence stems from that moment back in cosmic time when, somehow, compounds came together to form a self-replicating molecule and seeded the moon surface of Earth with life. Nevertheless, it is obvious to me that Carolyn's plea for a TV was an antecedent by many years to a new phase in our lives. We went to Sears and Roebuck, that great American institution, to buy the TV. It was two hours before I got to see the sets – we'd had to walk through the tool section to get to them and I was captivated, bewitched, lost. There were power tools for home use which you would only see in a professional workshop in England – and ridiculously cheap by our standards. When, eventually, I dug Peggy and Carolyn out of the coffee shop, where they'd gone out of sheer boredom, we went to choose Carolyn's TV; but I was already the proud owner of a large bench saw, a planer, a thicknesser, a drill-press, a bandsaw . . . all man-sized.

I was allowed to partition off a corner of the communal basement in the Wherry apartment and set up a workshop. Thereafter, the obsession I had always had for making things could be given full rein.

In the summer of 1952 I had to go out on a project to Dugway Proving Ground near Salt Lake City in Utah where chemical and biological warfare field tests were done. I thought we might drive out and take a holiday to follow, camping in the Rockies. Bert and Wendell, who were also on the Proving-Ground job, said they'd drive in convoy with us in Bert's new Lincoln. My diary was neglected on the trip but I remember it as a highlight in our lives. Oddly, it was a number of minor incidents that became part of our family stock of anecdote. We took a week driving out with the intention of staying overnight in motels, but one night we slept out under the stars in our sleeping bags in the desert. All was well until Wendell mentioned that rattlesnakes liked to creep into the warmth of a sleeping bag at night. Peggy and Carolyn spent the night in the car – I kept my head tightly cocooned in the bag.

Later, having pitched our tent for the first time in the mountains, I'd had great difficulty lighting a fire following a heavy shower.

Carolyn was in charge of making tea and she fetched a saucepan of water from the mountain stream nearby and I said:

"Okay, Carolyn, put it on the fire."

She did, with great glee, pouring from a height.

We also recall missing Carolyn while we were watching a Hopi Indian war dance outside our hotel on the South rim of the Grand Canyon – she had joined in the dance. And, we ate buffalo steaks under the eyes of the great stone presidents at the Mount Rushmore National Memorial in South Dakota.

We did a similar trip a year later taking Peggy's younger sister, Evelyn, who had come to the US for her summer holiday from school where she taught mathematics. Again, a fine holiday. Just one hiccup: we were often above ten thousand feet when, unusually, Peggy got very breathless and, on our last night in the mountains, she had a temperature and coughed a lot. She was all right in the morning but we dropped in on a doctor in Denver the next day. He took her temperature – which was normal – prodded and tapped and listened and said there was nothing to worry about, altitude did that sort of thing to people.

Three weeks later Peggy was in hospital in Baltimore with advanced pulmonary tuberculosis.

CHAPTER EIGHT

Autumn was watery in 1992 when we arrived for a champagne welcome at Stroat House in Gloucestershire for lunch with Mary and Geoffrey Watts. The lamb was delicious and was not responsible for my losing a front tooth somewhere in the sauce – it had been loose for months. We talked books with Mary, Europe and the stock market with Geoffrey and life-in-general with them both. Even as we chatted, we noticed with half an eye on Ceefax, silent on the TV screen, that the pound was in free fall. Even so, we got dewy eyed over Mary pictured in her wedding dress, and laughed at me in my Moss Bros. topper. Peggy was sparklingly humorous, and I whistled as I spoke. We stayed overnight.

On the way home the next day Peggy seemed dull, introspective, and took no interest in the radio report that John Major was about to take us out of ERM – base rates had gone up two percent and then a further three, unprecedented, in an attempt to support the ailing pound. We took a new route home and, with Peggy map reading, missed the way near Chippenham. I lost my temper and shouted at her. At home, I suggested she might like to write a thank-you note to Mary. She dithered, looking at me as though she didn't know what I was talking about. I blew my top again. I flounced out into the library, slumped into a chair and asked myself what the hell was wrong with me.

But I knew: I couldn't bear to see the effect of age on Peggy. There was no marked physical deterioration – her skin was smooth and clear and she was fit – rather, it was the snicks in the cutting edge of her intelligence, the veil over her brilliance. I wanted her up on her pedestal where I had found her half a century earlier. Peggy, as usual, was forgiving within the hour; John Major had us out of the ERM; and the Chancellor had backtracked a lot on the base-rate rise.

The next day, I dropped in to see the dentist about the mile-wide gap in my top teeth. With me resigned to having entered the toothless age, we drove to London, Teddington, to help Carolyn in her new flat. She was effervescent, delighted with the place, or perhaps more with the idea of having it. Peg and I mounted a wall mirror, hung some pictures, fixed up the TV, video and hi-fi, and put up a shelf. We pushed furniture around, tidied up generally. During all this, Peggy was fine, and Carolyn commented:

"Mummy seems better now. I have been worried about her."

And Peggy was better, but it didn't last. We drove back to Salisbury and that night she went to bed happy. But she woke up an hour later, terrified. Thereafter, nightmares and sleepless nights were increasingly the routine and she was markedly confused while dressing.

I felt I should get professional advice, but I was torn – the last time we had referred to the doctor we had suffered the sleeping-pill fiasco. On the other hand, lack of sleep was certainly changing my demeanour – unusually, I worried over trivial details. One thought, perhaps not in the trivial category, niggled me: for her glaucoma, Peggy had been prescribed two drugs. Timoptol was one, a beta-blocker. I must find out about possible side effects. The other one was pilocarpine, which I thought had cholinergic activity, increasing the production of the brain messenger, acetylcholine – although, from what I'd read, that might be a good thing in an ageing brain. I wondered about the possibility of an upset in the essential balance of that 'neurotransmitter' with others, perhaps giving rise to nightmares and other mental disturbances. I checked with my diary and found that the bad dreams had started around the time Peggy had first used pilocarpine. Also, the morning confusion occurred shortly after she applied her drops. Coincidences probably, but in my sensitive state the worry amounted to an obsession. I would ask the specialist. We were seeing him in a few days for him to check the results of the laser treatment on Peg's eye.

At the consultation, the specialist said the laser treatment had been successful and pressure in the eye was well down. As for the side effects of the drugs, he said pilocarpine was above suspicion –

it had been in use since 1875 and we certainly would have discovered by now any such undesirable properties. He took Peggy off Timoptol, however, and prescribed Betoptic instead to accompany the pilocarpine.

Nightmares and confusion didn't go away.

During December, Peggy seemed to lose interest in cooking – at least, she prepared only the simplest of meals rather than the *haute cuisine* we usually enjoyed. I said one day that if she'd show me how to do a fillet steak royale, I'd cook dinner. She said, "Oh, that would be lovely, Ken, would you? I'm so bored with cooking."

She helped, or tried – she chopped the mushrooms and flushed them down the sink disposal. I spent the next few days studying beginners cook books.

We had Mary Watts stay overnight just before Christmas and she told me that Peggy had confided in her that I never did anything in the house. She went on: "When I pointed out that you were in the kitchen cooking dinner, she wept. Is she ill, Ken? I thought she was a bit vague last night, not her usual humorous self."

Carolyn joined us for Christmas. On Christmas Day I took Peggy's cook's knife in hand and played chef. I cooked a lunch, light and expensive and asked Peggy to put the dish in the warming drawer while I fiddled with the sauce. She turned on the grill and my offering was cremated.

I told myself that it was time to stop clutching at straws. Peggy was ill and I must get proper advice. I talked to her about it and we agreed we'd make a date to see the doctor immediately after Christmas.

We had watercress soup and salad for lunch, but pheasant for dinner – to an Escoffier recipe, of course – with a woodcock stuffing using mushrooms instead of truffles and with all the befores and afters.

We enjoyed Christmas and there were no more lapses of any consequence on Peggy's part; nevertheless, a shadow had formed in my mind among grim memories, forty years old, of Peggy's illness in the States.

SITTING IN a soft chair, my coffee cold on a side table in a Baltimore hospital, I was given kindly smiles by one or other of several white-coated doctors huddled learnedly on the far side of the room in front of a screen illuminating X-ray plates of Peggy's shadowy interior.

My thoughts on that day in 1953, centred on the fact that tuberculosis was the world's greatest infectious killer and probably had been since long before the Ancient Egyptians built pyramids to house some of its victims. It was killing five million people a year across the modern world. Many cures had been attempted: herbs and kindness by the Ancient Greeks; centuries of magic transference of evil spirits; later, in more enlightened times, strapping a live fish to the chest, or feeding the patient with the blood of an executed criminal. Chemotherapy had included ingestion of mercury, copper, gold or even cyanide. Less obviously dangerous, for the patient anyway, was the process, much in vogue in the eighteenth century, of tucking up the patient in bed with a wet nurse to suckle her milk. More clinical, if less exciting, was the twentieth-century practice of long bed-rest, breathing freezing air in the Swiss mountains, which seemed no more successful. I didn't know whether there was any more enlightened treatment available, and I was tense with abject pessimism, my stomach in a knot. I was, however, jumping the gun. The doctor had only said so far that tuberculosis was one possibility. The doctors in conference over the X-rays were doubtless reviewing possibilities. My dejection wasn't improved by thoughts of an alternative.

The conference broke up, the screen was turned off and the senior doctor came over and sat in the chair next to mine.

He was solicitous. "You can rest assured, your wife hasn't got cancer." He went on to say they were pretty certain Peggy had tuberculosis, but we would have to await the results from cultures to be sure. He then explained that tuberculosis was no longer the horrifying disease it once was; antibiotics had been discovered which were effective against the tubercle bacillus. When he felt sure he had lulled me into a hopeful frame of mind he took me over to the screen and switched it on. I was immediately horrified. There was a blob the size of a walnut high in the left lung and a lot of tiny patches lower down. He waved his hand extravagantly over the little ones and said, "Bed rest and antibiotics and we'll get rid of those in no time at all". He turned off the viewing frame.

Hesitantly, I asked about the big blob and launched him into another flood of kindly equivocation – a cheesy mass of dead cells . . . tubercles for the bugs to hide in . . . doing no harm in there . . . and so on. He was vague, too, when I asked how long Peggy would need bed rest. He took his time arriving at, "A few months, I'm afraid." He told me I had better get X-rayed myself since I had been so much in contact.

Peggy was moved to a sanatorium in Towson, outside Baltimore, and I was summoned to discuss finances. The charges were a shock. Some careful sums showed that with all belts tightened we could just manage, but it was a great relief later to get a letter of condolence from the then Director in the London office saying, "Of course, we'll be able to meet all reasonable medical expenses."

Peggy had a pleasant room, a comfortable bed, and a soft armchair for me – they advised against Carolyn visiting. The contiguous bathroom was shared with the next bedroom, occupied, Peggy told me, by Mary-Frances, a ravishing brunette I was to keep my lecherous eyes off.

Peggy was introduced immediately to daily injections of streptomycin. I learned that a Nobel Prize had gone to its discoverer, Selman Waksman, the previous year, and I injected a mental 'thank you' into a morphic field. I learned too that another drug, related to aspirin and hidden under an acronymic cloak, PAS, was actually the first success in the field of tuberculosis cures. It was constructed rather than discovered by Jorgen Lehman who didn't get a lot of praise. I added my telepathic pennyworth, since Peggy had PAS in conjunction with streptomycin to inhibit the emergence of resistant strains of the tubercle bacillus. PAS had no serious side effects but huge doses were necessary. Peggy was to have her dose increased until she showed signs of 'gastrointestinal upset'. It wasn't long before she was swallowing dozens of tablets a day. The nurses called her The Ostrich – "Guess she could eat nails," said one.

Peggy rallied quickly, and after a couple of weeks she was looking healthy and scarcely coughing at all. One day when I went in she was radiant: "The doctor says I'm no longer infectious and you can kiss me." I did, with the fervour of a desert traveller reaching water at an oasis. A nurse came in, giggled, apologised and went out. She then knocked and poked her head round the door again. "You can lock the door, if you want," she said, winked and left. We wanted, and did.

Peggy was obviously doing well, we were full of hope and optimism and life was not at all unpleasant. I visited almost every evening. First, I would bring her up to date with Carolyn's sayings and doings. We would then watch TV – commercial broadcasting was new to us, and we were astounded while watching the Coronation of Queen Elizabeth when, as the Archbishop lowered the crown on to the Queen's head, just as it was about to make contact, the picture cut to a logo showing a crown and the invitation to 'Drink Crown Cola'. We played Scrabble, read our books, chatted, planned our future, sometimes locked the door, and generally acted like a married couple at home.

Carolyn was wonderful through all this. She would come home from school, we'd have dinner together, I would deliver her to one of our friends for the evening and collect her again when I got back from Towson. I'd tell her the news of Peggy as a bedtime story. Weekends, we would spend the days together before I went off to the sanatorium for the evening. She never once complained, but I didn't think it was much of a life for her.

Suddenly it all changed.

Ken Calder, our English friend in Frederick, rang me to ask whether he and his wife, Rene, could 'visit with Peggy' – he was already Americanized. I told him she was now non-infectious and I was sure she'd be delighted to see them. He asked whether I could be there too, they had something to discuss. The 'something' was that they wanted Carolyn to go to live with them for the duration of Peggy's incarceration. Peggy wept and I had to blow my nose.

I asked Carolyn that evening whether she would like to go – I knew she was fond of Rene and Ken. She said she wasn't sure, and went quiet. At bedtime she tore out my heart. She said, "I don't see Mummy any more and now I shall be losing you."

When I'd recovered, I explained that the school holidays would be a difficult time for us and that I would have to employ a stranger to look after her during the day. That made little impression. However, when I said that were she to go to Frederick I would come to see her every weekend, she threw her arms around me and said that was deep-dish apple pie.

It all worked out very well. Carolyn had only one complaint. She said that when she was naughty 'Uncle Ken' sent her into the garden to clear sticks from the lawn. I said I thought that would be preferable to a clip round the ear. She thought that was funny and didn't complain any more.

Soon after Carolyn moved out, I had a call from the Embassy in Washington DC. Dr Neville Creasey from Porton was being posted to Edgewood on an exchange, and they wanted to know whether I could recommend anywhere suitable for him to stay for six months. I knew Neville well and liked him. I said he could stay with me although I couldn't commit myself for the full time since I didn't know when my wife would be returning.

Neville moved in a couple of weeks later and we agreed that I would do the cooking and he the washing up – once on a visit to the sanatorium he told Peggy he had never imagined anyone could use so many saucepans making a sandwich.

At one stage my routine changed. I was bidden to join a Study Group under Professor E.O.Lawrence – Nobel Prize winner for his invention of the cyclotron – to assess the military effectiveness of atomic compared with biological and chemical weapons. We were closeted in the Chiefs' of Staff inner sanctum of the Pentagon, beyond the ultra-violet security beams – penetrated previously by only one Englishman, I was told, the then General, Montgomery. I stayed in a hotel in Washington for the period, but I could still quite easily get to Towson each evening.

Life went on smoothly in the sanatorium, but not uneventfully. One night, someone went round the bedrooms, apparently avoiding all the nurses, and slashed with a razor the pillows on the beds of sleeping patients. Peggy said she had woken up choking in a snowstorm of feathers. One old lady said she saw the man that did it and claimed it was Mr Schluter, one of the inmates. It so happened that Mr Schluter, sixty-ish, who had an inoperable cancer as well as a contained pulmonary tuberculosis, had been allowed out that night on one of his periodic jags and arrived back in the early hours after the slashing had been discovered. Mr Schluter was proud of his exploits on his free nights. He would show pictures of himself in a

Baltimore nightclub surrounded by scantily clad girls and at least one on his lap. He was not short of cash, and boasted you could get anything you wanted in Baltimore.

The slasher was discovered a few days later, a patient caught in the act of carving up his own mattress. He was removed for treatment to a more restrictive establishment.

On another evening, at Peggy's suppertime, we were each presented with lobster thermidor and champagne. It was courtesy of Peggy's neighbour, Mary-Frances, who was nearing the end of her term in the sanatorium and had been permitted an evening out with an ex-boyfriend, president of a large hotel chain, and rich. She had insisted he bought lobster and champagne for all her friends in the sanatorium. She told Peggy he had complained it was the most expensive bit of tail he'd ever had, but worth it.

"Well, y'know, honey," she said to Peggy, "Ah've bin locked in this calaboose since George Washington chopped down that cherry tree."

At six months, after one of Peggy's regular X-ray sessions, the doctor called me into his office and said, "She's going to be here at least another three months, but don't worry, we'll get there".

It was discouraging news, but the period so far seemed to have passed so quickly that another three months or so was not daunting.

At nine months I was called to the office again. This time there was no soft optimistic talk. The cavity was enlarging – it was the first time I'd heard the blob called a cavity. There was a choice. There were new antibiotics available – he mentioned isoniazid – which might deal with the problem. It didn't work on everyone and in any case we were talking of another long period, perhaps a year. The alternative was an operation, a lung resection, taking out the nasty bit.

I asked what, from the safety point of view, he would recommend.

"The operation," he said. "Positive solution, and life can start again for you both."

I wanted to ask what the percentage success was, but all I could manage was: "Is there a lot of experience in this procedure?"

He surprised me, saying, "We have the surgeon here who did the first one in this country, and he has done a great many since. He'd like to talk to you."

I needed little convincing. The disappointment with the long-term antibiotic treatment so far, which had seemed so promising, left me with little confidence in a new and relatively untried agent. The surgeon went into great detail about the operation and, heroic as it seemed to me in my inexperience, he impressed me with his candour about things that could go wrong and the way in which he would deal with such emergencies.

"I guess y'all'd like to discuss it with your lady?" he said.

Peggy had no doubts: "Let's get it over with, Ken, dear."

Back in the Baltimore hospital, Peggy had been in the theatre for four hours. I was in a long, arid hallway, occasionally sitting, more often pacing up and down. I was conjuring up mental images based on the surgeons talk of Peggy being cut almost in half, starting at the back of her neck, down and round under her left breast to the breast-bone, and of pieces being sawn out of her ribs to reduce the size of the rib cage for the smaller lung volume. Visualizing the bloody scene reminded me of the unexpected request from the hospital to either pay for gallons of blood from the blood bank or arrange replacement. I was touched that, in the event, every member of my OR Group at Edgewood volunteered to be drained.

I'd given up smoking some months before, and now the hallway echoed to my plodding back and forth wishing for the comfort of my old briar pipe. I occasionally broke the rhythm by walking along to the coffee shop. This meant passing a cigarette machine, which became more imposing and attractive each time I passed. For five hours I made do with coffee, but at six I gave in and put my money in the slot. I was opening the package just as the surgeon came out to talk to me.

He smiled as he walked towards me and I almost collapsed with relief. He said something like, "It all went very well, Dr James," – the title was the safety formula applied to anyone who seemed educated, as, apparently, anyone with an English 'accent' did. "Absolutely nothing to worry about. She's in recovery now and we'll be taking her upstairs in an hour or so. You'd better get home for dinner and a good night's sleep. Come and see her in the morning."

"I would like to see her before I go."

"She's under sedation and will be asleep for hours. We'll call you if there's any difficulty, but I'm sure it won't be necessary."

I dropped the cigarettes into a bin.

Ten days later Peggy was back in the sanatorium. A couple of weeks after that we went to dinner together at a local restaurant. It is difficult to express the delight of that dinner. I suppose I knew at the time what we ate, but my diary is blank for that night, of all nights, and memory only records euphoric haze. The following day we discussed with the doctor our possible date of departure. There was a boat leaving New York in three weeks, which had vacancies. Should we book? He thought Peggy would be all right to leave before then; but it might be better to take a holiday first and take a later boat, just so there would be no last minute rush.

A week later I had a call around midnight. Could I come to the sanatorium at once?

CHAPTER NINE

New Year's Day 1993 dawned to reveal swans swimming lazily in our garden in Salisbury, literally – the River Avon was in flood. One of the swans was black – doubtless an escapee – but there was no hint of racism. As Carolyn left for London she said she thought Peggy had been in good form over the holiday. I thought so too. I felt I had over-reacted to the lunch incineration, which was of course something anyone might have done. Certainly Peggy had been happy. We discussed again whether we should see the doctor but concluded we had nothing to add to our previous tale – there seemed little point in being told again we were getting old. We went out and bought a new hi-fi instead – our first with a CD player.

Until the Christmas break I had spent a lot of time on the Escoffier biography. Was Peggy's apparent improvement due to my spending more time with her? I decided that with hundred-and-twenty-thousand words written I could call the book done – the publisher was asking for it. I wrote the finale, got on with revision, reading list, glossary and the rest, mostly in the mornings before the larks had finished breakfast. Early March I sent off the ms.

Carolyn came down for a few days over her birthday in March – her fiftieth. She had taken up an old hobby again, painting, and did a fine canvas of a vase of daffodils, professionally modern. She commented that Peggy's improved demeanour had remained unchanged since Christmas. She didn't know that at night Peggy had been increasingly restive.

One morning in May I had one of my mad turns, sparked simply by Peggy's recurring insistence on trying to put in her eye drops several times during the night – they were not due until morning. She ranted at me for hiding the ampoules, which I hadn't, and, childishly, I ranted back. When I flew off the handle, I had a strange sensation of standing by staring in helpless amazement at myself out of control, going round the bend – rather as Peggy had said about dualism, like watching TV.

It was also the day Kenneth Clarke replaced Norman Lamont as Chancellor of the Exchequer. I didn't think that would affect our petty finances particularly. More chance of that from the visit of Mr Jeremy Wring of the J.Rothschild Partnership. He came to coffee to tell us we were paying too much income tax, and that Carolyn would be destitute by the time she'd paid inheritance tax on the pittance we'd be leaving her, or something like that. I had invited him to come on the recommendation of our accountant. Mr Wring had some interesting suggestions, and there was no hint in our pleasant chat that he had made an abiding entry into our lives. He did tell us he and his wife ran a nursing home in Salisbury but, despite such experience, he seemed not to notice anything strange in Peggy's behaviour – there was, indeed, little of it to observe. It was encouraging that she could still, and did, make that extra effort when other people were around. Her system was based on saying little, but pithily; she was an experienced hostess and knew how to say just enough to keep conversation flowing.

In June we went to Guernsey on holiday with Peggy's sister, Barbara – her youngest son, Michael, a bank manager on the island, lent us his house and a car while he took his family to Portugal for a holiday.

I think Barbara noticed for the first time that Peggy was no longer great shakes in the kitchen. However, despite her reluctance in that department, Peggy showed little confusion during the day and slept well every night. It was a good holiday and seemed to have a lasting beneficial effect on Peggy.

Later that month we went to Hereford for the wedding of Katherine Wood, daughter of Peggy's sister, Evelyn. Dad, the Reverend Peter Wood, took the service and as usual his talk comprised an entertaining mixture of Heaven and Earth. The hymns were to tunes I didn't know so I had plenty of time to consider the words – they seemed very deep but not worth the risk of the bends.

Peggy felt faint during the service and sat down, pale and peaky. She clung to my arm on the way out, but recovered in the car and was wonderful at the reception – in a country pub with a pleasant garden – quite her old self.

The next morning, however, she was much more confused than of late and was out of kilter for most of the day. Again, she recovered to near normality. She was nothing if not variable.

The following week we each had a medical check up for the Rothschild insurance. The doctor, chosen by the company, did not know us, and he spent nearly an hour with each of us. It was useful to get an independent check on Peggy – we answered all his questions as accurately as we could although we didn't volunteer anything beyond. He found nothing untoward. We went to dinner at the Three Lions at Stuckton. It was the night our favourite chef lost his temper over some kitchen catastrophe and exploded into the restaurant wielding his great knife under his wife's nose – stressful places, commercial kitchens. It was also Peggy's seventy-sixth birthday.

The restaurant kept an excellent cellar and I had a half-bottle of a fine claret to myself since Peggy no longer drank anything alcoholic. In the past we had taken turns to be abstemious for the drive home, but now it was usual for Peggy to drive back. She did on this occasion, but neither of us enjoyed the ride. Peggy had been driving since hansom cabs had horses, and was good, but this time she had my brake foot bending the steel floor. It wasn't exactly a fear reaction, resulting more from a return of an image I hadn't conjured up for years in waking hours of Peggy-One lying dead in the road, and which did a slow fade into that of Peggy-Two looking similar in the sanatorium in Maryland.

When we got home Peggy collapsed in tears, and said she didn't want to drive again. She saved my having to make the suggestion.

IT WAS one o'clock on a sultry late-summer night of 1954 when, having ignored all speed limits, I arrived in a cold sweat at the sanatorium in Towson. A nurse took me to see Peggy. She looked dead, lying sheet-white on a bed in an oxygen tent. The blood seemed to drain from me, too. Then her lips fluttered slightly as she breathed and I came to life again. The doctor was looking stern.

Peggy had collapsed in the bathroom. The fact that she was still alive was due to the chance circumstance that a night-nurse had just arrived on her rounds. Peggy had a pulmonary embolism, a blood clot in the artery between heart and lungs. She was dosed up with anticoagulant drugs, and the doctor said she stood a good chance of recovery: his doleful tone belied his optimism. Overnight would be critical and a room had been prepared for me.

I didn't sleep. I crept out several times during the night to check with the nurse sitting by Peggy's bed. In the morning, Peggy opened her eyes when I spoke to her, recognized me, and even managed a faint smile. The doctor said she'd probably be all right now, but it would be a long job.

Peggy was in the oxygen tent for a month, but after that, while remaining on drugs, she was able to sit out. On the first occasion, we sat together, clinging closely for some minutes without speaking. Then, as orderlies wheeled off the oxygen bottles, Peggy said quietly, "That wasn't very good, Ken, was it?"

A couple of weeks later, armed with a hypodermic, a case full of drugs, and warned to 'take things easy', we were ready to leave for an autumn holiday in Canada before boarding Cunard's *Scythia* for the trip home – the news was that food rationing had at last come to an end in the UK. We drove to Canada in the Mercury – which we were taking with us to England – first to Quebec and then into the mountains of the Parc des Laurentides. Carolyn, in all her waking moments, scarcely let go of Peggy's hand.

My job on return to Porton in November 1954 was labelled, extravagantly, Assistant Superintendent, Field Service Division. I was charged with setting up an Operational Research Group – overtly this time, the subject had become respectable. My boss, the Superintendent, was Arthur Hill, a nice man, but certainly no optimist. He once said to me when he had a pain in his back, "You know, Ken, when you get to my age every new pain is potentially terminal" – he was forty-five. He had taken over the job from my previous boss and friend at Porton, Edgar Bateman. Edgar had gone down in the Comet that had crashed in India, introducing the world to metal fatigue.

We bought a modern bungalow in Winterslow over the hill from Porton, on a narrow plot several hundred yards long. The garden was chalk downland which managed to support juniper scrub and wild strawberries, but the soil wasn't deep enough to grow a carrot sideways – a good excuse for not doing a lot of gardening. Peggy, in any case, was supposed to be 'taking it easy', although she had no such inclination.

We modified the whole roof space as a workshop to house my American machinery. It was a Heaven to climb to. By the summer we had the place in order and we drove to Austria for a holiday, Ehrwald again. This time we did walk the mountains, and Peggy, despite her depleted lung area, had no difficulty at all.

Back home, looking through the photographs we came to one of Peggy standing on a summit. She clung to me. Her eyes sparkled tears. She said, "It was wonderful, Ken. Just a few months ago I didn't think I was going to make it, much less walk mountains."

One night, as Peggy was driving us home from dinner with friends – it was her turn to have only one glass of wine with dinner – she said casually, "We are settling down a bit, aren't we, Ken?"

"Does it bother you?"

"It bothers me that I'm getting to like it."

"What shall we do about it?"

"I think I'd like to get a job."

"Not the infirmary again, Poomphie. You got tuberculosis last time. Anyhow, getting a job's no solution. I've got a job, yet I'm settling down a bit too."

We didn't pursue the matter, but later I felt I might be ignoring a *cri de coeur*. I, too, was getting to like the comfortable life and, I suppose, I'd been selfishly concerned that with Peggy out at work home comforts would be reduced. The next day in the Porton Mess I was talking to Dan Davis of Physiology when he asked after Peggy – they'd had professional contacts when she was working in the Infirmary. I took an opportunity: I told him Peggy was fed up with being a *hausfrau* and was thinking of getting a job. He called in at my office in the afternoon and said that if Peggy was serious about a job he had one for her. He was doing some research for the Ministry of Health on the microanalysis of blood using a tiny spot on a filter paper. He had just confirmed with the Ministry that he could take on a colleague.

A few days later the postman brought a large brown OHMS envelope. Peggy signed at the end of an incomprehensible document and became a contractor to the Ministry of Health at a salary not to be sneezed at.

After that, I didn't have to work at getting out of the rut, things just happened – it might have been that with our new mood we latched on to opportunities which previously we would have ignored.

Wansbrough-Jones, of course, had to get in on the act. No great domestic upset this time, he just wanted me to join a Working Party of the Defence Research Policy Committee which was to compare the effects of Atomic, Biological and Chemical Warfare. I'd been round that tree before.

The human race entered the Space Age on a Friday with the Russians' successful launch of their Sputnik. It was the very day Arthur Hill became Deputy Director at Porton and I was promoted to Senior Principle Scientific Officer to take over as Superintendent, Field Service Division – we used to say they gave us long titles to make up for not paying us much. The name was shortened later to Assistant Director but they didn't increase my pay.

A trifling act of mine in August 1959 joined that of my buying American machinery in setting the scene for the complete change in our mode of life, then still some years off. Sending for some screws by mail order from Whiston's of Stockport, a 'surplus' supplier, I noticed that the order form invited entry to a competition, so I put some numbers in the squares as directed. In October I had a letter saying, 'Dear Mr James, may I congratulate you on winning my Myford Super 7 lathe . . .'

When the machine arrived I rigged up a block and tackle and, with Peggy living dangerously, standing on a table below to guide it, we manoeuvred the massive lathe into my loft workshop.

That evening, sitting over coffee in the little TV room, Peggy commented that we sat in "this poky little room" every night and only used the nicely furnished living room when we had visitors. We were now getting suburbanized with a Victorian-parlour bias. She wondered whether we could change the layout to use more of the space. Carolyn, who was to change schools in a few months and go to the College of Art in Salisbury, asked whether we couldn't move:

"We're a bit out in the sticks here, Daddy."

I caught the glance between them and realized this was a prepared scenario, so I grunted noncommittally to see what they had in mind. I was not averse to a change. In fact, even as I waited, I felt my enthusiasm growing; it would be a great experience to design our own house – and have a large workshop on the ground floor . . .

Peggy was saying, ". . . and Mummy was on the phone yesterday to say that Daddy is back working in the shop again after his stroke, but he's retiring at the end of the year. They thought they'd like to move down to the Salisbury area. I think she was hinting they'd like to live with us, but I didn't bite."

I asked whether she would like that, wondering why she hadn't told me this earlier.

She said that there would come a time anyway when they needed looking after, and it would be easier if we lived together:

"We couldn't have them here, of course, we'd be on top of each other. Carolyn and I have been plotting. Cyril Trotman came into the lab this morning . . ."

It emerged that Trotman, who headed the Section responsible for the work on respirators and protective clothing, was building a house in Salisbury: he'd been extolling the virtues of a young prize-winning architect, Tony Stocken, who had designed it. This paragon, it appeared, was ahead of his time: underfloor heating, heat pumps and solar panels for water heating, ergonomic kitchens, and Swedish double windows – there were no phone-you-in-the-middle-of-dinner double-glazing salesmen in UK then.

A telephone call brought Tony Stocken to see us the following evening. We dithered at first but the clincher was that he had a lien on a riverside site in East Harnham, ten minutes walk through the Cathedral Close into Salisbury. He stayed to dinner, and we roughed out a house design on the dining table over the port. It had a 'granny-flat' annex. Peggy and I thought this masterly planning for the future: her parents would live in the flat and, when we were old, Carolyn could take over the main house with the family she would doubtless have by then, and we would retire with our Zimmer frames to the flat.

We were impressed with Tony Stocken and his quick thinking, as well as his apparent ability to keep down prices while not stinting on the many 'modern' features he wanted to build in – even the large workshop was to have underfloor heating.

Just before Christmas 1959 we completed the purchase of the land at the confluence of the Rivers Avon and Nadder, with its Constable-like view of the cathedral across the water. The builders were on site in the New Year and Peggy, Carolyn and I started clearing the ground that was to be our garden. It had once been an orchard but most of the fruit trees were decrepit and were interspersed with sycamore, hawthorn and other wild flora that had taken a fancy to the site. We pulled many of them out with the car, which had a caravan towbar. One large hawthorn resisted our efforts and survived many years. My diary in the nineties was expansive, with some licence, waxing poetic about its eventual passing. Peggy said the poem was a bit like the story of someone's life. That pleased me since I had intended it to be. It was much later I saw in it her own story:

THE HAWTHORN

Young strong tree bent to earth
as powerful motors strained,
clenched its roots, and won.
Sprang back in glee as rope slipped hook,
and lashed past frightened men.
The men went off to tea.

Winter passed and May's white scented flower
veiled proud and naked strength.
In Autumn, sap descended
to leave a ring of age.
But each year from sylvan rest,
bud-burst of Spring
renewed vitality.

Thus would surely always be
life's ever-constant cycle,
where only growing strength and grace
signed a tick of arrowed time.

But subtle were the thickening gnarls,
the scars of fallen branches.
And hidden too the fungal rot
powdering brown the woody grain,
until a weakened limb,
lashed in tempest, fell.
Men came and cut it clean
and then went off to tea.

The hawthorn stayed, and thinly
flowered another year.

Old now, and it showed –
sap could scarcely reach
the end of brittle, mossy branch,
and few leaves formed.
The misshapen hawthorn
stood there stark and grey
against the brightening sky.
Men tore out frail
and unprotesting roots
to free them from the fetid earth
for welcome shroud of air.

The men went off to tea.

CHAPTER TEN

It was Summer 1993: Peggy tripped over a hose in the garden; we lunched at The Manor House Hotel, Castle Combe, on Mary and Geoffrey Watts' first wedding anniversary; and my cousin, Geoffrey Bradburn, rang to say his mother, my Auntie Bob, had died, aged 94, 'peacefully in her bed'.

Peggy was embarrassed about her fall and said nothing about it until I noticed the badly bruised shoulder and hip. Nothing seemed to be broken, but I suggested we had better check with our GP and that we should ask him also about the periodic confusion and disturbed nights.

The doctor was very reassuring: No serious damage, and no sign of Alzheimer's or Parkinson's – that startled me; neither was a prospect I had seriously entertained. He said there was a possibility of mild hypothyroidism. Blood pressure a trifle high but no problem. He thought it was just that she was 'no longer 21'. He took blood samples and told us to see him again in two weeks.

As for my aunt's funeral, I'd felt it would be hypocritical to go, so I had made our excuses. Hypocritical? Well, I hadn't liked the lady. I hadn't liked the way she had kept her husband downtrodden – Uncle Arthur, who had shown me how to make a crystal-set, a 'wireless', when I was a boy – or how she had interfered with other people's lives, doing good always with an ulterior motive. She had given me my first bicycle, and had told the world about it for the rest of her life. Actually she had given me an old bicycle frame discarded by Billy, her then current lover. I'd then had to scrounge wheels, saddle and the rest to make it into a going affair. Nevertheless, I had been grateful at the time. It was years before I realized that she had merely been demonstrating to her sister, my mother, that she was neglecting her son.

That was a laugh. Auntie Bob gave her son, Bob, money towards a house in Australia and then went to live with him. She didn't stay long – she didn't get on with Irene, Bob's wife, who saw through her. She left for England and sued Bob for the money back.

My mother didn't like her. My father once said:

"Your sister's a whore."

"Oh!" said Mother, "What did she charge you?"

On our return to the doctor he told us that nothing had shown up in the blood sample, thyroid or whatever. He also went to great pains again to assure Peggy she was not abnormal for her age. What's normal? I suppose it was good news, but I felt I'd been left dangling. Good medicine for Peggy, however: she was immediately brighter – for an hour or so until our next telephone call . . .

It was Mary to say Geoffrey was in hospital with leukaemia. "I feel I've been here before, Ken," she said.

I wrote a few stilted phrases on a card to Geoffrey – what do you say to a friend who knows he's dying? and sent a short note to Mary. Peggy and I were pretty miserable for the rest of the day. I remembered Peggy's mother saying, "Worst thing about being old is your friends dropping dead around you".

There aren't too many ironmongers who get recognition for their fourth centenary, but one was recognized in September 1993. He had written, in his day, a biography of a local celebrity, George Herbert. I knew this because Christopher Rivett-Carnac, Barbara's eldest son, lived with his wife Sara and family in the poet's house, the Old Rectory in Bemerton. Oh, and the ironmonger had also written something about fishing: *The Compleat Angler*. Another author, a modern one, lived in the Cathedral Close, Leslie Thomas – *The Virgin Soldiers* and all that. His house was Walton Canonry and it was fitting that Leslie's wife, Diana, should organise an affair for Izaac Walton's fourth centenary in aid of a local water-meadows trust. We went along.

The party was on the lawn leading down to the Avon and Sir Edward Heath, who lived nearby, conducted the silver band for a few numbers. Peggy was wonderful. She discussed with him the question of the balance of instruments in the band – I was reminded of her spoof discussion with PLC on wine when we first met all those years ago – and she then walked around doing the social to perfection. It was difficult to think there could be anything seriously wrong when she could operate so well. Just as the doctor had said, perhaps, she just wasn't twenty-one.

I think Peggy might have been thinking along the same lines. At home, while things went on much as before, Peggy was much happier and, consequently, so was I. There was, however, no doubting the confusion, but it was still mostly about arrangement, the placing and sorting of things: keeping the knives, forks and spoons in their separate slots in the cutlery drawer seemed to present an insoluble problem; entries in her diary were placed regardless of date; and the dishwasher was loaded higgledy-piggledy. I suppose pattern recognition is one of the more complex functions of the brain.

Ian Pearce rang: were we thinking of skiing this Christmas?

"Skiing?" I said loudly, looking across the room at Peggy.

She nodded, grinning happily.

Later, I rang to invite Carolyn to come with us. She hadn't ski'd in the nine years she'd been with Derek and seemed delighted to join us. A telephone call to our favourite little hotel in Kandersteg, Switzerland, and the holiday was all fixed up.

By November I was beginning to worry whether we were being sensible to go skiing. Nights were getting difficult: Peggy had for some time been wakeful and restless in bed, but now she insisted in getting up several times. I thought at first it was symptomatic of her prolapse condition that she had to go to the lavatory frequently, but it was soon obviously not so: she washed and started to dress each time, and only with difficulty was I able to coax her back to bed. In the day, Peggy was becoming even less practical, and many quite simple manipulations baffled her – for our fifty-second wedding anniversary I bought her a watch with a clear analogue dial, since she was having difficulty reading her old one, but she couldn't manage the clasp. I made a bet with Fate: we were checking our ski gear, and I told myself that if Peggy could put on her ski boots and clip on her skis we would go to Kandersteg. She mounted herself on skis faultlessly in a few minutes, and if there had been snow she would have been away. So, we would go skiing.

November was an eventful month: Geoffrey Watts, who was still soldiering on, rang from hospital where he was getting his third chemotherapy course. He asked whether I knew where he could get a Geiger counter – he was convinced his leukaemia was associated with radioactivity from the power station over the river from Stroat House; Bunty, next door, died; and I wrote my obituary . . .

Obituary? Well, it wasn't put that way. The telephone told me that Professor Pat Rivett, the first professor of Operational Research, had been asked to do something towards writing the history of OR as seen from the OR Society. Could he drop in to see me to talk about my part in this. Of course, I said yes – not just because I was flattered, Pat and I were old friends.

Pat took what I thought were fragmentary notes while I reminisced in answer to his questions – I soon noticed these were all about me rather than OR. He went off the next morning and a few days later I received a scrappy, inaccurate version of what I was supposed to have said. Would I kindly correct where necessary, or rewrite it if I'd prefer. It was the old trick to get people to write about themselves. It was then I realized I was to write my obituary for the Society's archives.

I also made a decision in November. It followed my getting upset with Peggy. I'd cooked the lunch and she hadn't helped at all. Worse, about to serve the meal, I found she had cleared the table I'd laid, and had put the things, including the tablemats, in the dishwasher. It would have been a laughing matter if someone else had done it, but Peggy . . . I told myself – yet again – it was childish to 'lose my cool' on such occasions; I had to face up to the fact that Peggy needed a carer, and I was it. The dishwasher episode, not in the pattern-recognition category, was, I told myself, a bit of absent-mindedness we were all prone to. Nevertheless, my decision was to clear the flat, which I had been using as a library and study, and employ a live-in housekeeper. That would at least leave me free to be a carer.

The week before Christmas I still felt I was being stupid embarking on a ski trip, but we started sorting out stuff to take with us – or I did, while Peggy did the reverse. Not appearing to do much, she made chaos faster than I could make order.

I wheedled, explained, and shrieked all to no avail. Eventually I found jobs for her elsewhere and got the stuff packed.

Carolyn arrived with a huge case full of lead. I repacked her kit in a smaller case, saving about ten kilos and still leaving her with a good-sized pharmacy.

At Kandersteg, Ian and Mary who had arrived earlier had awaited dinner for us.

The snow was good and the weather kind and, despite my misgivings, we had a delightful holiday. Mary didn't want to ski, and Peggy, who did some skiing with Ian, Carolyn and me, went walks with her. I was glad Peggy didn't do too much, I was afraid of what might happen if she had a bad fall, she seemed to break bones so easily. She still ski'd with elegant style, seemed no less stable in action than she had ever been and, while she had once broken a wrist on a skiing trip, slipping on an icy pavement, she had never injured herself skiing. So, why was I worrying? Just because our eighties were in sight, perhaps?

Life was very simple on holiday, no complicated arrangements, nothing to sort out, and Peggy was at her best. Tired by bedtime, there was little of the disturbed nights we had experienced at home. But she was vague and sometimes lost her way in sentences. Ian and Mary asked me about her and I told them of the GPs verdict, that it was natural ageing, whatever that meant.

One strange incident: Peggy woke me in the early hours, switched on the light and, looking scared, said, "Do you know who I am?" I said, "Poomphie". She said, "Oh yes, of course," smiled, turned out the light and went to sleep.

I think that then, the end of 1993, was the point at which I stopped fooling myself. Call it ageing if you must, but it was clear to me Peggy was heading into some form of dementia. The future loomed: Peggy would need care and, as far as it was possible, it would come from me; moreover, our house in Salisbury was a pleasant place to live and I was resolved that we would stay in it together until . . . well, I didn't know.

THE HOUSE in Salisbury took well into 1961 to build – we were committed to having a Mr Fielden, the previous owner of the land, to do the work, and he had spread his meagre resources thinly around his various jobs. We moved in mid-June. We named our private road Watersmeet Road and as far as we were concerned it led to Paradise. Unfortunately it was not the route taken by Peggy's father who had suffered another stroke and died; it was a sad Mrs Dorothy Pratt who moved into the annexe.

Two months later I was posted to London.

I could have dug in my toes despite the carrot of another long title, Director, Chemical Defence Research and Development, which could be said in one breath as DCDRD, and promotion to Deputy Chief Scientific Officer, sighed happily as DCSO, but I went. Kindly, Peggy said it was a matter of ambition, but the real drive, I think, was vanity or perhaps conceit. There was an urge too to complete the circle, to return to where we started, Peggy and I; it was the job once held by a demigod, JDP, James Davidson Pratt. He was the first to telephone congratulations, inviting me to lunch at the Savage Club, which he subsequently sponsored my joining.

I commuted daily from Salisbury by train to Waterloo and, at first, it was pleasant being able to sit without interruption to read the newspaper, a book, or official papers. Some evenings, if a meeting went on a bit, I would miss the last sensible train home and I'd stay overnight at the Savage. That wasn't without its pleasures – the company in the club, if perhaps a little boozy, was highly entertaining. I would often play snooker with such people as Arthur Askey and Dicky Murdoch of radio fame, Wee Georgie Wood, who played his shots standing on a footstool, and that wonderful man "Professor" Stanley Unwin whose commentary during play kept us so diverted that he was bound to win. He might say: ". . .the fundamold of your snookhole chalky-tip is strikey-strikey not rippage clothly: zip, zip, holey black . . ." and the black ball would slam into the pocket.

I knew from my previous experience in the London office that I was taking on a non-job, but egotism said I would be in a position to change all that. There was a certain glamour in being a Director even though it was difficult to find anything to direct. There was glamour, too, in being a member of several NATO committees, which would take Peggy and me to various European venues. Also, I was to lead the UK team at annual Quadripartite Conferences on Biological and

Chemical Defence with the Americans, Canadians and Australians, in each of the countries in turn.

I had two bosses, The Chief Scientist, then Dr Walter Caywood, and The Master General of the Ordnance, in that historic job once held by the Duke of Wellington. One MGO in my time was General Sir Charles Jones, a nice man I got to know quite well accompanying him on a tour of the USA, visiting Defence establishments. As for 'changing all that', not a hope. Moves I attempted might have been stupid, but I never found out: they were steered around with, "Well, you know, Ken, the Chiefs of Staff . . . the Perm. Under-Sec. . . .the Secretary of State . . ."

The title of my post was shortened on one of the Defence economy drives. A post parallel to mine was Director, Biological Research, which was dissolved, and its responsibilities added to mine. I was then DBCD with an enhanced non-job with more of it to do in the same time.

As far as Peggy and I were concerned, the job made a mess of our life together; we were living virtually apart. I was in the job until 1965, a little over three years – it seemed interminable. I put up with the commuting for eighteen months or so. The crunch came in February 1963 when I was snowed up in a train diverted to Eastleigh near Southampton and spent a very cold night in it. Peggy and I had mulled over what we might do to get back to normal. We had talked about my giving up the job, but I'd chosen a career in the civil service for the sense of security it gave me – my childhood and youth had been distinctly insecure – and I didn't know what I could do otherwise while maintaining our standard of living.

To have asked for a transfer to something else would have been, I thought, to give up any career prospects I might have had – I'd seen several people consigned to the scrap heap that way. The cold night at Eastleigh settled one issue: we had to move to London. Perhaps the job would seem better if we could get our family life reinstated.

We bought a house on a second mortgage in Belmont Road, Twickenham. It was a pseudo-Georgian, early-Victorian house, detached in a cul-de-sac, with a small walled garden, a haven from the abominations of the motorized Babylon. Peggy's mother moved with us and shared the top floor with Carolyn. The ground floor we converted to open plan and built on a large workshop as a playroom for me. We let the Salisbury house.

On my last commuting trip back to Salisbury, the lifting of the tedium was almost visible, a mist dispersing on a Spring morning. This was the one such trip I was going to enjoy. Too spirited, I leapt into the carriage and fell over the legs of a passenger knocking his book from his hand. As I apologised and handed him his book, I noticed it was Fisher's 'Statistical Methods for Research Workers'. A teacher, I thought – he looked it. I am always intrigued, but not amazed, by coincidence – Fisher might have pointed out that while a particular coincidence could verge on the impossible, the chance of some sort of coincidence among the millions conceivable did not. On this occasion I settled in my seat to read a paper in 'Nature' on Professor Charles Pannett's research showing that radiation treatment of cancer worked not directly on the malignant tumour but stimulated surrounding tissue to produce a substance that killed the cancerous cells. Find the substance and you had a cancer cure. Glancing up from the journal I caught my man with the book on statistics straining to see what I was reading. He was embarrassed and apologised for being nosy. I showed him what I was reading and asked whether he knew the paper. He said, "I'm afraid I wrote it."

The journey as far as Basingstoke where he got out was most enjoyable. He told me a lot about his experiments at St Mary's Hospital: "I'm retired, you know, but they kindly give me space there". Then, with a giggle, "It's not always popular to take a new approach: the roof of the Medical Establishment fell in on me". He was learning statistics from scratch to design a crucial experiment to push it up again.

That summer we went on holiday with Neville Creasey – who had lodged with me in Maryland while Peggy was in the sanatorium – now married to Jenny, who, coincidentally, had been Carolyn's 'gym' mistress at school. We were joined by another couple, friends of the Creaseys, and chartered a yacht, a six-berth, thirty footer. The four of them were experts but it was a new experience for us. The trip was not without its excitements. We left from Chichester, our destination Treguier in France and Neville did a good job teaching Peggy and me the rudiments of sailing. A few hours out in the Channel we had to dodge as a submarine's periscope came up in our way. It swivelled, took a look, and went down. We sailed over the swirl of its wake. British? French? Russian! We'll never know. Neville at the radio reported then that we were heading into a storm. An hour later we were in it.

Frightening? It might have been, if we'd had time to think about it. Our four shipmates, having dashed around taking down sail, had retired to their bunks seriously seasick, leaving Peggy and me in the cockpit: "Just keep it pointing that-a-way," said Neville, before vomiting over the rail and going below.

His instruction was not easy to follow as we corkscrewed up and down huge waves, soaring first sky-wards and then plummeting into frothy green sea which came right over us. By the time the cockpit had drained, the cycle had started again leaving us little time for a glance at the compass.

When it got dark the sense of danger really set in. I had suggested to Peggy she went below but she wanted to stay; she concentrated on the compass while I struggled with the wheel. Then we saw a flashing light ahead. Leaving Peggy to hold the wheel and keep the boat pointing at the light I dropped down into the cabin, awkwardly in my wet oilskins. All four were flat out on their bunks. I shook Neville and asked about the light. He said something like, "Count it, but don't hit it," groaned and turned over, but then, turning back, said, "Christ!" and fished around for his boots.

Back in the cockpit, Peggy yelled, "There's something ahead, boats or something."

Topping the next crest, peering into the darkness, I saw them, or at least the white of the foam around them. Rocks.

Neville was just coming up, but we were too close to the rocks to wait. Adrenaline fired up my tired brain: would we capsize if I turned across wind? For some reason, I reached for the starter key to the motor and turned it. The motor started immediately, and I turned the wheel furiously to starboard.

I had no idea why I thought it necessary to start the motor, but we didn't hit the rocks or capsize. Neville took over, and in a quarter of an hour we turned to port into Cherbourg harbour. I'm sure I didn't take a breath from the time I switched on the motor until I sighed over the warm glow of a pink gin in the Yacht Club. Peggy said she didn't think much of this sailing lark.

It got better. We sailed around the coast calling in on various places Neville knew, where we ate – and drank – well. Neville taught me navigational arts, and the highlight of the holiday for me was making a landfall in St. Peterport, Guernsey, having sailed in fog from Treguier, and then on to that feudal offshoot of the Bailiwick of Guernsey, Swinburne's "small sweet world of wave encompassed wonder", the tiny island of Sark.

IN TWICKENHAM we settled down quickly: Carolyn got a job she enjoyed as a travelling window dresser, collected a boyfriend, Peter, and got engaged. I commuted to town from Twickenham station on the 8.30, hiding behind my Times; Peggy took Cordon Bleu cookery lessons; and Peggy's mother had visitors from Brondesbury Park, old friends she had missed while in Salisbury. We exchanged dinners with neighbours, particularly the Rowes next door – he was an avid collector like me, coins for him, items of postal history for me. I joined, on invitation, the Society of Postal Historians, and became president of the local philatelic society. We took holidays twice a year touring in France, either with our caravan or with Bunty and John Meades, our Salisbury neighbours, staying in Michelin goblets. Peggy and I joined the Richmond Film Society to make films, and that turned out to be the activity that eventually salvaged us from the slough of suburbanization.

The feel of my job in St Christopher House didn't seem to improve following our move. I was getting, perhaps belatedly, the idea that it was my fault, that I hadn't really grasped what the job was all about. And I never did. It wasn't long, however, before my working life suffered a radical change.

This time it was nothing to do with Wansbrough-Jones, now Sir Owen, a knight of the realm. In June 1964 I did join him at his club, the Oxford and Cambridge in Pall Mall for the Technical Officers' Association Dinner which he ran. He commented then, with a wry smile, that I seemed to have settled down in life.

A few months later I was surprised to be included in the Permanent Under-Secretary's list of invitees to a cocktail party, a farewell do for someone retiring. I was nobbled as soon as I arrived by Sir Walter

Caywood, the Chief Scientist (Army) who edged us through the forest of glasses and small talk to where MGO was talking to PUS. He purred a few words of greeting and then: "Glad you could come, James, MGO would like a word."

By this time I was feeling pretty edgy, wondering what was going on. MGO and Chief Scientist then did a double act, a sort of soft-soap opera. They told me at some length that Neville Gadsby, the Director of the Army Operational Research Establishment at Byfleet, was leaving and they needed someone with relevant experience to take over in a hurry. My heart was acting out a cliché: I could feel it thumping. There was a snag. The Royal Navy and the Royal Air Force both had similar establishments, and in a few months they were to join with the Army group to form a Defence Establishment. Would I mind very much taking on the job meanwhile?

"I come back to my present job afterwards?"

Walter Caywood looked, I thought, shifty. He glanced at MGO and said "No, Ken, you see . . ." He went on to say that Neville had been ill and that the job had worried him and they wanted him to have a less worrying post. They thought an exchange with me might be the best thing for him.

I recalled Peggy saying when I went to Germany with the Byfleet team: ". . . you never know where it might lead." I was now so pleased with where it seemed to be leading I almost forgot to ask what was to happen to me when Defence took over.

"Oh, we would like you to stay put at Byfleet as the Army deputy – at the same grade, of course. The director of the new Establishment will be at under-secretary level and will have to come from outside, someone obviously without a bias for any of the Services." He smiled broadly for the first time, obviously glad to have got that bit off his chest.

I left the party walking on air, and not entirely due to whatever it was I had been drinking – I hadn't noticed. However, there was something fishy about the sales talk. I knew Neville quite well and liked him. I knew he'd been off sick, but the implication that he'd had a nervous breakdown didn't ring true, and the idea that he needed a softer job – although you couldn't get one softer than a non-job – seemed ludicrous. Was it all a device for getting me out of my present post as nicely as possible? Or was that my guilt-ridden conscience at work? I knew I hadn't done much of a job – mostly because I couldn't find one to do – but I hadn't thought anyone cared enough to notice. On the other hand, perhaps they had noticed that I sometimes didn't quite toe the party line – there were aspects of the work at Porton that irked me and I hadn't hesitated to say so. But, cowardly perhaps, I could now escape. I had three reasons for delight: I was leaving the only job I'd ever wanted desperately to leave; I was leaving the macabre realm of Biological and Chemical Warfare; I was going into Operational Research, which I believed in.

Peggy, too, was delighted: "Pretty filthy business, B and CW. Different during the war, everything was filthy . . ." We had agreed in the past that a heart-stopping shot of nerve gas was a cleaner way out than a bullet in the belly or worse, but I think we both knew we were excusing ourselves.

THE WEEK before Christmas 1964, Neville Gadsby and I exchanged visits. When I'd introduced him to my staff in St Christopher House, we talked about the job. He said, in his clipped officer-style voice, "Army staff job, eh? That should be all right." I'd obviously missed out, not having had Army experience.

First impressions of Byfleet were from Neville's office, which I was to occupy for a time. It was a fine large room on the first floor, with panelled walls – turquoise, framed in white. The view from the wide sweep of windows was over the extensive terrace at the rear of the house and the impressive garden beyond. The building itself, a country mansion which had been the family home of the Charingtons, the brewers, was not beautiful, but it was a cosy place to work.

Neville took me around and introduced the staff. Several of the scientists I had met before in Germany and others at meetings of the Operational Research Society. I had also met some of the military officers who were on secondment. One in particular was Brigadier Paul Ward who was to be my military opposite number when Defence took over. Peggy and I were to find out that he was not only a charming man but could cook – he was later aide-de-camp to the Queen, but I don't think she allowed him in the kitchen. The

Storeman, an ex-sergeant major took me aside while Neville was taking a telephone call, and rasped:

"Yer got an 'ard act ter foller, sir. Neville was one of us, yer know. 'E kep' in touch pers'nal like. But we'll 'elp all we can, sir."

After that encouragement, I was introduced to the Porter. He'd won a huge prize on the football pools and ran a large Mercedes, which was left gleaming at the front door – ". . . to give the place some class," Neville said. The Porter told me he'd have gone on working until he dropped, but now Neville was leaving . . .

Looking back, I am surprised that I was not irritated by this reception. In fact, I was amused. He was expressing the sort of feeling we probably all have when the cold wind of change blows into the comfortable niche we have enjoyed. I doubt whether in similar circumstances I could have been that honest – but, then, I wasn't that rich.

Finally, we reached Mrs Brooker who was to be my secretary. She balanced things up a bit: "Hope you're better tempered than old Neville."

CHAPTER ELEVEN

Back from skiing in Switzerland in the New Year, 1994, telling myself I was now facing facts, I made a date to see the GP again about Peggy, determined to insist on a full examination. In fact, he took the initiative: he gave Peggy a physical examination while chatting to her, slipping in little tests of her comprehension and short-term memory. Peggy performed better than I expected but was still obviously confused. While Peggy was dressing, the GP took me aside and, after some appropriately soft words, said:

"I'm afraid we cannot discount the possibility of Alzheimer's. We'd better get her to a specialist."

I suppose I had expected nothing less, but his conclusion poured over me like a dumper wave while surfing. I croaked as I tried to speak but managed to say that I'd be grateful if he could fix it up.

A fortnight later we went to the Old Manor hospital on Wilton Road, an institution which, in our old-fashioned way, we had labelled the Loony Bin. There was nothing forbidding about the place; it was clean, bright and tidy; we were welcomed pleasantly and taken to an interview room with soft chairs. The doctor turned up immediately and she spent half-an-hour or so talking to us, learning the background, and again conducting the little verbal tests with Peggy.

Hope was restored: the doctor said Peggy was probably suffering from depression. She prescribed paroxetine which she said was a 'happy pill', the one safe for someone with glaucoma. She went on to say there was a possibility Peggy had suffered a minor stroke; she would fix for her to have an EEG and a CT scan to see if there was any obvious damage to the brain. There was a sting in the tail: she said the tests would also reveal any signs of dementia.

There were no immediately obvious effects from the paroxetine although one day we were sitting together over tea when Peggy, looking out of the window, said, "What on earth do they want?"

"Who, Poomphie?"

"The blackie-toppers out there in the drive."

I gathered no racist intent from the expression, which was one her mother used to describe anyone with dark skin, from a Congo pygmy to a sun-tanned Australian. I had never heard Peggy say it before. I thought she must be leading up to some sort of joke. I said:

"I can't see them, dear."

"Don't be silly, they're right there in front of you – long thin heads." She looked quite cross, and a little frightened, I thought.

Hallucinations, now. I didn't know how to deal with them. I said I'd go and speak to the intruders.

She got up as I did, clung to me and, in a tearful whisper, "Don't go, Ken, dear, I'm frightened."

"It's all right, Poomphie, they've gone now . . ." I hoped.

She looked, fearful . . . "Oh yes, there they go. Good." She sat down. "Sorry to be so silly, Ken. They looked so fierce."

I took a chance and said something like, "You realize it was only a daydream you had, dear."

"But they seemed so real."

"There really was nobody out there. It was just like the nightmares you have."

She looked surprised. "Yes, that's right, I do dream about them, the ones with the thin heads." She smiled. "Oh, I'm so glad. I won't be stupid about it any more."

And she wasn't.

Just occasionally after that she would tell me in ordinary conversation about the little girl over in the corner waiting for her mother, or laugh and say she those silly old ladies were back sitting on the sofa: "They never seem to talk." She was, I think, particularly fond of one vision, an Arab who careered around the garden on a camel.

The day came for the EEG. We drove to the Old Manor again. I turned into the car park opposite, scarcely knowing how I had got there; all the way I had been cocooned in chaotic, unproductive thought. Walking across to the hospital I made a mental plea, "Let something good happen, just for a change". To whom was I pleading? Just to nobody? To the great unknowable? It is on such occasions we need a God.

A nice man in a lab. coat stuck twenty-two electrodes on Peggy's head, and while he fiddled with his machine they posed there like opposing football teams waiting for the off.

"Right," he said, flipped a switch, and floating pens on his machine started spiking Peggy's neuronic fireworks.

He switched off, and I said, "Anything?"

He looked along the graphs: "Nothing unusual that I can see". What was unusual in his sphere of activity was a moot point.

He went on, "I hand these over to the experts to do an assessment."

The following week we went to the Salisbury District Hospital at Odstock for the CT scan. I wasn't allowed to witness these rites. Peggy was bewildered when she emerged and couldn't describe what had gone on.

Now we just had to wait.

Mid-February we had a surprise visit from Mary and Geoffrey. It was time for morning coffee, which magically turned to champagne – and Peggy risked a bubble or two. Geoffrey looked surprisingly well and had some hair re-growth after his gruelling therapy. Mary had done some remarkable bullying of the system to get things done, including maintaining sterility of Geoffrey's room during the crucial period of chemotherapy – apparently, most leukaemia patients die of an infection at this stage rather than from the direct effects of their cancer. She even insisted the doctors wore masks!

The next day our GP rang: "The tests show distinct atrophy. I'm afraid there's no doubt Mrs James has a dementia, Alzheimer's, or whatever . . ." adding the comforting remark, ". . .we can only be sure *post mortem*."

With that death sentence my world collapsed, although, strangely, I was calmed – it was the moment I stopped being sorry for myself. I had a new life to lead, to do what I could to make Peggy's life worth living for as long as it took. I'd read such sentiments in letters printed in the Alzheimer's Society Newsletter and had thought of their writers as putting on the noble act. Perhaps I was too. I said to myself out loud:

"So bloody well get on with it."

But I was still human, and events continued to raise emotions, which no amount of determined intention would control.

I told Peggy the tests had shown neurone damage in the brain, not mentioning the big A. I think she assumed she'd had a minor stroke and seemed quite untroubled. By day she could still give an appearance of normality but at times was happily muddled – I was the unhappy one, mentally beating my chest at every show of confusion, and outwardly, despite my resolution, not always able to disguise my frustration nor at times to control my temper. The nights were still bad – Peggy usually got up and dressed several times a night.

At Peggy's next interview with the eye specialist he found pressure had increased in one eye. He doubled the strength of the pilocarpine she was to use. A few days later, Peggy showed a marked increase in disorientation in the daytime and some increase in hostility at night when I tried to persuade her back to bed. Coincidence? Pilocarpine had been in use since 1875, the specialist had said. He hadn't mentioned that many medicines were in use even longer before being recognized as harmful – calomel, a compound of mercury, was used for constipation from the sixteenth century, and we were half way through the twentieth before it was decided mercury was a no-no. However, one pays experts for their advice because they are expert, and so I stepped down from the height of my inexperience and put my faith where my cheque had gone.

Whether or not pilocarpine had anything to do with it, we had certainly started into a new phase of Peggy's illness. She made tea without tea, and was quite happy about it – it was, however, the same day she prepared an excellent lunch without prompting; she had a conviction that we had a guest. She laid the table for her and when I corrected it back to two – I thought surreptitiously – she asked where I was going to eat. She got up and dressed one night at half-past two in a dreadful state, worrying about who owned the house and why they wouldn't let us stay. Another night I followed her downstairs when she refused to get back to bed. In the kitchen, she said it was time to go to bed and got upset because she couldn't then find her way back to the bedroom, while refusing to be guided. In the morning she was back to her happy state, long periods of almost normality with occasional mild confusion and short periods of hallucination – amazing variability.

From an article in the Saga magazine I gathered that clinical trials with a drug, physostigmine – an encouraging treatment likely to reduce the rate of deterioration in Alzheimer's – were about to start, and volunteer subjects were being sought. I wrote to our GP asking him if he could get Peggy in on the trial – if a straw floated by I was going to grasp at it.

I TOOK up my post at Byfleet on the 4th January 1965, apprehensive because of my lack of experience with a large staff. I needn't have worried, everyone was as helpful as the Storeman had promised. Peggy and I were invited to a welcoming cocktail party a week later, organised and paid for by the staff. Peggy was splendid as the Director's wife: she left me and went around to talk to everyone in a friendly, unembarrassed way. She told me afterwards that she thought I was going to like the job, there were such a lot of nice people. Also, a man – she thought he'd said he was the Storeman, had volunteered, " 'E's doin' all right, Ma'am."

Mrs Brooker, my outspoken secretary, said, "Your wife would make a good Director . . ." and added, in case I got the wrong idea, ". . . but I'm sure we can manage with you." She had been a secretary for a long time and was a good one – and sometimes quite tactful.

Now I had a real job, and I enjoyed it.

In April we joined the OR organisations of the Royal Navy and Royal Air Force to become the Defence Operational Research Establishment. The supremo was to be B.T.Price, then an Assistant Chief Scientific Advisor, Ministry of Defence, working to Sir Solly Zuckerman, Chief Scientific Advisor. What had been an anonymous bogeyman was now the Terry Price I knew and liked and, dare I say, admired – I had worked with him when he headed the British team of scientists, including me, sent to a NATO conference in Paris seeking to define the future of world conflict.

My job at Byfleet didn't change a great deal under the new label.

My main interest remained in Army studies, and I continued as father confessor to the staff.

We were now, however, a part of the decision making machinery of the Ministry of Defence, and plugged in at Chiefs of Staff level. Terry, working to the Chiefs of Staff Committee gathered in stratospheric studies of a strategic nature. The whole place acquired a more sophisticated air, which had me gasping in my naivety.

I learned a lesson at Byfleet that was to be especially important to me. High-level decisions were usually judgements made on information of dubious origins, filtered, condensed and opinionated on its long passage up through the many levels of the administrative hierarchy. In Operational Research we gathered our own information for objective analysis, quantitative if possible. Our difficulty was that important decisions were always urgent: waiting around for a study taking a year, to decide whether to scrap the TSR2 aircraft development, or stop working on ICBMs, might waste millions. And then, information used might well be out of date when the study was finished.

What could be done? I could only think that we needed an operational-research-like process behind the decision-making system the whole time so that information in useable form was always available, rather than waiting until a problem emerged before starting to collect it. That would need fundamental moves in the immovable rock of the administrative system, and advances in the model-building processes of OR which might be unattainable. Computers were getting better, perhaps they would give us the calculating power we needed so that a vast amount of information could be processed without the need for a hierarchy to condense it to manageable proportions. I sometimes got the feeling that the immense concentration of talent at Byfleet might be better employed finding how best to change the system rather than struggling to achieve untimely solutions which might be little better than the timely guesses usually made at the top.

In our new role, we attracted a lot of sightseers. One I remember for an odd reason: he stepped on my foot as he alighted from the helicopter that brought him. It was Lord Shackleton, then Minister of Defence for the RAF. It was a few years before we met again, at a time when he was poised to influence my future. Then, the tiny incident at Byfleet gave us an immediate reason to smile at each other.

One day, mandarins from HM Treasury visited: we gave them the red-carpet treatment. I felt I didn't speak the same language, but Terry did, and they seemed impressed with what we were doing. We showed them our million-pound computer (less powerful than the one on my lap I'm typing on) in its purpose-built, air-conditioned, dust-free building and enjoyed their gasps as they mentally added the sum to the next batch of gilts to be auctioned.

Over lunch, one of them, Bert Creamer, too bluff and burly to be easily recognized as a mandarin, said – and there was a distinct twinkle in his eye – "We've started doing Operational Research: we have a scientific officer in our Organisation and Methods Section, O&M, you know." I jumped in, saying something about OR being a team effort, a mix of disciplines, synergism . . . Terry was faintly shaking his head and I shut up.

As we walked with them to their cars, Bert Creamer said quietly to me, "Why don't you come and join us?" I thanked him and said that I didn't think I'd be any use to them, I didn't see OR as a branch of O&M – thinking to myself that there went any career I might have had in the civil service.

Terry was in London a couple of days later, and when he got back he said that on the escalator at Leicester Square tube station he'd met a man from Bert Creamer's empire in HM Treasury. He had told Terry they had decided to expand their OR group. Terry said to me:

"He asked whether I could recommend anybody senior to take it over. How about you, Ken?"

I'm not sure why I didn't tell him I had already turned down the suggestion. I said I was rather fond of my present job and that the idea of trying to do OR at Treasury level with just a couple of bods under the O&M banner was not too attractive, but I'd think about it.

He must have passed on my sentiments. The following day I had a call from Bert Creamer: "All right," he said, "you can have it your way. We want to start a new OR Division in parallel with O&M, not under it. Would you like to come and run it?" He went on without waiting for an answer. "I've spoken to Price and he's happy . . ." adding, kindly, ". . . but reluctant, of course. Your personnel people in Defence will release you on temporary secondment . . ."

He went on talking – I got the feeling he was giving me a chance to think twice before saying no again. I also got the impression he was quite keen to get something going. I said yes. Was it possible that I could get in a position to change the system just a little?

Free time at home was centred then on the Film Society. Peggy and I had entered wholeheartedly into film making, not only the team efforts of the Society but making our own. Most of the films made by the Society or individuals were aimed at prize winning in the various national and international competitions for amateurs. I had bought a sixteen-millimetre ciné camera and the necessary editing equipment so that we could work at home. We had made a few very short films to learn the processes, and we were working on a longer one starring my sister's boy, David, aged ten. In the story, he and some friends had found an unexploded wartime incendiary bomb which, for fun, they were going to drop off Hammersmith Bridge on to a passenger steamer passing underneath.

On the bridge, early one Sunday morning, Peggy on sound and me on camera, David, with his fellow conspirators, was leaning over the parapet about to drop the dummy bomb – made, quite realistically, from a quart beer bottle. It was to drop into the water harmlessly – we had previously shot scenes of a pleasure steamer approaching and going under the bridge – we could splice in an explosion later. Peggy, with her microphone boom in position from a stand, had switched on to record and was standing with the clapper board poised to mark our crucial shot . . . There was an explosion of sound, screaming sirens of police cars racing in from both sides of the bridge. I couldn't resist starting the camera so as not to waste the exciting noises we were recording. The cars screeched to a halt and a dozen policemen rushed to grab David. They flattened him on the pavement while one of them, bravely, took the bomb and was about to rush off – I couldn't imagine where. I intercepted and explained. They were quite nice about it – Peggy did a good job charming the sergeant, and "You might have told us," was the worst we got. In the film, the police scene cut in neatly after the bomb had been dropped.

The Society's sound-dubbing facilities would have embarrassed Heath Robinson. Most needed was a film recorder – essentially an outsize tape recorder and player running in synchronization with a film projector – far outside the financial resources of the Society. One of the members, Alan Lavender, an instrument engineer in his mid-twenties, said he could make one if he had a well-equipped workshop. I said he could use mine.

Standing high on his apprenticeship certificates, he said:

"Thanks, Ken, but it would need a professional shop with lathe, milling machine, drill press . . ."

"Better come and look," I said.

And that's where my American machinery and the lathe I had won graduated from making the odd sink-stop to doing what they were designed to do.

Alan came to look and brought a friend, Glyn Powell-Evans, a sophisticated seventeen-year-old who was set on being a millionaire before hitting his quarter century. For several weeks we worked long hours together in the evenings and weekends making the film recorder – midnight was just the time for a second supper break for us.

Alan was very good, not only at making things but also in designing them. He was a genius with mechanism, and his design of the film path and control on the machine was complex and very efficient; moreover, it was beautiful. My own modest skills in precision metal work improved a lot under his tuition.

We were rushed at the end because the Society had somebody from the BBC coming to give a talk on film editing and he needed to use a film recorder. We made it with a day to spare, the machine fully tested, and stainless steel gleaming against its background of new paint.

Talk done, the BBC man said to the society's chairman. "That's a splendid film recorder, not one I recognize. Who makes them?" Quick as a flash, Peggy said, "The designer is here tonight . . . where's Alan, Glyn?"

Glyn, and the rest of the people around, looked towards the darkroom door, just as it opened. A girl emerged, stopped and blushed to see everyone looking in her direction. Alan following her out, stopped for a moment to take in the scene, and said to the girl as he turned back into the dark room:

"I'll be with you in a moment, I'll just hang up the prints."

Alan spent half-an-hour or so, explaining the finer points of the recorder to the BBC man, interspersed with a phrase he often used – more from enthusiasm than braggadocio – "And then I had another brilliant idea . . ." He finished on, "This is only the prototype of course."

"Our people at Bristol would be interested," said the BBC man. "He gave us a name."

Back at Belmont Road later, Alan and Glyn were bubbling. Alan said we should start a company but he didn't know how to raise the capital. I pointed out that they had quite a lot – a workshop to use, a prototype machine and free labour.

Alan said, "You mean we can carry on here? And where's the free labour?

"You two, for a start, but keep your day jobs. And there's me as odd job man."

"And me, said Peggy, "I'll make the tea."

We talked on well into the small hours on ways and means, and finally on what we would call ourselves. Alan was keen that we should creep gradually into the film making business – he had a prestigious British award for a film he had made and was picking up prizes for it around the world. We agreed the name should have 'Films' in it, and settled finally on 'PAG Films Limited, initials of Peggy, Alan and Glyn – no K; it didn't fit; also I wasn't sure that as a civil servant I'd be allowed to go commercial on the side. The official board would be the three of them, but they'd have board meetings in the evening and invite me. Glyn volunteered to start things rolling, getting clearance for our name and registering the company.

CHAPTER TWELVE

At the end of the first week in March 1994 the daffodils were dancing sprightly in the garden and the camellia buds were blushing, but the post brought a letter from our GP regretting that recruitment for the physostigmine trials was complete. He suggested we apply for entry to Glaxo's trial of Ondansetron, a drug used to counter nausea after radiotherapy for cancer, which was another candidate for slowing the progress of Alzheimer's Disease. The trial was to start in a couple of months conducted by the Thornhill Research Unit at Moorgreen Hospital near Southampton. An alternative straw and I grasped it.

I was running into a difficulty at home. Nights were largely taken up with attending to Peggy getting up several times and dressing, often in bizarre fashion where in other circumstances I might have been amused – she once had tights on over her shoes, and on another occasion no tights, but a low-necked vest as knickers. Persuaded back into bed she was likely to have frightening nightmares, which woke her and me. I might then doze for half an hour before she'd be out of bed again. I tried hiding her clothes, but she then merely took off her nightdress and searched the house for something to wear.

When it came to the normal time for dressing in the morning she seemed quite different and would dress herself without problem. Oddly, too, she had little difficulty sleeping during the day, which she often did. Only rarely did she have frightening dreams at such times, but if she did she was likely to wake in a distressed state and behave in a deranged fashion. So, I couldn't join her in a daytime doze for fear of what she might get up to when she woke. It was

Peggy 1917

Peggy 1918

Mr and Mrs Pratt with Peggy and Barbara 1922

Mr Pratt and his shop 1932

Peggy at Paignton, 1928

The author's mother, Jessie, 1936

Author's sister, Georgina, 1942

Peggy and Carolyn with the author, 1944

Barbara (Rivett-Carnac) – John in evidence. Mrs Pratt, Evelyn, Mr Pratt, Peggy, Douglas R-C, Christopher R-C, Carolyn, the author. 1947

Peggy, popular with the schoolchildren in Tokyo, 1978

Evelyn and her husband, Rev Peter Wood, on the occasion of the Queen's visit to Chile where they were missionaries, 1968

Terry Price, Brig. Paul Ward, the author, Lord Shackleton who has just trodden on the author's toes, 1967

The author with Peggy near Kandersteg, Switzerland, 1986

Peggy and the author – Golden Wedding, 1991

Peggy and Barbara in Guernsey, 1993

Lawrence, Carolyn and Peggy, 1994

some time before my dulled brain thought of tying our shoelaces together, but the first time I tried it I awoke to find Peggy engaged gently untying them:

"Sorry, Ken," she said, "I was trying not to wake you."

For the most part, however, daytime was less strain than the nights. Most days, Peggy had long periods of lucidity when there appeared to be little wrong with her, when we were able to enjoy our life together. The shadow of the next lapse was always there, certainly for me, and, I think, for Peggy – often I caught a hunted look, which she quickly smiled away if she noticed my glance. It was almost an encouragement that she was usually able to keep out of the shadow when friends called – although it seemed deeper and more prolonged afterwards.

In other ways too there was suffering after joy. Jeremy Wring, the man from Rothschild's, now our friendly financial advisor, took us to dinner one evening to Chewton Glen Restaurant, one of the gourmet centres of the South. From the outside you could see the food was good – squeezed into the cracks between Rolls Royces and Mercedes in the car park was a fair sprinkling of family cars too decrepit to be owned by expense-account holders. Service was superb, if showy. Peggy, who told a waiter she was cold, was provided with a personal electric heater beside her chair; three waiters wearing pristine white gloves synchronised their flourishes removing the covers from the dishes. It was a splendid meal, and that was the joy.

The suffering was overnight. I had severe indigestion – having had my gall bladder removed, rich food did that to me – and Peggy was so frightened by her nightmares she was at one stage cowered at the top of the bed gibbering.

Early April there were changes in Peggy's behaviour. We still had most of our daytime together in harmony, but mornings, usually very early, Peggy was not only unclear where she was, but, in particular, who I was. On one occasion, when she dressed soon after midnight, she said she didn't like the man in her bed and got quite belligerent when I tried to persuade her to get back in. After that she became obsessed with 'them': "What are they trying to do to us?" or, "Why can't we go home and leave them." One early morning when I was trying to stop her leaving the house in her nightdress, she called me a pig and said I was in league with 'them'. Despite all this she would usually recover to near normality around breakfast time. She still had daytime hallucinations but they were benign.

I don't know whether she was watching her favourite vision, the camel rider, at the time but once when we were gardening she tripped and plunged headfirst into a ceanothus bush which had been pruned back hard. She lacerated her nose and broke her glasses. I was increasingly worried about her tendency to fall about, but I didn't know what I could do about it, short of wrapping her in cotton wool or chaining her down.

There was another worry creeping into our lives. Mid-morning, Saturday, April 9th, overnight snow had turned to sleet. I turned from the window where I had been contemplating icy stair-rods slanting into the river, and went out to the freezer to see what I could find for lunch. The telephone rang while I was searching. It was Carolyn to say she had pains in her lower back and abdomen again. The doctor had given her some pills but they had given no relief. On such occasions one tends to think dire thoughts. I told her to ring the doctor and tell him, and to let me know what he said. I suppose I would normally have panicked and rushed up to London to see her but . . . well, things were different now. I didn't tell Peggy – I felt she had enough on her plate. I forgot about lunch until Peggy asked what we were having. I made a salad.

In the morning Carolyn rang again. The doctor had been to see her the evening before and was pretty sure she had a kidney infection and had started her on a course of antibiotics. I rang her in the afternoon when she said she was feeling a lot better. She had been able to eat a good lunch. A bit relieved but still apprehensive, I went out to the freezer to get something for dinner. The freezer door was wide open as I had left it in the morning and the floor was very wet. I now had more cooking to do than I had bargained for.

A week later, Carolyn was a good deal better although there was still pain lower back and front. The doctor was puzzled and was fixing for her to have a scan, but thought she could go back to work. So, the worry wasn't over. I felt pretty low that day. I had a cold, which was dragging on, and lack of sleep at night was putting a nasty edge to my temper. I thought it best to find reasons for keeping at arm's length from Peggy. I did the week's washing and ironing, mended the cistern in the downstairs loo, cut down and edged a super-king-sized blanket, repaired our neck-pillow cases, all the while keeping in touch with Peggy with passing comment or shouts from the next room. She volunteered to weed the rockery while I mowed the back lawn.

We had a poor night, but I didn't feel too bad in the morning. We went shopping. Peggy tripped going into Debenham's. A woman with a huge shopping bag dodged in front of me as I dived to save Peggy, who fell heavily and broke her arm. Again we were an expense on the hard-pressed National Health Service.

I JOINED HM Treasury 15 January 1968 and found myself on the discussion circuit for the many interesting subjects that came to the department for decision or advice. On my first day I had a paper for comment on the problem of financing the Health Service, thought likely to be critical by the end of the century, another on the possible catastrophic flooding of London by the River Thames and the need for a Thames barrier, and one on the need for a Channel Tunnel. I'd certainly have no difficulty finding problems to work on – I could just grab them as they went by if I had something useful to offer. The immediate difficulty was that I had only two scientific staff and a secretary and I couldn't tackle anything of any size.

A Deputy Secretary had said to me when I first arrived:

"O and R? That's like O and M, isn't it? Of course, the main value of doing that sort of thing in Treasury is as an example to spending Departments. But it would be nice if you could find a way to save a penny or two."

But that wasn't what I had in mind. However, if we were to be taken seriously I had to get among the millions and show results: that would need a sizeable team of good people. The trouble was, the Treasury prided itself on its small size for its enormous job, and even administrative staff was cut to the bone. As for scientists . . . What! In HM Treasury? Oh, reform according to Lord Fulton, eh? I suppose we have to show willing and house-train a couple of 'em.

Clearly only success would ease the constraints. I gritted my teeth and hacked a way through the thicket of small tactical studies that had grown up around us. Penetration led to some small savings and people started to talk to us.

Suddenly, in November 1968, the going got easier. A new government department was commissioned to act as a management body for the whole Civil Service, 670,000 souls. The new Civil Service Department, CSD, was under one Cabinet Minister, then Lord Shackleton, working direct to the Prime Minister. The Treasury was split to staff the new organisation and my MS(OR) was one of the emigrant divisions. Early on, I was invited to have a chat with the Permanent Secretary of CSD, Head of the Home Civil Service, Sir William Armstrong. I confess to being surprised at the obvious interest he showed in our subject and what it might do for Government. He was complimentary about our small successes to date and, there and then, we plotted to set up under his chairmanship a seminar at Nuffield College, Oxford, to consider the future of OR in the Service.

The seminar, 4 January 1969, brought together: mandarins from the upper strata of Departments; senior people from the groves of Academe; senior managers from the various centres of OR that had sprung up since the war, including The Coal Board, ICI, and British Steel; representatives from the OR Society, management consultancies, and the Defence OR groups that had started it all. I was a little perturbed by the fact that a few of those from the private sector, senior people who had been vocal in the past urging Government to do something about OR in Departments, seemed to be treating the affair as a bit of a jolly. To be fair, they would have had little reason at the time to think otherwise. However, I think that William Armstrong's opening talk and some potent introductory presentations changed a lot of attitudes and, from my point of view, the seminar went well.

A month later I had a meeting with Sir William Armstrong and Lord Shackleton. I covered my nervousness with a light-hearted greeting to the Minister. Recalling the incident when he had alighted from the helicopter at Byfleet, I said he had already trodden on my toes and that I was wondering what was he going to do to me now. After the meeting, Sir William wrote to all departments advising those who hadn't already done so to start up OR groups. All such groups were to be centred professionally on mine in CSD.

The next day I initiated the setting up of an interdepartmental committee, which I was to chair to oversee the new OR organisation.

That was the take-off point, and gradually we got most departments without an operational research group to start one of their own. It wasn't too long before we even had a group of substantial size back in HM Treasury.

At home, we had new neighbours, Margaret and Stuart McHardy-Young. Margaret was a GP locally, while Stuart was a clinician of the Harley Street variety. They were not only fun, but had tastes similar to ours for wines. At the time, however, we didn't have a lot of time to indulge ourselves with them. Peggy was now an unpaid director of PAG Films Limited and I an unpaid worker, allowed to talk at board meetings held in the evening and chaired very efficiently by young Glyn Powell-Evans. For us, the venture was a hobby. I had always liked making things, obsessional – Peggy told friends that in our house "if you can't make it, you can't have it", and there was something in what she said. I was intrigued with the idea of making a hobby pay, and Peggy was wholeheartedly in favour of us taking the new hobby seriously.

Our main product was the film recorder of which we now made several versions, but we also featured a number if simpler devices for film makers. We worked long hours after our 'day jobs', including weekends, but there were numerous things which could only be done by day when normal people were around. Peggy was our saviour: she collected metal fabrications from the sheet-metal factory and took them to the sprayers; picked up our machined parts we'd had plated; delivered finished items to customers; dealt with the printers on our publicity pamphlets, and so on. At night she did various assembly jobs and kept us fed and refreshed. She told Margaret, next door: "We live in the passage between the bedroom and the workshop". Nevertheless, she professed to enjoying the life: "Never a dull moment, and I meet so many interesting people. I feel sorry for housewives who are stuck with a boring old husband day after day". She caught the cushion and threw it back.

They were busy years, but I did find time to get my prostate seen to.

Sometime during all this activity Neil Armstrong made his 'giant leap for mankind' on the surface of the moon. I wasn't in the least disappointed that my bid in New York to go on the mission had not been successful – in any case, we were arranging for Carolyn's wedding to Peter at the time. We were resigned to it, the marriage, that is. I didn't think much of Peter and I didn't think Peggy was over keen. She said we must not interfere; it was Carolyn's life, and she wouldn't thank us for destroying her illusions. I told myself that my attitude was normal for a father towards his daughter's suitors. I put on a happy face.

The wedding turned out to be a happy occasion. It was good to see the two of them so delighted with each other. Peggy's mother, Mrs Pratt, thought so too. At the ceremony at the church in Richmond, she was trying to hide the fact that she had tears in her eyes, not a reaction she was prone to.

PAG's sales grew and we couldn't cope. For my part, working by day and a lot of the night was getting to be a bit of a strain. Both Alan and Glyn had left their day jobs and we had started to take on staff. Soon, space was a worry. Glyn's father, a GP in Raynes Park, retired, and we took over his surgery as an extension. Then we bought a shop opposite the surgery that we turned into a factory.

Peggy and I returned to an almost normal life. We still had staff working in the workshop at home and, when the pressure was on, I did a bit in the evenings. Peggy spent more time with her mother. Mrs Pratt was seventy-six, kindly, and good company; I thought her a most unusual mother-in-law and we all got on very well together. Peggy still did a lot of running around for the company during the day, and took a small salary, but we had most of our evenings and weekends free. If we were home on a Saturday, Mrs Pratt would invite us upstairs for roast beef and Yorkshire pudding, a regular Saturday meal for her – which she must have cooked a couple of thousand times in half-a-century, even allowing for holiday breaks and war-time rationing. She would usually have Sunday dinner with us, she having first cooked a succulent meal for Zippy, her ginger tomcat.

APRIL SHOWERS of 1994 were dying out and the sun was beginning to warm the earth. Peggy's sister, Barbara, came to tea, which we were able to take *al fresco* in a sheltered spot in the garden. Peggy made a bit of a mess pouring the tea and pretended it was because of the wrist-to-shoulder plaster on her left arm. Barbara, from her puzzled expression, had obviously spotted that it wasn't.

I struggled with my thoughts: to tell Barbara, or not. I hadn't told anyone yet, not even Carolyn who was the only one until now who had noticed Peggy's confusion. Peggy's ability to cover up was amazing: she smiled a lot and said little; concentrated on answering, laconically, rather than questioning; agreed instead of arguing – a lesson, perhaps, for us all. Somehow, too, she was now able to differentiate between the real and her hallucinations – she would sometimes look down into her lap, but not before I had seen the vagueness in her eyes and realized she'd had a momentary switch to Dreamland. To tell anyone of her illness, I felt, would be to go against her obvious wishes, and would be a final admission that I was taking over for her. I only wished I could discuss the matter with her, but I felt that would in itself be a finalising step.

In the end I had no choice. Barbara took me aside and, looking cross, said:

"Ken, what's wrong with Peggy?"

I told her.

The next morning, after the usual up and down sort of night, I was sitting with Peggy on a sofa having coffee. I dozed off. I awoke with a start. Peggy had gone.

After the initial shock, I calmed myself and called her. No response. She had obviously gone to the loo. I checked the loos and the rest of the house. No sign of her. Then I noticed that the front door was not quite closed. I rushed outside, checked front and back of the house, ran down to the river and back. No sign. Then I panicked. I got in the car and drove madly around Harnham, searching. Near the Old Mill I saw an old lady I knew walking painfully with a stick. She was from the nursing home down the Harnham Road from us, and was, I knew, demented, and yet there she was taking her usual walk to the Old Mill and back.

That calmed me. Peggy was in much better shape, quite able to find her own way home and to ask if in difficulty. I went back home intending as a precaution to notify the police. The telephone was ringing as I went into the house. It was Jean Crichton, a neighbour:

"Just wanted to let you know Peggy's here. She was a bit upset but she's all right now."

Jean opened the door when I arrived and said that Peggy had been in an awful state when she arrived. She had told them that some people had taken over the house and that I was in league with them. Jean went on to the effect: "She has calmed down now. I'm so sorry, Ken, I didn't know she was ill. Come in and have a drink."

David Crichton was there talking to Peggy. He had been a colleague of mine in the old days at Porton, a RAF doctor – he had retired an Air Vice-Marshal.

Peggy was sitting back on a sofa looking quite relaxed and happily chatting.

Relief poured over me in a flood and I sat down quickly, feeling I might faint. I tucked myself with ill-mannered speed around the large sherry Jean poured for me. She smiled and poured me another.

We had a fairly sleepless night, and I was miserable at breakfast. Peggy, with a kindly smile, like the Queen talking to the kitchen staff after a meal, said, "Do you work here?" and later, she really did ask me whether I took sugar.

We had a kip after breakfast, Peggy in my arms on a sofa – I contrived to sit on her skirt as a safety precaution. The telephone woke us, nicely timed for morning coffee. It was Carolyn to say that her tummy trouble was reckoned to be referred lower-back pain. The scan had shown she had three deteriorated vertebrae at the base of the spine. Almost good news after the scare about what it might have been.

I picked up the post that had been sitting on the mat while we slept. It, too, bore good news – a letter from Thornhill Research Unit about their trial with Ondansetron, giving us a date, mid-May, for Peggy to be assessed on her suitability as a guinea pig. The trial was for people in the early stages of the disease; I hoped Peggy would not be considered too far-gone.

At the Thornhill Research Unit we were welcomed by a white-coated young lady, a clinical psychologist, I think. She sat us at a low table in soft seats with coffee and magazines. After a while, White-coat whisked Peggy off into a little room for interview, having explained that it was for assessment of cognisance as a starting point from which to judge any improvement. Peggy was in good form and, if she maintained the standard during her assessment, the new drug was going to have to go some to show any improvement. Later I was also subjected to inquisition, both, I suspect, to judge my likely proficiency as a reporter of Peggy's reactions, and to establish a baseline for my future evaluations of her behaviour.

When all that was done, the doctor in charge of the trial came to see us and told us that we could be accepted and explained what the work was all about. He stressed that it was a 'double-blind' trial so that neither the researchers nor we would know whether the tablets they would give Peggy to take were the real thing or placebos – I said my little prayer to the unknown again, that please, let us not get the inactive look-alikes.

On the way home, Peggy said she had told the doctor who had interviewed her that she had given up drinking wine and asked whether that was the right thing to do. The doctor had told her that there was no harm at all in her having a glass, or even two, of wine with her dinner, if that was what she enjoyed.

That evening we dined out with friends, and Peggy was delighted to be able to join in sampling a splendid bourgeois claret. She had less than a glass of the wine but by the end of the meal she was behaving badly, even rudely, to the others, and they were obviously put out. I was able to explain to them on the way out, so we didn't lose any friends. Peggy was calm going home and we cuddled on the couch with a milky drink before bed.

Peggy was in and out of bed a dozen times during the night. She got up finally, very quietly, around six, and was on her way downstairs carrying her clothes when I awoke to the sound of her dropping her shoes. She was in a fine old state. I was the enemy again and she got quite belligerent when I tried to stop her leaving the house. I stood away, but fortunately the secondary lock was on and she couldn't find her keys. She did eventually sit down to breakfast and then quickly recovered.

I didn't refer again to the morning's events but I tried to discuss the occurrence at the restaurant. She had no memory of it, and was appalled. As far as she was concerned it was an enjoyable evening. Did I think it was due to the wine? I said I didn't know; it could have been coincidental. She declared she would give up alcohol altogether, "Just in case . . ."

I was inclined to favour coincidence, especially in view of the small quantity of wine she had drunk. I couldn't think the overnight activity and the outburst in the morning were connected, particularly in view of the calm break before we went to bed. I thought it safer, however, to trust Peggy's instinct and keep tempting wine out of evidence in future.

The District Nurse came in to give us 'over 75s' our annual check-up. It seemed that neither of us was at death's door according to the standard tests. She took me aside as she was leaving and told me I must get help with Peggy: "You have your own life to lead, you know."

She was kindly and caring and was giving me good advice. I nodded acceptance – a lie, since I felt that I was living my life where I wanted to be, close to Peggy. I did, however, tell Jeremy Wring what she had said wondering whether in recruiting for his nursing home he might come across a suitable housekeeper for us.

A week or so later, Peggy and I went to dinner with Barbara. She made a rather splendid salmon kedgeree accompanied by a Saumur white wine. I was brought up short when Peggy suddenly said she thought the wine went very well with the dish. She had already drunk half a glass. She saw my look:

"Oh Hell! I forgot."

The night followed the pattern of the last alcohol incident. Peggy got up a dozen times and at six o'clock, she was at the front door in a tracksuit, and belligerent. It was difficult to avoid the conclusion that alcohol was the cause of the instability, although without it Peggy's behaviour was nothing if not variable – in minutes she could change from Zombie to near normality. She recovered over breakfast, and we went off to the hospital at Odstock to have her arm-plaster removed. She was given a light removable splint to wear in the daytime for a couple of weeks.

That night was a good one – we each had about five hours sleep. In the morning, after breakfast, Peggy was happily contemplating her latest vision, a leopard with its kitten. She admitted she wasn't sure who I was, but gave me a running commentary on the animals' activities, which included the little one peeing on the carpet. Then, unexpectedly clear minded, she asked me about her life expectancy with Alzheimer's Disease.

I was astounded since I had never mentioned Alzheimer's to her, and nor, I thought, had anyone else. I said that the doctor had said it was not possible to tell if someone actually had Alzheimer's. All we knew was that she had suffered brain damage of some sort. In any case, at our age the disease was unlikely to be the deciding factor since people lived with it for ten or fifteen years. I didn't go on to say that they probably didn't know they were surviving. But Peggy said just that.

Peggy's sudden jump from confusion to clarity was now typical behaviour. The periods when we could have reasonable conversation during the day were still much longer than the difficult patches. I wrote about a day, early in June, when Barbara joined us and we went to Kingston Lacey, a National Trust show house. Peggy was in good form all day, taking a lot of interest in the pictures, Van Dykes, Rubens and so on. Back home, we had a light supper in the garden and Peggy slipped from her good form a little and asked where we would sleep that night. Then, suddenly, her talk was vague and difficult to understand:

"I want to know what it's all about."

Naturally, I asked what was what all about.

"You're supposed to be the expert in dealing with patients like me. You ought to know."

I apologised.

"And what about the others?"

I changed the subject – or rather, changed to a definite subject – but she wasn't having that:

"I also want to know how we got here, and who's going to pay for the food."

Barbara then tried to change the theme by inviting us to dinner the following evening. Peggy said:

"That will be nice, thank you, dear." Then to me, "Will you be coming with us?" She smiled. "Sorry, Ken, that was silly. Of course you will." And we were back to normal – except her hands were twitching and she was fidgeting.

I took her hands and she gripped tightly. "What's wrong, Poomphie?"

"I don't know, Ken dear, I feel all shaky inside."

CHAPTER THIRTEEN

By the Spring of 1969, Operational Research had settled into Government. In my Group we had more major projects than we could cope with, even with our now much expanded complement and teams of management consultants we employed from the private sector. The trick was to use outside people, do a successful study, and then point out that it was cheaper to use insiders, and get the complement increased – perhaps I should have put that in code.

Peggy usually called for a 'debriefing' over dinner on my day's activities. Even her mother, Mrs Pratt, took an interest when we got to planning the change to decimal currency.

"It was scandalous when they got rid of the silver thr'p'ny bit, our little Joey. Now they want to get rid of our sixpence . . ."

In jest, I told her I would speak to The Earl of Halsbury about it. He was Chairman of the Decimal Currency Board to which we reported on that study. We were concerned not only with getting the coinage right but also in keeping costs down on the changeover. When we'd finished the study we had a final meeting with the Board. Lord Halsbury walked from the room with me afterwards and said, quietly:

"How sure are you, James, we've got it right?"

Tony Halsbury was no slouch and his question was not one from a lofty figurehead to mysterious technician. He was a chemist and an engineer who had recently been elected a Fellow of the Royal Society, and you can't get much more eminent in the scientific world. Moreover he had been president of our Operational Research Society. My mental processes stuttered. How sure was I? I said something lamely to the effect:

"Well, I think we've made the best assessment possible on the evidence we could unearth."

"What about adding a little more to the budget just to be on the safe side? What do you say to that?"

"We have safety factors built in, and the model would show, on present evidence, you'd have any addition as a surplus at the end – and that's almost as bad as spending it."

"Would you take it amiss if we added, say . . ." and he named a relatively small sum.

"Not at all. Shall we split the surplus afterwards?"

He laughed, but he did recommend the addition – HM Treasury did something with the resulting surplus.

Mrs Pratt did keep her sixpenny piece for a time, the 'tanner', which as 2½ new pence, was an anomaly in the decimal system. It was a political decision in response to public appeal, and it made sense once the inclusion of the tiny halfpenny coin was admitted as an anti-inflation device.

A fuss was made, too, over some of the new coins because, it was said, the poorly sighted would be unable to distinguish them. At a meeting I was at, the chairman was called to the telephone:

"No, sir."

"No, sir, that wouldn't work either."

"No, sir, you can't drill a bloody hole in it, the Queen's face is in the way."

Back at the table, he said, "That was the PM." He grinned. "I retire in a couple of months, anyway – wouldn't be surprised if he did too."

At home that evening, Peggy had taken delivery of her Austin A40 and she took me for a ride around Richmond Park. We had dinner in Richmond, and I told her about the telephone call from Harold Wilson, coin recognition and retirement.

We went on to talk about my retirement: seven years away, it seemed remote and we didn't treat the matter very seriously. I was vaguely looking forward to it, but I hadn't thought out what I might then do. I was clear on only one aspect: I would not hang around after sixty taking charitable consultancies and the like. Peggy verged on the macabre quoting two friends who had prepared for years for their retirement: large pension contributions, holiday homes abroad . . . One died a year before retirement and the other a month after. She also wondered whether we enjoyed life as we were because we were not falling over each other all day.

"Don't you notice," she said, "now we have extended our summer holidays to a month, how we enjoy getting back to the grind?"

"You mean you get fed up with having me around?"

"Not really. You're more exciting when I sometimes can't get at you."

1970 was an interesting year: Edward Heath took over from Labour's Harold Wilson as Prime Minister; the one cent postage stamp of 1856, British Guiana, sold in New York for the record price of $280,000, and, to add to my postal history collection, I paid – a record for me – £150 for the world's first stamp error, a Victorian penny red of Great Britain with a corner letter missing; I had a stand-up argument with Wedgwood Benn at a talk he gave to the top hamper in Treasury and Civil Service Department, and got disapproving glances from the Permanent Secretary. Nevertheless, I was promoted to Chief Scientific Officer and invited to join the Cabinet Office Mess. I had to wait for the wall-to-wall office carpet I'd become entitled to, but I was surprised to learn that the rank gained me automatic entry to 'Who's Who'. Bert Creamer told me about it before the forms arrived. He said, "Won't do you much good, but your kids'll love it."

There was an eerie, end-of-the-road feeling about that promotion.

Early the following year the Civil Service Department moved up Whitehall from the Treasury building to the Old Admiralty Building next to Horseguards Parade. There, I got my all-over carpet in a suite of interconnecting offices for myself, my secretary, and a senior principal, my personal assistant – I had a sneaking suspicion that dear Jim Tuson, was there to keep an eye on this strange scientific chap to save him putting a foot too far wrong. He was certainly invaluable and probably kept me out of a lot of trouble. There was one slight difficulty over my lavish accommodation: the officer responsible for the allocation of rooms came to tell me, most apologetically, that I'd have to move elsewhere since it had been noticed that my room was bigger than that of the Permanent Secretary, Sir William Armstrong. I didn't think Sir William would have worried too much about that, but I thought the problem more easily solved, without my moving. I had them by put in a partition across the large office to give me an entrance lobby and library – which could also house my badge of rank, a bentwood hat-and-coat stand. Peggy said, "When they make you king, you can have a velvet-covered lavatory seat."

It was during this period the Central Policy Review Staff in the Cabinet Office, Edward Heath's Think-Tank, was doing its forward thinking. The Director of the group was Victor Rothschild who had taken over my office at Porton during the war. His quick summary of the situation he found when he took office was: "I never realized the country was run by two men I'd never heard of," meaning Sir William Armstrong and the then Secretary to the Cabinet, Sir Burke Trend. I suppose I hoped he wasn't now going to overshadow my efforts to get objective study into government policy making – he was a scientist, an inspirational leader, and he had collected a powerful team of very intelligent people sitting top-centre, and could have a strong influence on central decisions.

What seemed strange, if not downright heretical, was that such a group had been set up. The great machine of the civil service, whose executive task kept it in detailed touch with reality, existed essentially to advise political ministers. Was it expected that just a few brilliant people could replace this complex system? And, how would contrary advice between the large and the small be resolved? I had once been asked a similar question concerning my own aims, and I said that my arrogance didn't extend to thinking I could outbid the system; I aimed not to give advice, but to produce a tool to strengthen the system.

In the event, there was no conflict. I don't know what Edward Heath thought about the many brilliant ideas he was fed – perhaps they merely added a little salt to the bubbling stew of advice he got from the system. Certainly, Margaret Thatcher, later, preferred to take her nourishment unseasoned. One of the CPRS team joined my group in CSD for a while. She was scintillating in discussion and contributed several bright ideas. I formed the opinion in fact that CPRS was indeed an ideas machine, better for raising issues than resolving them.

PAG Ltd was slowly improving its sales, and Peggy and I were still doing our bits to help. I was a little worried about the film side of the business. Sale of a recorder for several thousand pounds was always a notable event but all too rare, and it seemed to me that without the auxiliary business from batteries and chargers we wouldn't survive. Glyn, who was looking after the numbers, assured me, however, that we were on an even keel, and that at a recent exhibition where they had unveiled our latest recorder there had been a lot of serious interest. He and Alan were also pressing on with arrangements to start up the intended film-making side of the business.

We did get involved in making a film, 'Hunted', a short, starring Edward Woodward and June Ritchie. Peggy and I went to the premiere in Soho and quite enjoyed it. PAG only had a tiny part of the financial action – not that it mattered, the film made very little. After that, film making died for us.

The year was then routine – except that I was so entranced with Segovia's guitar playing at a concert in the Festival Hall, on the South Bank, that coming out after the recital I fell down the stairs. Peggy was as embarrassed as I was. "Get up, you silly ass," was her sympathetic comment. I had a few grazes and a bruised hip, but no serious damage.

Peggy started 1972 going on a freezer course. She said she had learned that if you put things in the big box and switched on, the things got cold.

Out of routine in the year was an interest in sharpening up our very elementary French conversation. We arranged with the Twickenham Technical College that they would introduce their French *assistants* to us – they came to the school for short periods, mostly from France, to improve their English and to teach French at the school. We would invite the current one to dinner and conversation. With one exception they were young women. The young man was

Abdy, an Arab from Tunis who felt the cold and came to us in the winter, thin and bony, looking miserable in ill-fitting European summer wear. On his first visit, Peggy forgot the cream for the pudding. She fetched a half-pint carton and handed it to Abdy with an apology for not putting it in a jug. Abdy's eyes lit up. He said thank you in three languages and drank the lot from the carton. We did manage, under the guise of practice conversation, to advise on warmer clothing, but he wouldn't hear of us going with him to the shops. The next time he came, he looked even more miserable, a scarecrow, broomstick arms sticking out from a woollen sports coat several sizes too small, and it took three or four visits for us to get him up to a reasonable standard of dress.

It was several years later we had a telephone call from Abdy: could we join him for dinner at his hotel in Piccadilly to meet his new wife. He no longer looked miserable, filling well his Savile-Row suit. He was in Shipping, he said, smiling happily at his beautiful young wife.

Our summer holiday was in the Pyrenees. We drove down with our caravan and parked it fairly high beside a lake. We had done this before, but this time we took off on foot for the high mountains with backpacks, including in mine a Norwegian lightweight tent. We were particularly aiming to climb up over a col and down to a glacier we had seen on our last trip and couldn't get to in a day. We had really worked on getting the weight down in our packs – even cutting the handles off the toothbrushes – and climbing, well, rock scrambling, with them was no problem. We enjoyed the experience because of the sense of freedom, as Peggy put it – being able to carry on, enjoying views in a leisurely fashion, without thought to getting back to base by dark. What we didn't much enjoy were the long nights cramped into a tiny tent in the rain. We got to our glacier and back all right, but it was a great joy on our return to the caravan to sit under our awning in comfortable chairs, sipping cold white wine, while the chicken was roasting for dinner – exotic suburbanization! We went back to day walks – more suited to the dignity of our advanced age.

Back home, Peggy finished the year going to the Tutankhamen exhibition at the British Museum. "Not too many eighteen-year-olds get remembered after thirty three centuries," she said. "Mozart might have been a candidate, I suppose, if he'd had a tomb full of gold."

CHAPTER FOURTEEN

Our next visit to the Thornhill Research Unit at Moorgreen Hospital was mid-June 1994. Peggy went off to the little room to be assessed again while I was questioned about her behaviour at home. The doctor in charge of the research also had a word with me and asked whether I had noticed any changes in Peggy since the last interview. I told him about the fidgeting and the feeling of shakiness, and how variable her behaviour was, from near normality to demented. I took the opportunity to ask about the possibility that alcohol, even in small amounts, might be adversely affecting Peggy. He too thought it very difficult to tell because of the innate variability. To be more certain we would have to try a week off and a week on a few times to see whether there was an obvious pattern.

We were to go through the interviews again with an independent assessor, but the assessor would be a little late – she'd had to take her dog to the vet. Meanwhile, what could they get us for lunch?

We went off after a lunch of Marks & Spencer's sandwiches, with a month's supply of pills. One slight difficulty was that we'd had several restless nights and we were both tired. Peggy went to sleep almost as soon as she was settled in the car and I found it hard to keep awake driving. Dangerous. I should have stopped for a kip. At home we both slept for a couple of hours on a sofa, with me sitting on Peggy's skirt.

The next day, Saturday, Carolyn arrived with her new boyfriend, Lawrence, to stay the weekend. Lawrence was Carolyn's age and was obviously looking at her with serious eyes. He was bright, intelligent, a pleasant chap, and we were delighted. In the afternoon we had tea in the garden and, later, the Farant Singers of Salisbury came down the river in a boat singing madrigals. We went along to the Rose and Crown just down river from us where they were to tie up to sing some more, and we could have a barbecue supper.

I hadn't intended starting the alcohol trial the doctor at the Thornhill Research Unit had mentioned, but we ordered beer and Peggy wanted to join in. She enjoyed the singing, her supper and her small glass of lager.

She said afterwards she had enjoyed seeing the chaps walking on the water, they were so clever. She had a terrible night. Again the now familiar pattern – up dressing half-a-dozen times, and belligerent at one stage, accusing me of preventing her phoning Barbara to get her to help.

"Help with what, dear?"

"To get rid of the man in my bed."

"Perhaps I could help."

"You're on his side."

That was the end of any thought of an alcohol trial.

Peggy had recovered as usual after breakfast and we spent a pleasant day of domesticity together, both of us sharing life happily with her imaginary people – the Arab on the camel was still around. We did three loads of washing and Peggy helped with the ironing – she was all right on the plain things but left the shirts and blouses to me. She did some tidying in the garden while I mowed the lawns. As for the cooking, I had a certain love-hate relationship with it – I enjoyed doing it but resented the time it took. While trying to avoid the packages or dull simplicity, I was learning fast the simplest approaches. We had lunch by the river – salmon and prawn with chopped spring onion in a proprietary seafood dressing, with a mixed salad. I did a pork fillet casserole for dinner served with Jersey Royals and baby sprouts. For pud we had yoghurt in two colours supporting a pair of peach halves, flat side down, with a small raspberry balanced suggestively on each – not original: Escoffier did it with a cream base for King Edward VII at the Carlton in London.

My sister Georgie came to see us the following week with her husband, Dennis. It was hard to take in the fact that my kid sister had just passed her seventieth birthday – she had worn well despite her endless list of allergies and ailments. Dennis was my age, and Georgie complained he was getting senile – but she had always had a deprecatory word for Dennis's behaviour. I couldn't risk cooking for Georgie since I wasn't familiar with the tortuous path through her jungle of allergies, so we went to lunch at a riverside pub a couple of miles up the Nadder from us. Georgie was a ray of sunshine and Peggy basked in it. She was splendid; there might have been nothing wrong. We were a couple of weeks into the Ondansetron trial and my spirits rose. She crumpled a little after Georgie and Dennis left, but that night she slept right through and woke up friendly. It was so marked a change that I couldn't think I was only seeing it with an eye of hope.

Barbara and Evelyn came to lunch next day and Peggy prepared lunch without prompting and with only husbandly help. I was trying hard not to be desperately pleased – we'd had similar long periods of near normality before the experimental treatment. The next night was only marred by a bellyache – Peggy's. I rang the Research Unit about it and was told to change the pill schedule for Peggy to take them with food, and that I was doubtless pleased since this side effect indicated that we had the real tablets and not the placebos – so much for a double-blind trial.

The good nights went on, but the days had slipped back a bit. On Peggy's birthday, 3 July, she said there had been a man in her bed, did I know who he was – she seemed to have a down on the poor chap. I had concocted a huge birthday card for her and propped it in front of her at the breakfast table. She sat in its shadow and didn't notice it. She said to all the people she alone could see around the table, "Why don't you speak?" I don't think they answered. She said to me:

"One of them has stolen my shoes."

Then the nights went bad again. By the time we were due at the

Thornhill Research Unit it was clear there had been no lasting improvement. Whether we had real tablets or placebos, I could only think the early rally had been the so-called 'placebo effect', Peggy thinking as wishfully as I was. It was a plus point, I suppose, that she could still rouse herself in this way – rather as she could with visitors.

At the Research Unit, Peggy had blood and urine checks only. It would be the same next time – psychological tests the following month.

Peggy was now vague for somewhat longer and had little bouts of tearful misery, which I think were caused by her recognition of her condition. She spoke for twenty minutes on the phone to Barbara and then asked me who she was. But she was still reasonable most of the time, even if worse at doing things – not being able to locate the cold tap at the sink, or find a light switch. She was, however, still intent on trying to do her bit – she always cleared up after a meal, and usually quite well. She still dressed herself in the mornings with a little guidance.

As for me, I needed to improve. When Peggy was particularly confused I was liable to break down and shout at her. I hated myself for my behaviour, but I didn't seem to be able to prevent it – I seemed suddenly to reach the end of a rope and there was no alternative but to drop off.

We did our August visit to the Thornhill Research Unit, Peggy had her blood pressure measured and we collected a new supply of pills. Back home we had a bad night and a repeat of a previous episode. We got to sleep probably around five o'clock in the morning. I awoke about nine and Peggy had gone. I did the panic tour of Harnham again and then did what I should have done first, rang Jean Crichton. Peggy was there and quite happy.

There was a call on the answerphone when we got back, from Jeremy Wring: he had a candidate for the housekeeper job. It gave me a good feeling. No more cooking, and some relief from the constant watch.

Friday night, and Carolyn arrived with Lawrence in time for dinner to stay a few days. Carolyn said it was the nineteenth anniversary of her divorce from Peter. Her back was now much worse, she was scarcely able to walk, although she managed to get around using a stick. Lawrence was very attentive and over dinner he said they were engaged to be married and hoped that was all right with us.

Carolyn was taking early retirement from the civil service and they wanted to move to Salisbury. Carolyn could certainly do much worse as far as the marriage was concerned – and had previously done so with Peter – but I didn't put my answer quite so baldly.

Lawrence went flat hunting and found a suitable one in Bouverie Avenue just over Harnham Hill from us. When they left for London it was difficult getting Carolyn to the car. Her legs seemed paralysed.

Lawrence rang the next day to say that Carolyn was in Atkinson Morley Hospital. The specialist had seen her. There was something on the spine compressing nerves, probably a tumour; hence the immobility of her legs. She was in theatre.

In the post that morning was the Alzheimer's Disease Society's Newsletter for August, and a report on current research was about Diffuse Lewy-Body Disease. While my mind was mostly tensed for news of Carolyn, almost subconsciously I recorded that symptoms ascribed to the affliction were closely matched in Peggy – hallucinations, high sensitivity to tranquillisers, episodes of acute confusion, and mild Parkinsonism. Considered a rare disease in the sixties it was now thought that about a quarter of those diagnosed Alzheimer's in fact had LBD.

I tried to get information on Carolyn from the hospital from eleven o'clock onwards, but it wasn't until four in the afternoon that I was told she was comfortable in intensive care and that nobody was free to tell me more. I tried several times to get the surgeon who had done the operation but without success. I did get a message from him saying Carolyn's operation had gone well and she was recovering satisfactorily.

Lawrence rang early in the morning. A lot of tissue had been removed from Carolyn's lower spine area and a sample sent to Pathology. The surgeon had told Lawrence that it was almost certainly malignant and likely to be a secondary rather than the primary tumour. She would be going to the Royal Marsden hospital for radiotherapy. He said Carolyn was in fine spirit and could bend her legs again and wiggle her toes.

We drove up the next day. Carolyn was bright and cheerful in her bed on a morphine drip. She couldn't quite lie on her back because of the staples in her incision. She said she was like a zipper. Lawrence was very attentive and caring. I felt a heavy sadness. Just when a future was opening up for the pair of them, it had been snatched away. Peggy and I looked across the bed at each other with tightly compressed lips, holding on. Peggy turned quickly, switched on a broad smile and chatted away to Carolyn in wonderful style, no sign of her own affliction.

I didn't know what they would now do about marriage, but it could no longer be the grand opening to a new life for them. I wished I could give them something to look forward to.

Inspiration!

"Lawrence, what about taking Carolyn on a cruise for her convalescence?"

His eyes lit up but I could almost hear him counting the pennies.

"To New Orleans?" I suggested – Lawrence was a jazz fan.

"Wonderful," said Carolyn, looking as though she'd jump out of bed and go immediately.

Lawrence was looking at her with soft eyes.

"Can you fix it up then, Lawrence, when Carolyn can get around? I'll send you a cheque."

It wasn't difficult to see I'd done the right thing.

I tried to get to see the surgeon before we left but he was out for the day.

On the telephone the next morning I got little more out of him than confirmation of his opinion that it was a secondary malignant tumour he had excised – the biopsy results were not yet available. Carolyn was going to the Royal Marsden Hospital where they would try to locate the primary but it was unlikely to be found. She would have radiotherapy there. He was no bundle of joy, but perhaps surgeons don't need a bedside manner. At the time I suppose I appreciated his frankness.

Peggy said she felt she was in limbo just waiting for something awful to happen – I felt it already had. We drove out into the country, had lunch in a country pub under an acacia tree, and went to Hillier's to buy some shrubs for the garden. It was soon obvious that neither of us was able to concentrate enough to decide on such purchases, although we did buy some lettuce seed.

We shopped at Tesco's on the way home and drained their petrol storage into the Jag, and went home to tea. It did Peggy a lot of good to get out and about and, despite our new Damoclesian sword, she had been quite happy all day. She had a spell of vagueness after dinner and asked where Barbara lived, why did we never see her, and would she be coming to France with us this year. She was then tearful but would give no reason – not that it wasn't obvious.

It was a couple of days later that Lawrence rang to say Carolyn's biopsy results were in. It wasn't cancer.

FROM 1973 the years to retirement seemed to spin by. With the generous leave from the civil service Peggy and I were able to take holidays two or three times a year, which we mostly spent in France or Italy, with our interests divided between food and mountains. My diaries are detailed on our exploits, but in memory the holidays mostly blur into abstract pleasure. Some memories are clear-cut, often for frivolous reasons. A climb in the Alpes Maritimes in late October stands out, not so much because we got lost in a sudden snow storm, more because back in the hotel we broke the bed. Peggy said it was dangerous for me to be so enthusiastic at my age, but I thought it was Peggy really – or perhaps we were both celebrating an escape from a freezing night on the mountain.

Sign of my advancing age, I became a member of the Board of the Science Research Council and its Mathematics Committee, and Chairman of its Operational Research Panel. We allocated government funds for research – and I wondered, when so much personal opinion went into the decisions and success of an application depended so much on who happened to be on the committee, whether tossing a coin might not have been a fairer system.

I resigned from the Savage Club that year when I was elected to membership of the Athenæum – no pretension, I think (well, perhaps some), just that so many of my day-to-day contacts were with members of the Athenaeum. Perhaps my election had resulted from members I'd lunched with at the club thinking it was time I paid my whack. It was the day I first paid for lunch there that the IRA detonated a 'bomb' in New Scotland Yard. My office in the Old Admiralty Building faced the blast across Whitehall. The windows were blown in – there were daggers of glass stuck in my desk. In my secretary's room, the whole frame was blown in and projected past her sitting at her desk to smash into the far wall. The exploding car had excavated a large crater in the road opposite, but nobody in our building was hurt.

In the summer, Peggy and I went back to DOAE at Byfleet for their annual cocktail party; we had a new roof on our house in Twickenham, and then another year started. In this one, we, that is, PAG, bought the shop next door to our existing one in Raynes Park to add manufacturing space; Peggy and I went to the OR Society's Banquet in the Guildhall; and we celebrated our thirty-third wedding anniversary at a wine tasting and dinner on Peggy's old stamping ground, the School of Pharmacy in Bloomsbury Square. In December we ran quickly through my fifty-ninth birthday and the year dissolved into 1976.

It was the year Carolyn came back to live with us, the year of the divorce. We were never quite certain what precipitated the final break. Carolyn just said things had not been right from the start: there were no children. Peggy and I had mixed feelings: pleased she was clear of Peter, sad for her – she was a lonely young lady.

Zippy, the ginger cat, died in January, and Mrs Pratt was forlorn. We took her out to dinner at a rather nice restaurant in Sheen. It was another of those small events that led to bigger things. We sat in the lounge area of the restaurant and had an aperitif. I picked up a magazine and glanced through it. There was an advertisement by the Ramblers, something like, "Learn cross-country skiing – if you can walk, you can ski". I showed it to Peg:

"Fancy that, Poomphie?"

"What, at our age? They wouldn't take us."

"Shall we try them?" I don't know why I said it, I had never been attracted to skiing.

"Where is it," Peggy said.

"Switzerland."

"Never been. Let's go."

I don't really remember the meal, but Mrs Pratt thought the turbot wasn't as good as the coley she used to feed Zippy. A telephone call in the morning brought us the pamphlets, and in February we went to Münster with the Ramblers.

The Ramblers' advertisement needed editing. It should have read, "If you can walk *on skis*, you can ski". The skis tend to go faster than you and leave you with no support other than your behind.

Our first lesson was inauspicious. Our leader, a strapping, young lady in her mid-twenties, Mary Hill, took the ten of us across the road from the hotel to the top of a gentle hill down to the stream bordering the local airfield. She showed us how to clip the skis to the toe piece of the soft, comfortable boots. Most of us slipped on to our behinds in the process, but when she'd got us all vertical she said:

"OK, you lot, just push off with your poles and slide gently down the hill."

Most of us managed to get away as fast as our skis. As speed built up, which it did alarmingly, I realized I had no idea how to stop. Peggy was ahead of me and crouched over, with obvious confidence, her poles under her arms in an impressively expert-looking stance. She'd been watching the skiing on TV, so perhaps she did know how to apply the brakes. Mary came past shouting some sort of instruction, but at that moment the man in the lead of our bunch, doubtless not wishing to test the ice of the stream at the bottom of the slope, sat down and slid on his back. We piled into him to form a writhing mass of skis, arms, poles and legs. We were all shrieking with laughter – such was our relief at not being dead.

"Well, you made a mess of that, you lot," said Mary, when we had untied ourselves.

By lunchtime she had shown us how to snowplough and had us all, with varying degrees of confidence, skiing up and down gentle slopes without falling about too much.

I sat next to Mary at lunch and she confessed to being a downhill skier: she had never had cross-country skis on before. She was surprised how fast they went on a gentle slope.

There was another Mary in the group, Mary Pearce, a soft and gentle Mary, and her husband Ian, interestingly computer-wise and argumentative. Mary Pearce had broken her wrist in a fall in a skating rink before she came on holiday and was still in plaster – she said she would feel safer skiing if the other wrist were plastered too.

It was Ian Pearce, later in the holiday over a goodnight glühwein, who asked me about a bump on my forehead. I said: "What bump?" But sure enough, I could feel one.

"I should get that looked at, if I were you," he said.

The comment might not have gone down too well with me from others, but Ian somehow made it an expression of a personal worry sincerely felt for me. I saw Peggy watching me, worried too, I suppose, about the bump; but also about how I might respond to Ian.

"Thanks, Ian," I said, "I hadn't noticed it. I'll see the quack when we get back."

Later, Peggy said, "What lovely people."

At the end of the holiday most of us were getting around quite well on our skis and wandering out of the cut tracks into the hills, a wonderful freedom. I was hooked, and Peggy, too – with some reservations, I think.

Holiday over, the fact descended on me of 1976 being my last year in the civil service – papers awaited me in the office revealing the details of my retirement pension. With the realization came relaxation and as a result I seemed to get a lot more done – I certainly enjoyed doing it. I was advised to put in for a university fellowship to retire into, and I applied for one at Nuffield College Oxford. I was a bit half-hearted about it. Although there were some aspects of OR I felt would be interesting subjects for research, I couldn't see myself as a university don. Apparently, nor could the assessor. My application was not accepted.

At home, Peggy and I were at our happiest, and that too might well have been due to my more laid-back attitude.

June was a memorable month for me. First, I went to an Invitational Conference sponsored by Sussex University, Professor Pat Rivett, in fact. There I had lunch with Pat, Sir Derek Ezra who was running the Coal Board at the time, and Sir Marcus Seiff of Marks and Spencers. At the conference I met James Davidson Pratt again, JDP. He was as handsome as ever, the jet-black hair now gleaming grey. He asked after Peggy. I also chatted to Sir Malcolm Muggeridge and to one of my scientific gods, Sir James Lighthill. I learned that day why famous people are interesting – besides providing names for name droppers – they *are* interesting. I had more than a sneaking suspicion they would not be decorating their diaries with my name. I also suspected that retirement would reduce my opportunities to meet erudite celebrities.

Then Peggy and I went to Brussels where I had to run a conference on OR under NATO aegis. We discovered that Brussels could produce *cuisine* at least as *haute* as anything available in Paris. Unfortunately, on our last night, it seemed to have produced the most intense bellyache I had ever experienced.

By the morning it had settled to a grumble and disappeared on the trip home. At home that evening it was back. Peggy called in Stuart and Margaret, our doctor friends from next door. When I'd described my symptoms – which took just three words including the expletive – I caught one of those pursed-lipped glances from doctor to doctor. He prodded around my abdomen a bit, gave me some painkillers and then got on the telephone and fixed for me to see a mate of his in Harley Street in the morning.

A few minutes in the waiting room with Peggy and several hawk-faced Arabs, and I was led gently by picturesque starched femininity into clinical cleanliness beyond the panelled oak door. There, X-ray machines took full-frontals, back-and-sides, and slices. Half-an-hour and two cups of coffee later, I was visited in an interview room by a charming fellow who had an air of being rich, not disguised by his wrinkled pin-striped grey suit – or perhaps I just felt he must be, with all those Arabs sitting outside. He had his arms full of X-ray plates, which he talked me through, demonstrating there was nothing of diagnostic importance to see. I could read in his eyes that he thought I should be pleased, but actually I hadn't thought I might have cancer.

It was several days before I had the pain again. This time it was much worse; I was rolling around on the floor. Peggy called on Stuart again and he arranged immediately for a bed for me in the Masonic hospital, Ravenscourt Park. So unfair: think of all those people out there waiting for operations. I didn't.

Gall bladder removed, the nurses made me sit up in bed; the pain was indescribable – they did the operation the hard way in those days with a great slash up through the navel. They allowed me to stay sitting up so that I didn't have to suffer the procedure of getting that way again to eat dinner. Three days later I was back home, a nicely crafted navel healing well, and doing a little work in the workshop. The month of June was over.

December had to come, my last commuting month. I was

enchanted one day early in the month when my secretary, after a few inconsequential remarks said, shyly, "I want to ask you out to lunch before you leave. Would you come?" I said that of course I would be delighted but felt I should be taking her. "So that's settled then, I asked first."

On the day, she collected me and asked if I'd mind walking.

"Where to?"

"Not far."

It was to the Commonwealth Club off St James's. Inside, I was puzzled. We seemed to be expected. Our coats were taken and we were shown immediately into an empty room curtained off at one end. The curtains fluttered and Jim Tuson materialized like a genie, accompanied by Peggy, radiant. Jim had a red-covered book with him, which he opened, looked at, and said:

"Ken James, this is your life."

The curtains parted to a burst of applause from a couple of hundred people assembled there. Mostly they were from the government OR groups but there were representatives from all the places I'd worked in the past twenty years. It was a wonderful party. Peggy and I sat together for the banquet and we were then entertained by a series of stage shows by MS(OR) staff. I didn't even have to make a speech. When I mentioned to Peggy that I ought to at least say thank you, she said something like:

"I expect that's what they're celebrating, not having to listen to you talk any more. Actually, Ken, I've been told to make sure you don't spoil your lunch thinking about having to make a speech."

I think that party gave me more sense of fulfilment than . . . well, anything else since Peggy and I married.

My 'official' farewell party was some days later in the Treasury, the usual drinks affair in the evening. At what seemed the right time I walked out alone, a little hazy, thoughtful, but contented. I was stepping out into a new world. How fortunate I'd been to spend the past ten years in contact with that elite intelligentsia that runs the country and influences the world. True, I had kicked against the pricks of its arbitrariness, but how otherwise could it act? Wait around for months while scientists poked stuff into a computer? Even with my religious fervour in chasing the future – where the hierarchical decision machine would be replaced by the flat organisation, where information would be fed in all the time, to be handled in all its complexity at the decision level, rapidly and accurately, without the need for great armies of people sequentially filtering, condensing, and emasculating it with judgement – I hoped those who eventually replaced the mandarins would be chosen with similar care for their high intelligence and ability to acquire wisdom. There were no absolute truths; in the end someone had to judge.

I had taken a couple of breaths of the cold December air of my new world and it stirred my party-fuzzed brain. I was walking out to nothing. I walked back in.

First I rang Peggy, then Glyn. I'd be joining PAG full time in the New Year. I went home for Christmas with a bounce in my step.

CHAPTER FIFTEEN

It was a showery, cool, September day of 1994 when we drove to the Thornhill Research Unit. We were in much better spirits than usual: Carolyn had been unstapled and was getting out of bed and already able to walk a few unpainful steps.

We had a long session at the Unit, going through the double set of interviews again. Rather hesitantly, when it came to the talk with the doctor in charge of the trial, I raised the issue of Diffuse Lewy Body Disease, expecting polite response indicating I was hanging on to anything that led away from Alzheimer's. I was even rash enough to ask, LBD being a sort of extended Parkinson's Disease, whether treatment with levodopa might be indicated.

To my surprise and delight he took immediate interest and talked to me in technical terms about the disease. He then took Peggy off for examination leaving me with the technical papers on his own trial to read.

Half an hour later they were back, and he said he agreed with my diagnosis – I was now on a professional pedestal. He thought the chances of the Ondansetron doing Peggy any good at the dosages being used in his trial were remote. It would be better to take her off the trial and put her on a regime of levodopa.

Again he surprised me. He said he would write to our GP, but meanwhile here was a prescription for a levodopa preparation, Madopar. We were to return in two weeks to see if it was working.

It felt good to be doing something positive. I just had a slightly uneasy feeling: I wished it hadn't been my lay diagnosis.

Mid-September, and Carolyn was in residence at the Royal Marsden Hospital starting on her radiotherapy courses. Even though the tumour they had removed was not cancerous, she would, we were told, be having another operation when she was strong enough, to remove any last vestiges of it so that it didn't grow again. I was not clear why she was getting radiotherapy if the biopsy had shown the tumour to be benign. Perhaps they were not that certain.

We were expecting the Baumfields to luncheon – that seemed to be more suitable for them than lunch – on their way to West Bay where they had a cottage. I had spent the morning on my feet preparing the meal, wondering why I went in for such complication when Marks and Spencer's was ten minutes away. We had suffered a few poor nights in a row and I was tired anyway, but now there was a new difficulty, a painful back. It had come on during the morning, and I hoped it was just from standing around so long, but I'd run the gamut of death thoughts – not an uncommon pastime at my age.

Peggy was not showing any overall improvement from the Madopar treatment. However, internal 'shakiness' now only occurred about four hours after a dose – and, I noticed, invariably accompanied by cold hands and feet – and was relieved in half-an-hour or so by the next pill. She seemed more variable, both worse and better than before. It was sometimes more difficult to get her to understand a simple direction: "Put it in the fridge, dear," had her fiddling with the light switches. However, for the Baumfield's visit she laid the table faultlessly, without prompting, something she hadn't achieved for many months. She went on then to make 'coffee' for us both while I was cooking, using several tea bags in one teacup.

As usual, she perked up wonderfully when our visitors arrived, and we had a most entertaining luncheon with them – the lunch itself was all right too.

The Baumfields left soon after the meal, and I rang Carolyn at the Royal Marsden. She and Lawrence were planning to get married in Salisbury in November. She was leaving hospital in a few days.

My back was still troublesome. That night I crept upstairs to bed like a very old man – which, come to think of it, I was.

We had a reasonable night once I found a position with no daggers sticking into me. Peggy insisted on getting up early; she was more than usually confused. I wasn't anxious to get up to drag my back around and I tried persuading her to stay in for a while, but she was adamant. I got up too, staying in my dressing gown to oversee Peggy's dressing, breakfast and pills. She was obstreperous and wanted nothing to do with me. I managed all right up to the time she refused to take her Madopar pill, clenching it in her hand. I tried to retrieve it but she fought like a wild cat.

"Ken," she shrieked, "Come quickly. He's trying to poison me."

Then I lost my temper and went a bit berserk trying to force her hand open. I even bit her finger when she poked it at my mouth. That stopped me, and I recovered enough to go back to gentle persuasion, but without success. Not surprisingly, Peggy was much affected by my fury and went to all the doors in the house calling for help. In the end, however, I got through to her that the pill was medicine and that I was not trying to poison her – I pretended not to notice when she secreted the pill and popped it surreptitiously into her mouth.

That was probably a summit or a ridge in my climb to total frustration, a watershed, perhaps. I couldn't imagine that I could behave worse.

Then came the good bit. Half an hour after the pill, a complete transformation, a total change of personality back to the normal Peggy I knew – normal for those days, that is. Would it have happened anyway – there had always been a tendency to some improvement after breakfast – or was it the pill?

My back was still pretty troublesome – I did the ironing sitting down. I heated something from a packet for lunch and involuntarily dozed off in a chair after the meal for about two hours. I awoke in a panic, but Peggy was asleep in another chair nearby.

It was fine and breezy the day we drove to the Thornhill Research Unit again. The doctor thought, as I did, that the Madopar had improved Peggy's alertness. He increased the dose of Madopar a little and we were dismissed from Thornhill and the Glaxo trial.

Back home I cooked a celebratory dinner. To cool down from the kitchen, I walked out on the patio in the dark, stepped over the edge. It was a drop of over two feet, but on to grass and I managed a roll.

No damage. Both of us had now gone over the edge; I would have to add a balustrade.

September had been quite a month: Carolyn's cancer scare (I hoped it was just a scare since we now knew there were still some results to come from the Royal Marsden) and Peggy's new diagnosis – who would have thought having some form of Parkinsonism a cause for rejoicing; and Carolyn engaged to be married again.

Good news at the end of the month was that Geoffrey Watts, Mary's husband, was still in remission from his leukaemia. He was engaged in a full-time refresher course for instrument rating at the level for airline pilots.

October started with me in a foul mood – back troublesome, computer, too; and there was the washing to do. It all started with my finding one of Peggy's precious pills on the floor. I didn't know whether it was one she should have taken or not, but I was suddenly incensed with the thought that I had to keep an eye on her day and night – and I was so tired. Then I finished the washing and ironing; solved the computer problem; cooked lunch; felt better.

Dr Maggie Cormack, a skiing friend, came to see us in the evening and cooked dinner. She said I should get help. I said we already had some in the form of a cleaning lady who came in twice a week and took over the house and our lives. She put on her professional-medico smile and said I was a hopeless case. But I knew that.

Our problem was in fact soon eased. Our GP referred us to a physician, a specialist both in Parkinson's disease and in the aged.

He too thought Lewy Body type dementia the most likely explanation of Peggy's condition. He recommended unchanged dose of Madopar for the present, and introduced us to slow-release Madopar capsules for night use. As regards the reported association of the glaucoma drug, pilocarpine, with dementia, he was, I think, dubious, but thought it would be a wise precaution to take Peggy off it – he would write to our GP.

I liked our consultant – sensible fellow, agreed with everything I said! But I was uneasy again – was he, too, just going along with the poor old chap? However that might be, the new pills certainly seemed to ease our night problem – we got more sleep, and Peggy was more inclined to be friendly in the mornings.

If the Madopar was in fact working, it wasn't clear to me why it affected Peggy's mood. In Parkinson's disease proper, cells in the brain stem produced insufficient dopamine needed as a 'neurotransmitter' to carry signals between brain cells, which then activated motor nerves controlling movement. The levodopa in Madopar was used by the brain cells to make dopamine to make up the deficiency, and so alleviate difficulty in voluntary movement, reduce involuntary shakes, the shuffling gait, droopy jowls, and falling about, typical of Parkinsonism. Peggy was affected in such ways only to a small extent, although she did experience her 'internal shakes', accompanied by slight quivering of the arms and hands, and involuntary fidgeting – skirt kneading and 'pill-rolling' with her fingers, for example. Most marked was her tendency to lose her balance and fall. Perhaps it was simply that when the pills gave her relief from all that, she was happier. On the other hand, in her variant of the disease, as I understood it, cells in parts of the upper brain were involved, and perhaps dopamine was involved in some way in other more subtle brain functions.

Barbara, Peggy's sister, had decided to move from her place in the New Forest closer to civilisation, as she put it, and she was in the process of buying a small house among several being built just over Harnham Hill from us. Peggy and I walked over to see it. Peggy was amazing: she had no difficulty going up over the hill at a cracking pace – she was not even breathing hard at the top, and it must have been almost a year since we did anything as strenuous. Although my back was now almost repaired, my knees didn't like the climb too much, but I made it without screaming loud enough to be heard.

That night, at home, around eleven o'clock, Peggy was sitting on a chair, rummaging in a cupboard under the spiral staircase in the living room. She stood up and hit her head on a metal stair tread. Disorientated, she went to sit down again, but missed the chair and fell backwards hitting her head hard on the sharp corner of a doorframe.

There was a lot of blood, and for a moment or two I panicked, dashing around like a headless chicken – I was looking for something to make a pad. I calmed down when I thought of the freshly ironed tea towels in a kitchen drawer. After a few minutes pressure the flow slowed to an ooze. I then got to the first-aid drawer, strapped a padded dressing over the cut with a triangular bandage, wrapped her in a blanket and drove to Casualty at Odstock. We were back not long after midnight, the cut cleaned up and stitched – it was about three inches long but closed nicely with half-a-dozen or so stitches. Peggy was wonderful through all this – kept her sense of humour. When the doctor said he was putting a saline dressing on temporarily she asked if she could have the oysters that went with it.

Back home we had a cup of tea and went to bed.

I KNEW that my request – decision rather – to join PAG full time would cause a bit of a stir – what are we going to do with the old chap? There was an obvious solution that I hoped they would see. The proposal would best come from them – certainly Glyn would recognize the awkwardness of my working to him. I told Peggy I thought Glyn and Alan were rather intent on the film-recorder side of the business – we were all in love with our machines which were so efficient as well as elegant – but I felt there was more future in the TV accessories we made, particularly the specialized camera batteries and chargers where there was trivial competition in UK. I said I would like to grow the company in that field rather than fight the big battalions in the reducing market for film recorders.

Peggy said that Glyn was a wily young bird and liked being the boss: he would make sure I didn't usurp him.

At a board meeting on Friday, 31 December 1976, Glyn said he and Alan were so pleased I was joining them full time. After all, I had started the company and it seemed only right. He was sure I'd want something to get my teeth into, something with a challenge. Now, the battery side needed a push. He knew that might seem a bit mundane to me, but he was sure I could make something of it . . . What did I think about starting a separate company for that side of the business?"

The new company, PAG Power Ltd., was formally registered 20th January1977 with Glyn, Alan and me on the board along with Nigel Gardiner, a young engineer who had joined us in the Belmont Road days. I was elected chairman of the board and voted a salary, modest until we knew what we could earn.

We started trading officially 1st February. Previously, I had opened a bank account for the company and negotiated a facility with the bank manager; discussed factoring our invoices with Alex Laurie Ltd (later 3i plc) to ease cash flow; visited the Department of Trade and Industry's Small Companies' advice centre; transacted a discount structure on battery cell purchases from SAFT and Varta UK; and had been around drumming up trade.

Overseas Films & TV Ltd was PAG Power's first customer, closely followed by Ciné Help, a hire company, Westwood Television, Rank, and a Dutch company, Olde Delft, already a customer of PAG Films through a BBC colleague of Peggy's. RCA who had a UK facility in Jersey was developing a new shoulder-borne (ENG) TV camera and showed interest in us supplying the batteries for it.

One thing, it seemed to me, which was desperately needed for use with the new ENG cameras, which were voracious power gobblers, was a means of recharging their nickel-cadmium batteries rapidly. All chargers on the market purporting to do this had the nasty habit of exploding the cells; the only safe chargers took some fourteen hours to recharge a flat battery. Dr David Hamill, an electronics graduate, joined us and was soon on the track of a novel method.

Carolyn, between jobs, was helping out at Raynes Park as a typist and general help. Peggy had taken on the role of buyer for PAG Power, but she was still on the board of PAG Films and still active, dashing around picking up and delivering – not a function normally associated with a company director, but she enjoyed the contacts with people it involved. By mid-April, the new company was trundling along nicely and Peggy, Carolyn and I took off on a walking holiday, first on Corfu and then in the mountains of northern Greece near the Albanian border.

The morning after we got back, Carolyn went to her new job at the National Physical Laboratory in Teddington. I had to make what was now a rare sally into Town, for lunch at the Athenæum with Sir Charles Goodeve, one of the early stalwarts of Operational Research, and one of the few Silver Medalists of the Operational Research Society. We were to discuss the trends in OR – were these youngsters getting it right?

While we were on holiday, David Hamill had constructed a working model of a computerized fast charger, which we immediately demonstrated to RCA. We landed the contract to supply both batteries and chargers for their new camera, the break-through for PAG Power. They were launching the camera at an exhibition of TV equipment in Montreux, Switzerland, in June.

The shock came on a Monday morning in May: a call from RCA in Montreux where they were preparing their stand at the exhibition. Urgent: they had to have batteries on Friday a week before opening day.

We could have said it was impossible since deliveries weren't due until a couple of weeks later and that was going to be difficult for us. But we were noviciates and the great god RCA had to be propitiated. I did ring Glyn, who was at the exhibition hall with Alan preparing our stand, to see whether he could persuade RCA to use some of the batteries we had there to show. No use: RCA had a potential customer who wanted to see what he was actually going to get.

We pulled out all the stops we could find. We finished the batteries – built into moulded-leather belts with chargers incorporated – by three o'clock Thursday morning. Peggy and I grabbed two hours sleep and drove lickety-split with them to Montreux. We got there late evening, draped ourselves with the packages and dragged our weary bodies into the exhibition hall.

The huge RCA stand was still having nails knocked into it. The sales director was there:

"Hallo," he said, and, as he turned away, "Are those our batteries? Put 'em over there, would you." A great welcome.

It turned out to have been worth the effort. RCA's customer bought, and we had our running contract doubled. As for the exhibition, we got ourselves known to many major companies, potential customers, and we engaged several other organisations as overseas agents.

There was one curious incident on the opening day of the exhibition. Peggy had just walked around to look at the stands of the companies with which we had or wished we had dealings. She was steaming. She said to Glyn:

"I thought you had arranged to have our batteries shown on most of the ENG cameras on show here,"

"I did," said Glyn, obviously surprised at being attacked.

"Well, they are all fitted with and labelled with . . ." and she named our chief competitor in the USA.

"The bastard," said Glyn and stormed off. We followed. On the way to our competitor's stand we looked at various cameras on show, like Sony's and Hitachi's which were supposed to be showing our wares. They were fitted with American batteries and labelled as such. The assistants confirmed that they had put ours on and had no idea how they had been changed.

I caught up with Glyn, fearing the worst. "Take it easy Glyn," I said.

When we got to enemy terrain, the boss, perhaps fortunately, wasn't around. Peggy nobbled one of the assistants and said:

"I think you have some of our batteries. Could we collect them please?

"Oh, er . . ."

"They're over there."

Sure enough they were, and the affair ended without ructions. I was astounded to meet such back-street behaviour at an international exhibition.

By the end of the show, Peggy and I thought we had earned another little holiday and decided to spend a few days in France, Guillaumes in the valley of the Var. There we spent our time walking around our old haunts and even went a little way up Cîme de Pal, a mountain which in our younger days we had scrambled up to stand on its sharp summit – this time we were happy to wallow in our memories.

Back home, we had no difficulty delivering the rest of RCA's batteries and Speedchargers on time, and we had our contract increased yet again.

We had bought another shop in our row in Raynes Park, but we were running out of space once more. This was just as I heard a rumour that the factory opposite was coming on the market. Peg and I went over and saw the owner. She showed us around and we drooled. It was ideal. Looking over the diamond rings on her hand, she told us the price, and, in the approved fashion, we smiled regretfully and went away. She rang that afternoon with ten percent off the price and I said I might be able to manage with fifteen. She said yes – rather quickly, and I wished I'd said twenty.

The other members of our two boards had a look and mostly drooled too. Alan wondered whether it wasn't rather large for us; Glyn wondered whether we could afford it; Nigel thought the parquet flooring too good for a workshop; Peggy said it was so cheap, what was wrong with it? But they were token objections and I went to see what the bank manager had to say. His objections were more than token: he said it was unwise to go into the property business, as he put it. But then, he wasn't in the risk business which, as manufacturers, we were; and since property was less risky than flogging batteries to (then) an even riskier business, TV, I fixed a mortgage elsewhere.

My first year of 'retirement' was a very good one. Peggy and I had been busy and happy – being in the cut-and-thrust of the business world was new to us and exciting. Turnover in Power products had increased tenfold, and we were exporting through agents in a dozen countries.

In November, Peggy's mother died. She had suffered a penetrating peptic ulcer and had bled catastrophically. A week after surgery, recovering well, she collapsed in the lavatory with a pulmonary embolism and died before she was discovered. The parallel with Peggy's near-fatal collapse after her chest operation in the US was striking.

CHAPTER SIXTEEN

Peggy's head wound from her fall under the spiral staircase at home had healed nicely and had given her little trouble – she hadn't even had a headache. Hallucinations still diverted her during the day, but they were mundane, mild affairs compared with her earlier exotic fancies – "He doesn't seem to want any coffee," of a non-existent chap sitting next to me; or "What are all those children doing in the living room?"

On Carolyn's wedding day, 21 November 1994, Peggy was up before six o'clock in the morning and had rustled Carolyn and Lawrence out of their beds for fear they would be late. We all managed to laugh about that, and the four of us drove to the simple ceremony at the registry office, and then on to Stratford Lodge where a lunch had been prepared for us – a memorable one – and a cake. We went home for photographs and a cup of tea. Carolyn and Lawrence then went off to New Orleans. It was the simplest – deference to Carolyn's convalescence – and the most enjoyable wedding, apart from a rather similar one back in 1941, that I had ever attended. Peggy glowed the whole day.

She was still relatively brilliant in the evening when we were alone together. Later she was tired and put herself to bed in the wrong room. I joined her there, collecting her shoes from where she had 'hidden' them from thieves, and recovering her knickers – they were usually to be found in a wastepaper basket, but this time I eventually found them behind a radiator.

It was mid-December before anything of note occurred. Barbara came to tea: she came frequently to be with Peggy while I went shopping, or to my Writers' Circle, or had a quick snooze. I was feeling particularly low that day. At one stage I was disorientated and for a few minutes I didn't know where I was. I came-to a bit apprehensive, but décided I was just tired. It wasn't so much not sleeping at night – Peggy was very much better on the new Madopar regime – but the constant vigil. I felt drained. Barbara noticed when I suggested she stay to dinner, and she said we had better go back to dinner with her. We did.

Barbara poured a Loire white as an aperitif for her and me, and a lime and tonic for Peggy. I was feeling ethereal again and decided to leave my wine until dinner. I left it behind when the three of us went into the kitchen to talk to Barbara while she cooked – or I thought I left it behind, but when I went to collect it for dinner it wasn't there. I was still feeling a bit muzzy but I looked around for where I might have put it, and eventually decided the empty glass on the draining board in the kitchen must be mine. Now I knew I was slipping: I didn't remember drinking it.

I had water at dinner.

Peggy was quite cross with me when we were driving home. She said I'd been a bore all the evening, hardly talking to either of them. I apologised and said I wasn't feeling very bright, and she said it was because I'd been drinking too much.

I didn't respond – that was just how it felt to me.

Peggy woke at three in the morning, flashing her torch in my eyes. She fought with me when I tried to take it. She got up and put on her dressing gown. My entreaties for her to get back into bed were met with "Why should I?" and "Who are you? Why are you trying to stop me?" and so on. I followed her downstairs and tried to persuade her not to go out in the dark in her dressing gown. I put an arm round her and then lost my cool when she fought with me. I carried her back to bed while she pounded my back shouting for help. She wouldn't stay. She got up, opened the window and again shrieked for help. I followed her downstairs again, feeling ashamed of myself for losing my temper. She went round trying to get out of the windows. When I asked where she wanted to go, saying I'd take her if we could first get dressed, she said she wanted "to get out of this nasty place and go home". She went to a cupboard took out some Genoa cake and tore it to pieces, eating chunks of it. In the end I persuaded her to sit down at the table while I made a cup of tea. It proved a difficult task because as soon as my back was turned she was up trying the doors and windows again to get out. But we did get tea. She calmed a little and we sat together on a sofa. She went to sleep in my arms.

She was still a little obstreperous when she woke about six o'clock – my arm had 'gone to sleep' and I'd had to move. However, she did come upstairs with me and we got into bed again. She slept until nine o'clock. Gradually during the morning she improved, but she was fairly scatterbrained until after coffee. She was then almost back to her normal self, and we conversed as though nothing had happened, but I now had no doubts about what had happened to my glass of wine.

Our Parkinson's specialist rang a couple of days later to say that he had not been able to find any evidence of pilocarpine triggering dementia; he was inclined to agree with our eye man that it was safe. On alcohol, he confirmed that it was not incompatible with Madopar, but he would not be surprised if Peggy was sensitive to anything adding to confusion, and it might need only a small dose of alcohol to show effect.

Christmas came and snow settled a little on Christmas Eve but it had been rained away by the morning. Carolyn and Lawrence had moved into their flat but they came out with us to a restaurant for lunch on Christmas Day. They first came round with loads of presents for us, including a bar of Toblerone chocolate for me in the usual triangular-sectioned box – stood on end it was as high as the table and it weighed ten pounds. Peggy was good company all day with a couple of small bits of creative memory, and one minor lapse – she asked me what was the name of the strange fellow (me) who had been driving the car.

We went to dinner with Carolyn and Lawrence on Boxing Day. Lawrence had done most of the cooking and it was nicely produced with wines to match, finishing with port and hi-fi. A very pleasant evening. They must have worked furiously to get the flat into such a civilised condition for our visit. They were a happy couple taking life as they found it. Their New Orleans trip had been a joy and, if the shadow of Carolyn's pending second operation was darkening their horizons, it wasn't obvious.

The year 1994 came to an end. It was the year of Carolyn's wedding and of her tumour on the spine. It was the year when Peggy's illness took shape; the year of struggling to get something done about it; the year that saw Peggy deteriorate to the point where she couldn't really do very much, although there were long periods of lucidity when it was still Peggy and Me.

It was the year we didn't go skiing.

JUST ABOUT the time I left the civil service – I hesitate to use the term 'retired' with its air of finality – the current tenant of our house in Salisbury, was about to leave and we decided we would not re-let. We drove down one weekend in January 1977 to survey the wreckage wreaked by half-a-dozen families over thirteen years. Our reactions were 'What a lovely place to live,' and 'God! What a mess,' in that order. We spent the weekend messing around in the house, cleaning and rearranging, gagging over the filthy cooker, and giving up hope that we could live with anything left in the house. I said we should throw the whole lot out and start again, but Peggy, with her usual penetrating wisdom, said there was more than just the furniture and fittings to consider: the house was designed years ago for two other people we wouldn't recognize if we met them; it didn't fit us, and we ought to reshape it. She thought, however, we should live in it for a while to be sure we knew what we really needed.

And so it was that we started a shuttlecock routine between Twickenham and weekends in Salisbury. After about three months of that we plucked up the courage to call in Tony Stocken again, our original architect – now almost as bald as me. We told him what we wanted. He then told us what we wanted; we said yes, and went off to buy furniture while builders came in and tore the place apart. They hadn't quite reassembled it early December when the furniture arrived. One of the builders, we assumed it was the boss, liked our new bed so much he was impelled to give it a test run with a girlfriend – they left evidence under the bed.

We were gradually picking up with old friends we had neglected in the London years. A great pleasure was to have them stay with us over the weekend. We picnicked on the riverside, paddled canoes, pop-philosophized, got our visitors to help us fiddle around in the garden we had redesigned for ease of maintenance in old age, enjoyed Peggy's memorable dinners, and often exceeded the advised two glasses of wine a day. Essentially we had come back to live in Salisbury and the Twickenham house was a *pied à terre* for our work with PAG.

In 1979 there was a flashback scene in my life, I was presented with the Silver Medal of the Operational Research Society. Suddenly, from looking down my nose at such things, pride welled up unbidden. The presentation was made at the Royal Society and there was an impressive turn out both of old colleagues and anonymous young men and women with shiny faces. I really felt old that day, particularly while making my ponderous speech and noticing the rapt faces of the young people looking up and seeming actually to be listening to what I was saying. Even Sir Ian Bancroft, Cabinet Secretary and Head of the Civil Service, who had so kindly come along, looked as young as a policeman – if not exactly rapt. He came along to the lunch afterwards at the Athenæum. A day of great flattery.

In the summer, Peggy and I discovered Kandersteg, an unspoiled little village in the Bernese Alps, Switzerland. We thought it would be pleasant to ski there and went back after Christmas to do just that. We went with the Ramblers again, and Mary Hill was our leader – she knew how to do it this time. There was no health warning on the Ramblers' package and we became addicts: went at least once a year thereafter. On this ski trip, we met a lone soul, erudite, around forty, and worried about his weight: Brian Baumfield – he corrected our pronunciation, 'aw' not 'oh'. He was knowledgeable on wines and literature and he was good company, although not destined to become a devotee of this form of skiing. On the other hand, Maggie Cormack, a young clinical psychologist, was adept and taught us a lot of tricks.

The people we met cross-country skiing were different from those I usually had contact with in government, or in business: not necessarily better or worse in any way I could define, but different and, to me, and I think to Peggy, appealing.

In particular, with Ian and Mary Pearce and Mary Hill, and now Brian and Maggie – and later Christine, Brian's charming wife – we developed friendships, which have spanned the years.

I did get worried about Peggy once when we were up high, skiing over a frozen lake: Peggy got very breathless to the point of cyanosis. It was the first time since her operation twenty-six years earlier that One-and-a-Bit-Lunged Peg had shown any signs of her reduced oxygenation area. Mary Hill, ever resourceful, got behind Peggy and, holding her around the waist, skis outside and parallel with Peggy's, she took all the strain and ski'd Peggy to a cable car we could descend on. We were high and, except cruising downhill, cross-country skiing is energetic; after that we kept lower and had no repeat of the difficulty.

We didn't entirely neglect London in our leisure time. We made occasional forays into theatreland; we saw Star Wars at the Dominion; and we went to hear Ella Fitzgerald and Oscar Peterson at Grosvenor House. PAG itself was exciting – it was now just PAG Ltd since we had folded the Films side to concentrate on power products. Our customer list continued to grow in the UK, and we had substantial running-contracts with Hitachi (UK), Sony (UK) and Sony Broadcast. Our agents overseas were also doing well – the one in the USA had renamed itself PAG America Corporation. We had bought in a sheet-metal fabrication company, renamed PAG Sheet Metal Ltd.

Not all our adventures were crowned with success. We started a company, Comprehensive Video Ltd., to resell video accessories of other manufacturers. That was Glyn's little folly – it didn't do too well. Perhaps we should have called it PAG Something. On the other hand, my folly did get the PAG insignia. It arose from my interest in solar panels, free electricity from the sun and all that. I joined forces with an expert in the field who wanted to leave the company he was with and start out on his own. Glyn and Alan were not keen, but did agree we should start up PAG Solar Ltd – later Photon plc – with a factory in Abingdon. That didn't do too well either – with BP as its chief competitor in a small market – and was eventually wound up. One interesting diversion while the company was functioning came from a dynamic Dane, Lesse Hassel, who was seeking to market condoms designed for women, and wanted us to make them. We had a hilarious lunch in a restaurant in Abingdon with Lesse explaining, not exactly *sotto voce*, how the devices were worn, and brandishing his wares like Christmas balloons.

In March 1981 our good friend and neighbour in Salisbury, John Meades, died while we were away skiing in Kandersteg. One sparkling facet of our life died with him.

That year we had a peep into films again. A company called Lightflex Ltd had a system of ciné photography where shining a light into the lens of the camera increased contrast in the picture at low external light levels. We were asked to design and supply the portable power supply for the device. The film, 'The French Lieutenant's Woman' starring Meryl Streep, was made using the system, and the external night shots without subsidiary lighting were most impressive.

That year, too, we bought our first Jaguar – a Daimler Sovereign in British Racing Green. Peggy thought it almost as impressive as our Riley Kestrel of just forty years earlier.

We were now running out of factory space again. Fortunately, there was a piece of ground for sale behind the factory, which we bought even though we were aware we would be unlikely to get planning permission for a factory on it. We did, however, erect four thousand square feet of 'temporary building'. We called it Tardis since with its small frontage the huge area inside came as a surprise.

The following year I was invited on to the board of a company specializing in solar panels for military purposes. It was an ill-fated company, which had to be wound up when its managing director forged a letter purporting to show support by the Ministry of Defence for the company's products. He sent it to Hughes Aircraft in the US who were going to buy anyway. They ducked out, he went to gaol, and the company folded. Our PAG Solar (by then floated as Photon plc) was geared up to manufacture the panels and the loss of the contract contributed largely to the little company's demise.

Peggy and I settled down to business life and enjoyed particularly being able to work together. Overseas exhibitions were interesting to plan, design and attend – and we usually managed to tack on a holiday. Most memorable was a trip to Japan when Glyn, Peggy and I set up and manned our stand at a trade exhibition in Tokyo. Glyn went home via Taiwan, while Peggy and I went on holiday and to seek business in Hong Kong, Thailand and Singapore. We came back in an afterglow of pleasure and with contracts in our brief cases.

By December 1987 PAG had been in being for twenty years, and I for seventy-one. It was time, for me anyway, to do something else.

CHAPTER SEVENTEEN

The evening of the first of the year, 1995, was tingly cold and you could reach out and touch the stars. We went to dinner with friends. An old-fashioned evening with stories and music. Peggy was in good form and happy in an unsophisticated manner. She told us several quaint little stories of her childhood – typically, how her mother, rather proper, had given the clue 'hen's bottom' in a Christmas fireside game about places in London and around, the answer being, of course, Hatch End.

We were home by eleven, and Peggy, still in happy mood, went straight up to bed while I cleared the dishwasher, put out the milk bottles, set the breakfast table, checked around and locked up. When I got upstairs, Peggy was in a hell of a state. She was wandering around in her vest, utterly lost. Worse, she didn't recognize me, and refused to be comforted. She wouldn't take her bath, her pills, or get into bed.

It was after two o'clock when I finally got her to take her Madopar, and soon after that, persuaded her into bed – still in her vest. Then, for more than two hours, she was in and out of bed, babbling nonsense, extremely miserable and inconsolable. She wouldn't have the light out. No question of my cuddling her to sleep; it wasn't the night for strangers. She went off to sleep around four o'clock and I switched off the light. I was still tense, and it must have been an hour before I slept myself.

Something woke me. Peggy had nearly finished dressing. It was six-thirty.

"Sorry to wake you, Ken dear," she said, and came over and kissed me.

It was as though at dinner she had switched to a reserve tank of control she had for use on special occasions, but which then had to be refilled from dementia before she could go back on to the main tank. Whatever the process, it allowed us to socialize – it was reliable, although the refill had not previously been so demanding.

Her behaviour this time had been similar to her reaction to alcohol and I wondered whether she might have taken a glass of wine in error at or before dinner – it's almost a reflex to reach for a glass while chatting on such occasions. We went visiting several times in the next couple of weeks with only much milder, wind-down reaction on our return.

The period of very cold weather of early January was replaced with incessant rain, and the river flooded the garden. At dinner with Carolyn and Lawrence in their cosy flat, I noticed how tired and twitchy Lawrence was. I understood – Carolyn was still groggy and needed constant attention night and day. On that occasion, Lawrence cooked an excellent meal, but Carolyn was very poorly with back and belly pains. She retired to bed without dinner. We three settled to watch TV over our coffee, or Peggy and I did for a while: Lawrence slept soundly in his chair. After a while we crept out and went home.

At the end of January, Peggy had her routine visit to the Parkinson's-disease specialist. He reduced the dose of Madopar she was to take. I was surprised, but I appreciated that it was advisable to keep the dose as low as possible – or so it was said – to prolong the period over which it remained an effective treatment.

The next morning, Peggy was fairly aggressive, but after breakfast she relaxed to the stage of, "Do you enjoy your job here?" and "Why do you call yourself Ken?" Later she was more friendly, and indeed, she was concerned about the possibility of my being upset about Carolyn, who was soon to go back to the Atkinson-Morley for the clean-up operation on her spine. Until she spoke of that, I had assumed the upset to be due to the change in her pill regime, and that she hadn't yet adjusted to it; but it was more likely she was worrying about Carolyn. I knew I was.

Peggy continued in her deteriorated state. Nights were bad again, and lucid periods during the day were less evident. Her hallucinations were more intrusive – "Strange, ugly people . . ." who were in some way menacing. She couldn't place me at all: she thought I was very much like the Ken in the picture of the three of us at Carolyn's wedding.

I didn't know what to make of this phase. I was getting taut again as well as tired, and sometimes despairing, feeling that if I didn't get help soon I'd blow my top – blow it, that is, more than I did already. Jeremy hadn't come up with anybody, and I couldn't bring myself to do anything about it – it was a three-way dither between the urgent need for help, not knowing how to judge that someone would be suitable, and the instinctive need for privacy.

After a week or so with no improvement in Peggy's behaviour, the idea of a period of adjustment to the reduced Madopar dosage evaporated. I couldn't understand why Peggy now hallucinated before the dose as well as after. Was the overall dose now too low? Tremors too were more marked, but again not fitting pill periods. Was this a sudden jump in her inevitable deterioration, or was it to do with the Madopar dosage. The specialist had been positive in his action and he had a lot of experience. Mine was limited to one evolving case.

I tried a few times to telephone the specialist but without success. I changed back to the old dosage pattern. It worked almost immediately – the eye of pessimism sees coincidence, but most of the time I'm an optimist.

The first morning after the new dose was a friendly one, which we reinforced by a trip to Peggy's favourite shoe-shop in Christchurch. A couple of pairs of new shoes had Peggy beaming, and even the lunchtime pizza at a melamine-topped table was not terrible.

There was a break in my stream of euphoria. We had a dreadful morning February 6. Peggy was up and down in bed until just after six when I gave in and got up. She was wild and uncontrollable, fought to keep me out of the shower and hit me over the head with a shoe as I went downstairs. It was interesting that she had dressed herself without help despite her maniacal condition. She did say later something about "acting mad," as though she were standing beside herself watching the performance. She insisted she wanted to go for a walk, but when I took her out she rushed indoors again:

"They're out there," she gasped.

We repeated this procedure several times, with minor variations, Peggy getting more aggressive with me each time. I managed tolerance for an hour or so, then lost my temper and insisted in a very loud voice that she came in to breakfast. She gave up violence and resorted to insults. One of my chief difficulties was physical – I needed to go to the lavatory but couldn't leave her long enough to do so.

She was calm by coffee time and I risked a visit to the little room. While Peggy ate her belated breakfast, I stood with my coffee looking out of the window towards the cathedral over the sad scene of the flooded garden, and felt hard-done-by. It was then I remembered it was the morning Carolyn was to go into Atkinson-Morley for her second operation.

A call to the hospital the next day brought the relieving response of Carolyn being "comfortable". Peggy was contained but, understandably, unhappy. I rang the hospital the following afternoon and, to my surprise, Carolyn was in a fit state to be telephoned. I did so, and Peggy and I with a handset each had a long talk with her. Carolyn was still hooked up to a morphine drip, and to catheter and drain tubes, but she could sit up in bed. She spoke strongly and with confidence, and gave us an account of the operation, which the surgeon had described to her in detail. She had been told that she would probably be able to leave for home in two weeks or less. When we rang off, Peggy came into my arms, smiling, with tears in her eyes. Outside, the sun was shining and swans were floating peacefully on the flooded lawn.

Barbara moved into her new little house, but she couldn't live in it, it was chock-full of furniture from her large house in the New Forest. Her eldest son, Christopher, was organising a disposal operation.

Peggy had again returned to the state she was in before the dosage change – I had forgotten to tell the specialist about my changing back to the larger dose and felt too embarrassed to contact him so long after the event. We were getting more sleep and were happier as a result. All was well until Peggy tripped in the garden again and damaged an ankle. It was badly bruised and, although she could stand on it, the GP was fairly certain there was a break. We visited our friendly casualty department at Odstock again.

X-rays showed that a ligament had broken away from the heel bone, not a common occurrence, it appeared – the consultant asked if he might keep the plate as a specimen. He thought it best not to operate but to let it heal as it was. She would probably have a stiff foot.

"It might interfere with your skiing a bit, my dear," he said, laughing.

"I was thinking of giving it up, anyway," Peggy said, po-faced.

Carolyn and Lawrence, back from London, rang in the afternoon inviting us to tea the next day. Carolyn was cheerful. She was largely chairbound but could walk confidently across the room with a Zimmer frame. Lawrence said she was improving rapidly.

For the first time in a year she and Lawrence were discussing the future – Lawrence was keen to start a small hotel and be his own chef. They were still planning when we left.

The next morning Peggy and I sat outside for coffee, sheltered from the northerly wind, quite warm in the sunshine of late February. The garden had been flooded for over a month, but the water, harbinger of gloom, had at last receded. The telephone rang in the house. It was Lawrence. The water had lied.

Carolyn was in Odstock Hospital with angina, probably a blood clot following her operation. She was on oxygen and heparin. He rang again in the evening to say there was no change on Carolyn. He was speaking in short gasps.

"Are you all right, Lawrence," I said.

"Just tired," he gasped.

I said I'd ring Barbara and ask her to come down and sit with Peggy and then come over with a bottle of wine for a chat.

He said he thought he'd better go to bed, he'd been very short of sleep.

He rang the next morning from bed only it was in Odstock Hospital, in the same ward as Carolyn.

IN 1988 I started my second retirement. Other things happened too:

famine in the Sudan, severe drought in Texas; numerous ferry disasters; Piper Alpha oil-rig explosion; Armenian earthquake; Clapham Junction train crash; Lockerbie Pan-Am Jumbo-jet bombed . . . Also, we sold our Twickenham house, got rid of three skips full of junk and made Watersmeet our home again. We discovered that our old-age pensions had been wrongly calculated and recovered £5000 between us. We took a leisurely holiday in June driving around France, but inevitably wound up in Kandersteg.

Back home, I started to write what I intended as my best seller, something a bit philosophical. My diary recorded: 'The thoughts I had, which seemed to me profound, splodged on to paper like cold porridge from yesterday's breakfast.' – or they would have done except they got no further than distorting magnetic fields on a floppy disk. I read bits to Peggy and she said:

"You were obviously born to it, Ken."

"My mother told me that when I was born, during the Great War, she had no clothes for me. The mid-wife had wrapped me in newspaper and put me on the mantelpiece. Do you think the print rubbed off?"

Mary – the one who taught us to ski – and boyfriend Martin, came to visit us, fished a body from our river and revived it. It was a man of about eighty, a neighbour, who had fallen in. Mary was good at that sort of thing. A girl in a party she was leading in the Himalayas, fell off. Mary climbed down and spent the night with her on the ledge she had snagged on, and sewed up a great gash in her head with darning wool – using the morphine fluid from a bottle of diarrhoea mixture as anaesthetic.

Another Mary, Mary Lovell (the one who was to marry Geoffrey Watts), following her best selling biography of Beryl Markham, had finished one on Amelia Earhart, and had been commissioned to write a third. She had been made Master of Hounds in her local Hunt, and we were invited to the Hunt Ball. We felt a bit out of place, but we enjoyed the evening as an experience. And, it is always a great pleasure to reflect the glory of one's talented friends. I'm sure Peggy felt that – her eyes were soft and glowing while she watched Mary acting the hostess with such aplomb. Otherwise, I think, Peggy was quietly amused at the whole affair.

She said:

"Are these things a bit *passé,* I wonder?"

She wondered further, saying she thought Hunt Balls were devised originally as fishing competitions for predatory mothers and their daughter-bait. These days, the daughters were man-eaters in their own right. Unless you were young, she felt, you must find a modern Ball boring, as she did, not even knowing what the dancers were supposed to be doing. But youngsters, who should enjoy such happenings, spent their time trying not to appear foolish to their peers, and must be in tension the whole time. Middle-agers were mostly trying to prove, to themselves and others, that they were still as young as they had been. Other than that, they put on an air of wise tolerance to the cavorting youngsters, and pretended to enjoy their outlandish music.

"They are the future of humanity," I said.

"I know," she said. "Lovely, really, aren't they?"

"What about oldsters?"

"Here's one who'd like to go home to bed."

As a would-be predatory old man I did get something out of watching prancing nubility, so long as the wine was good. I didn't tell Peggy that – but I don't suppose I needed to.

When the music was approximately suitable, Peggy and I indulged ourselves in a little proper dancing – which we were told was improper, 'dirty dancing'. The youngsters moved aside for us, with that half-disparaging, half-compassionate, poor-old-dears look. We got home just before the milk.

In September we went to Birmingham for Mary Hill's wedding. She was marrying Martin Campbell the boyfriend we had met, a like-minded, mad mountaineer who could cook.

The year went on, and others followed. Friends and family spent weekends with us, as we did with them all over the country; we went canoeing on our river; I was conned into becoming the Co-ordinator of the local Neighbourhood Watch; we suffered surgery on our receding gums, but kept most of our teeth; we drove into France, Switzerland, Italy and elsewhere in Europe to walk in mountains in Spring and Summer, and went skiing Christmas and early March; we sailed with Mary Lovell to Cowes Week; we did the Mediterranean islands and went on Saga holidays for the over fifties – Kenya was memorable and I have sketches of lions and elephants to prove it. We became more and more like all the other retired people we knew, truly suburbanized, although we were not yet playing bridge – but we did grow bonsais.

Then came the Spring of 1991 when Peggy recalled Peter Lonsdale-Coombes CMG and had bad dreams, and our life together began to change.

CHAPTER EIGHTEEN

The last day of February 1995 and both Carolyn and Lawrence were in hospital. Was it never going to end for them? Angel Barbara arrived within ten minutes of my telephone call and we were having a quick cup of coffee before I took off for the hospital. I had lied to Peggy, telling her Carolyn was in the hospital for a check up. Even so, she was agitated and wanted to come to. Her hairdresser was due in about half an hour and I used the excuse. Then the telephone rang again – I was getting to fear the thing: what was I going to hear next?

It was Lawrence. He was just leaving the hospital to go home. He told me he had passed-out at home just after he had phoned me. He had come-to and rung for an ambulance. Nothing had been found wrong with him: it was thought he had been hyperventilating due to stress – understandable after all he'd had to put up with. Carolyn was out of the wood and would be home in a couple of days. She would stay on an anti-coagulant for some time.

We went to tea with Carolyn, March 23, her fifty-second birthday. She was in a bad way. She feared moving an inch, and stayed hunched in her tip-up armchair all the time dreading the next time she had to go to the loo. She was cheerful enough as long as she could stay still, but life was scarcely fun for the poor dear.

However, things were moving to get her proper attention – that is to say, the Salisbury people were in communication with the surgeon and others at Atkinson-Morley. I felt sure nobody was going to let anybody else off the hook.

I had worried about Peggy seeing Carolyn in her present condition and she was obviously shocked. For a moment she babbled incoherently. She recovered quickly, and turned the babble into a throat clearance, smiled and gave Carolyn a gentle hug. She turned her head away, but not before I'd seen the tears.

They talked together then, and were soon light-hearted and laughing.

Lawrence was a worry. He had prepared tea having baked a fine cake, and he maintained a happy veneer, but he was haggard and looked desperately tired.

At home, Peggy and I had a very short night. Peggy wasn't restless in the usual way, and wasn't particularly confused. She wanted to talk – mostly about Carolyn. She got up occasionally and hobbled about the room without dressing, and was quite rational, discussing what we might do about Carolyn if she were to be permanently disabled. At five o'clock confusion set in. She refused her medication and started to dress with the intention of walking over to see Carolyn. I tried to dissuade her, both because of the early hour, and since she wouldn't yet be able to walk that far – her ankle was still sore. She persisted and raved a little; I had to skip my shower and dress at speed – I didn't realize at the time I'd dressed over my pyjamas. I did then persuade her to have her Madopar and breakfast. She calmed down and we drove over to see Carolyn for coffee mid-morning.

News from USA was that a new drug, Tacrine, was sometimes helpful for Alzheimer's-disease sufferers. I wondered why it was only sometimes. Reading around I learned something of its action and that only about a quarter of those treated benefited. Bells rang. The action was such that it seemed reasonable to suppose it would be useful to those with LBD, that is, to a quarter of those previously diagnosed Alzheimer's – I was grasping at straws again. There was a snag: serious side effects in some people, interference with liver function, but that could be monitored and the drug withdrawn before serious damage. It certainly seemed worth a try on Peggy, but it emerged that it had not been approved for use in this country. We went to see Peggy's specialist about it. He thought it was scarcely worth the positive risk, since only a small proportion of those treated got any benefit, which, as he understood it, was not dramatic. I don't think he thought much of my conjecture that it might be that those benefiting had LBD like Peggy – couldn't say I was surprised, it was an unsubstantiated guess. Nevertheless, he said he would see who made the drug and get some for us on a 'named patient basis'.

Carolyn's problems became acute again. Before anything happened following the liaison between Salisbury and London, Carolyn was again paralysed in the legs. She was taken back to the Atkinson-Morley for another operation. From the scan, the problem, it was thought, might have been due to a blood clot at the site of the previous surgery, an infection or, less likely, regrowth of the tumour. The surgeon said there was no guarantee she'd walk again after the proposed operation, but there was no sensible alternative.

The operation was successful and, immediately, Carolyn had feeling in her legs and could wiggle her toes: the expectation was that she would be able to walk after a while. The Atkinson-Morley was still not sure Carolyn hadn't regrown a malignancy, and more tests were going on. The surgeon, on the other hand, felt that the pressure on the spine had come from bleeding due to the anti-coagulant treatment she'd had. In any case, she was going to the Royal Marsden again for a course of radiotherapy over a period of six weeks.

Peggy, now that we had an effective Madopar routine established, was much more stable and, with the exception of the night when Carolyn went into hospital for her operation number two, we'd had no excessively wild escapades. She was still very changeable and sleep at night varied from a couple of hours fitfully, to five or six at best. There were some strange, even humorous episodes. One night after we had cuddled intimately, she said:

"I was expecting Ken tonight."

I'm sure women are fundamentally wanton: come to think of it, so are men – some anyway.

In the daytime, Peggy was again taking interest in matters domestic; she would still help with the ironing, perfunctorily dust, and push the vacuum cleaner around. She had never been a great lover of television, but she would retain her concentration for a thirty-minute program. A new twist was that she would sit and listen to me playing the organ, ask for particular pieces, and even express appreciation. Conversation, except in her very confused periods, was almost normal: she would sometimes get as far as the verb in a sentence, and not be able to express the noun, but she was usually able to find an alternative route to completion of the thought. She was upset by such difficulties. She wept one day because of her inability to connect clear memories. She couldn't understand the relationship between Barbara and her grandchildren, nor could she connect the Barbara of today with the sister she remembered from her youth – although she recognized Barbara as her sister. Another time she was puzzled about her own relationship with her two sisters and thought it a remarkable coincidence that the three of them had been to the same school.

Peggy was certainly ashamed of her condition, and she went to some lengths to hide manifestations of it, even from me. One day she went around with her handbag tightly clasped to her, clearly fearful that I would take it from her. She still had it with her at bedtime. In the bathroom I noticed her two-tooth lower denture was not in place. When I asked about it, she said she hadn't wanted it in. I searched the house for it before the penny dropped – the handbag. I managed to sneak a quick look. Sure enough, there was the plate zipped up in an inner pocket.

I'd been so pleased that morning because she had dressed herself quite well without prompting, and I could only assume she had wanted to conceal from me her inability to get her plate in without help.

Mid-April, Lawrence rang. The tests at the Royal Marsden had confirmed that Carolyn's spinal tumour had not been malignant. I was instinctively riled that for the second time the Atkinson-Morley had kept us hanging on the brink of despair with false warning, but doubtless I would have been equally indignant had dread news turned up without warning. As it turned out, it was great news, although I couldn't share it with Peggy since I had kept the possibility of the alternative from her.

With the hope that Carolyn was now on the mend, our lives returned to their somewhat distorted normality. Except when Peggy had slipped into one of her confusions, and when we were not too tired, we did a lot of the things we were used to doing. One thing we did at irregular intervals several times a year was to meet our friends Peggy and Jack Chapman – dubbed the Chapmen at home – for a meal at one of several restaurants about mid-way between Salisbury and their home in Milton-under-Wychwood. Jack and I would split the bill between our Visa cards. For our meeting on May 5, we were to meet at 'Raffles' at Ogbourne. I went suitably daubed with ashes, wearing my dingiest sackcloth – the last time we were supposed to have met, we forgot, that is, I forgot. It had been on one of Peggy's bad days, but I couldn't tell them that. This time we made it, and for me it was a notable occasion; Peggy was in fine form and it was 'just like old times'. It was noteworthy too for a more mundane reason – I noticed a week later I had Jack's Visa card. He had mine, and we had both used the cards heavily since our meeting. So much for card security.

The day after Ogbourne was a beautiful English-summer day, as befitted the 155th Anniversary of the issue of the world's first adhesive postage stamp, the Penny Black of Great Britain. We had breakfast in the garden and watched the Heath-Robinsonish weed-cutter at work on the river. Our resident swans seemed convinced the scant early harvest was entirely for their benefit. Peggy said something like:

"They've got a neck, but it saves cooking."

I got the general drift of her thought.

I went back to reading The Times of the previous day. I turned a page and a paragraph jumped out at me. Geoffrey Watts had died.

Mary's letter was in the morning post.

CHAPTER NINETEEN

Early May, 1995, a letter came from Peggy's specialist saying that Tacrine had been turned down for the second time by the National Committee for the Safety of Medicines and that he couldn't get any. I determined to go on the warpath – if I could find it.

First I went to see our GP. He ducked out, saying he couldn't interfere, the matter was entirely in the hands of the specialist. That released me to work directly with the specialist. It had just been reported that in an investigation in the USA, patients who had responded to Tacrine were found, *post mortem* – death presumably not attributable to their chronic complaint or the treatment – to have been suffering from LBD, and not Alzheimer's disease. Suggestive, but not proof positive that Tacrine was the stuff to get specifically for LBD. With that as a basis I wrote to the specialist – copy to our GP – putting again my lay but somewhat technical arguments, and wondering whether it would be useful to contact Professor Wilcock at Bristol who had experience of both LBD and Tacrine. I asked also whether he could order the drug directly from the manufacturers. He rang a week or so later and said he was fixing to get Tacrine through Parke Davis – he was trying to do this under NHS first, but we might have to buy the tablets privately. He was referring Peggy's case to Professor Wilcock.

Jeremy Wring came to coffee to talk about some of our trifling money affairs: I was anxious to maximise our income against the time when we would need to pay for care for Peggy or me – or for both. He said he was advertising for staff and he would include a housekeeper for us.

Peggy was very good with Jeremy and joined in conversations convincingly. She remained bright all day but faded towards evening. After dinner she said she didn't know where she was – although she did offer to show me where the loo was when I said I was going there. She also asked me how I knew her name was Peggy. She was back on board by bedtime, having shown her normal variability. But it didn't continue that way . . .

I had often wondered whether I was deluding myself that Peggy's medication, Madopar, was beneficial. Perhaps her deterioration when the dose was reduced had been coincidence and again part of her random variability. Experienced professionals had diagnosed her ailment as Alzheimer's disease, and the idea was introduced by me, a layman who had read a few papers, that Peggy was suffering from the Parkinson's-like LBD. Were the doctors merely going along with the stupid old man? After all, they didn't feel they could do anything about Alzheimer's anyway. True, Professor Wilcock who was well acquainted with LBD had confirmed the diagnosis, but on my description of symptoms. But we were about to have a crucial test.

That night Peggy talked and shouted gibberish and kept getting out of bed aimlessly and falling around. She thrashed about in complete bewilderment and also messed the bed – something she had not done before. By four-thirty she still had not slept. I was desperately trying to stay awake fearing what she might get up to without my hearing her. I switched on a bedside light intending to turn on the radio and listen with an earpiece. It was then I spotted the slow release Madopar capsule still in its little plastic cup by the bed. I had forgotten to give it to her. I gave her an ordinary fast-acting capsule. She was all right again in half an hour and slept until ten o'clock.

Having noted that with considerable relief, I was still puzzled – I had not read anywhere that levodopa relieved dementia. I could only think that, while there was some dementia, the exaggerated behaviour without the drug was an added, but to some extent conscious, reaction to an incomprehensible loss of motor control – like a child jumping up and down screaming with a bellyache it didn't understand.

When she woke, Peggy was calm and in her usual morning state of mild confusion, of the type, "What am I supposed to call you? Where's Ken?" She did ask when I was going to meet my uncles.

Since all my uncles were dead, I said I hoped it wouldn't be for a while yet. She looked surprised but didn't comment.

After Madopar and breakfast she was rational, but worried: "I can't understand what's happening to me, Ken," she said. "I feel so queer. I'm not even sure I know who I am."

It was the end of May and I was sitting with Peggy in the garden, a computer on my lap, attempting a little writing. I was in fact having a session of feeling sorry for myself. I think the mood was triggered by the fact that Carolyn was coming home from the Royal Marsden the next day. She would be in a wheelchair, and it wasn't yet known whether she would ever be able to get around without it. There was also the point that I'd been getting flashing-light migraines with increasing frequency, and they were always a sign for me that I was overdoing it. Peggy was snoozing in the warm sunshine under a broad-brimmed hat and looked peaceful and, damn it, adorable.

Optimism returned and I took stock. Carolyn had survived an enormous ordeal and could now, presumably, look forward to a life without constant pain. And, if I knew anything of her guts and drive, she'd get pleasure from small gains in her attempts at mobility. As for Peggy, she was, if anything, somewhat better than she had been a year ago – thanks to Madopar – and, despite ups and downs, we still had something of a life together. In her relatively unconfused periods – which didn't seem to have decreased much – she only had hallucinations to contend with and she was resigned to living with them, as was I. There were the tall thin chaps with the long necks in the front garden, a new batch replacing the thin-headed 'blackie-toppers', a chap in a white hat across the river, numerous children, and an old lady with a dark-coloured, folded face. There were also inanimate things, like the suitcases piled under the stairs, although these were clearly a misinterpretation of the CDs in their racks. It might well have been that many of her visions were imaginative renderings of real objects, like faces we see in the clouds. Children on the sofa were cushions; the man in the white hat was a tree-trunk reflection in the water, topped by a white plastic chair brought down river in the floods and trapped in the willow branches dipping in the water. No reason I supposed why brain cells concerned with interpretation of visual input should not be part of the necrosis.

Peggy had an interesting view of me. I'd always thought of myself as having something of a split personality, but she clearly thought of me as two separate people – one, the kindly old chap who did things for her with a smile and patted her affectionately; the other, the ferocious old man who lost his temper and shouted at her. She often asked one about the other: "What's Ken doing now?" she might ask, and go on, "No, not you, the other one." It was an escape route I hadn't the gall to take. I had improved a lot with experience but it bothered me that I still occasionally went off the deep end, not because of what was actually happening, but because it was happening to Peggy. It was a foot stamping, a tantrum against the unfairness of life.

My reverie was interrupted by a telephone call. Jeremy was bringing a candidate housekeeper for us to vet. Great! I put down the telephone and it rang again. It was Peggy's specialist. He had heard from Professor Wilcock who thought Tacrine "suitable for Mrs James". We could go ahead when the tablets were in.

Barbara came to help us interview the candidate housekeeper. We were impressed. She – we'll call her Erika – was a slim, blonde Nordic type, vivacious short of gushing, and looking ten years younger than her mid-fifties. She was a very experienced housekeeper and carer and she 'loved' cooking. How could we refuse her? We didn't. She joined us mid-June on a three-month trial and took over the flat.

It wasn't long before the snags began to show. It felt good to be free of the chores Erika had taken on, but I didn't yet feel any freer. I still had to spend my whole time with Peggy – who was quite demanding. I actually wanted to be with her, as things were; I suppose I just wished they weren't as they were. Poor Peggy took fright if I was out of her sight for a few minutes.

We had also lost the privacy we'd had for half a century: adjustment wasn't going to be easy. Compounding this was a fact – not revealed at interview – that Erika had a 'boyfriend', a man of mature years she was trying to save from the bottle. I had made the mistake of leaving twin beds in the flat and it wasn't long before they were both in use. I finally had to axe that when Peggy was frightened to screaming gibberish when accosted by the 'boyfriend', lolling drunk, coming out of the cloakroom by the front door between flat and house.

What to balance against all this? What had we gained? Well, I didn't have to do the cooking, the washing and ironing, or make the beds. We still had disturbed nights, but I could safely snooze after lunch with Erika on watch. Erika shopped well, if extravagantly – three pounds to park in the Cathedral Close because it was a five-minute walk closer to Boots than the forty-pence car park.

She cooked well, and she was pleasant. At first, it was obvious Peggy resented the intrusion of another female, but in a few days they had made friends, and after a while they went together on shopping expeditions, for afternoon frolics to tea, or perhaps to visit a National Trust house. And so, some free time for me began to creep in. I thought I could probably last out the trial period and not rush a decision.

I was already feeling better disposed to the world, and I felt sure my happier demeanour was reflected in Peggy. She, too, seemed calmer during the day, and the usual early morning confusion mostly resolved itself into a pleasant, if somewhat fanciful, conversation. One morning, she told me at some length how Ken was keen on philosophy, but was really a disappointed man who felt he should have done more in life. I felt I had to stand up for the poor chap and said that he probably didn't have the time these days to feel disappointment. She said that if he had more time he'd be even more disappointed. I changed the subject.

Carolyn was back home, and we went to tea. She was in a wheelchair, but she could stand, with difficulty, if helped. Peggy and she embraced and wept, each for the other. At tea, Carolyn and Lawrence were full of optimism and we talked of their ideas for the future. They assumed Carolyn would be able to walk, but they had back-up plans.

On our next visit a week later Carolyn could stand up in a Zimmer frame without help. The next time, she could move a halting couple of steps and, with Lawrence lifting her into position, she had practised going down stairs on her behind.

I expect there were Americans in the UK who had thoughts elsewhere on the Fourth of July, but for most Brits the interest was in John Major's 'confidence' vote in the Commons which he won convincingly. We watched the TV at Barbara's where we had gone for tea and in the excitement I forgot to give Peggy her Madopar dose and she had a shaking-misery spell. She had recovered by dinnertime but suffered a strange lapse of memory – her short-term memory had so far not been bad. On this occasion, she couldn't remember who Erika was. When I'd explained she said, "Lives in the flat? What, with you?"

The summer went on smoothly and we had fitted the new household system around us. Erika worked five days with weekends free – for which she left us prepared meals. She was still obsessed with her drunk, and he absorbed a great deal of her mental energy. He no longer had entry to the second bed in the flat, but was often to be seen sitting in the garden in a semi-conscious state awaiting Erika's return from shopping or elsewhere. Peggy was used to seeing him around now, and I was so pleased with the way Peggy now related to Erika – there had been no return of the green-eyed monster – that I did nothing. I just hoped for some sort of resolution of Erika's hopeless problem.

Early August, on a scorcher of a day, Peggy went off with Erika and Barbara to Stourhead and thoroughly enjoyed the outing. Erika said, however, that Peggy had become breathless and pale after climbing a few steps, as though she might faint. The heat, Erika thought. The next day, getting up rather quickly from a snooze on a sofa after lunch, Peggy did faint. I was there to catch her and she recovered quickly with no apparent after effects. I rang the GP. He said he would like to look at Peggy's notes. He rang back saying that her recent general checks, blood pressure, and so on, had been very satisfactory and there was probably nothing to worry about. It wasn't unusual for old folk to faint, exercising in hot weather. I was to let him know if it happened again. Meanwhile, he'd get the District Nurse to call. Odd, old as we were, I wasn't used to us being referred to as old folk.

At dinner with Carolyn and Lawrence we learned that Carolyn had been swimming and had managed two lengths of the pool with some effective leg movement in the crawl. Her back still gave her trouble, however, and sitting at table was a trial. Lawrence enthused about a device at the pool for lowering disabled people into the water. It was an ingenious device invented by Ken May, a friend of mine who lived locally. He and I had made bits for it in my workshop but I'd had no premonition that it would later be aiding my ailing daughter.

Peggy's specialist rang mid-August. The Tacrine tablets were in. Peggy had a blood sample taken for a liver profile and started on the tablets immediately, at four a day – caviar would have been a lot cheaper. I had rung BUPA to which we had subscribed since its inception, but they weren't interested.

For a few days Peggy was a bit queasy after her dose, but the effect didn't persist. It was a week before I noticed what I thought might be improvement. We spent a pleasant evening after dinner just wandering in the garden, picking up sticks, watering shrubs, or just sitting and chatting. Peggy would have seemed normal to a casual observer and she was certainly quite bright. Later we tried Scrabble, but she wasn't that normal.

We had a fairly restful night, but in the morning, Peggy, if calm and friendly, was back to her usual confusion: "You're a very nice man," she said as she snuggled down in my arms. "Who are you?"

Women!

After that it was back to the variable round of lucidity to confusion; from friendliness to aggressiveness; calmly happy to tearful misery.

So far, I couldn't see that Tacrine was having any beneficial effect. The slight improvement at first was probably seen with my now well-trained eye of hope. Perhaps, in any case, we could only expect it to delay deterioration. How would we know that it had done so? I wasn't even disappointed when the specialist rang to say that Peggy's latest liver profile was dodgy. No problem at present, but it would be wise to take her off Tacrine.

Sunday, August 27, and it was a bit cloudy and comfortably cooler, a nice day for some perfunctory gardening. I didn't know it was going to be a significant day in our lives. We had coffee on the patio and then fiddled about on the rockery. I was forking a small bed to clean out the weed when I heard Peggy call softly:

"Ken, can you come?"

I looked around but I couldn't see her. She called again, the voice was from the front of the house, now with a note of urgency:

"Do hurry, dear."

She was lying on the paving propped on one elbow. I went to help her up but she yelped.

"What happened, Poomphie? Where does it hurt?"

She felt around her left hip and thigh. "I'm not sure, somewhere here. I fell over the flower trough."

I told her to stay put without moving, went into the house and used for the first time the emergency ambulance button on our burglar-alarm system. I took out a blanket and some cushions and made Peggy as comfortable as possible. There was no pain apparently if she remained still. I made some tea. The ambulance arrived as she started to drink it, and in a couple of minutes Peggy was stretcher borne into the vehicle and away. I followed by car to the Odstock Casualty Department we knew so well. We arrived just before noon. X-rays almost immediately, and this under emergency staffing on a Sunday.

She had a fractured upper femur.

I accompanied Peggy when she was wheeled to the pre-op room about four in the afternoon. The surgeon, a charming young Indian, explained to her what he was going to do: pin a metal strap across the break, as he put it. As he turned away, Peggy winked at me and whispered:

"It's all right, Ken dear, he hasn't got a thin head."

It was remarkable that through all her troubles, Peggy had always retained her sense of humour. At times it even shone through in her confused periods, like the time we were surveying the mangled remains of a spoon she had dropped into the sink 'disposall': "Modern rubbish," she'd said. "They don't make 'em like they used to."

The anaesthetist gave her a shot and they wheeled her off.

I went home to lunch at five o'clock and to collect Peggy's effects and her medicaments. She was back in the ward at seven, looking tired but smiling, tubes sprouting here and there. I sat with her for a couple of hours by which time she had dozed off. The ward sister assured me that all was well.

In the morning, I found her a little dopey but in good spirits. I went home for lunch and back in the afternoon until about seven o'clock.

At home, Erika had cleared dinner and I had taken my coffee into the library and switched on the computer intending to do a little writing. The doorbell rang.

Erika showed in Lawrence, deathly white faced, eyes staring: "We've lost her, Ken," he said.

CHAPTER TWENTY

Carolyn died at seven-thirty in the evening of 28th August 1995 – a pulmonary embolism, just the way Mrs Pratt, her grandmother, had died after her operation, and as Peggy had narrowly survived after her lung resection in the USA.

Lawrence having delivered his message collapsed into an armchair shaking his head as though in disbelief. I wanted to go to him; I also wanted to go away for a few minutes to . . . well, just go away. I compromised:

"Whisky?" I said.

"God! Yes, Ken. Thanks."

In the kitchen, I stood for a moment wondering how I felt about Carolyn. I didn't really feel anything. Numb. Empty. I should at least have felt sorry for myself, but I didn't. I didn't seem to be a factor in the equation. Peggy was. How was I going to tell her, or rather, when? Certainly not while she was herself recovering from an operation. Then tears ran down my face. It took me a few moments to realize the sob came from me. It seemed a bit false, as though I was doing it because it would be expected of me – or to convince myself. I shook my head and fetched the whisky.

Our GP arrived as I poured. He came to commiserate, and it was from him we learned the probable cause of death. I seemed to stand outside myself as I listened to him, noticing how sympathy induced self-pity in my other self. Lawrence wept too. He stayed the night.

I went to the hospital after coffee in the morning. Despite the whisky the night before I hadn't slept well. As I approached the ward I could hear Peggy calling loudly for Ken. I saw the sister on the way in and she told me Peggy had been most difficult, fighting the nurses, and calling for me since breakfast. I wondered; had some special mother's sense told her something, or had the news been leaked to her somehow?

She was still rampaging when I went in, literally tearing up the bedclothes, and it took quite a time to calm her. I hadn't been able to determine any particular cause for her behaviour. She ate most of her lunch and drank well. I went back home for my own lunch and to collect a few things Peggy needed. Panic. Barbara was visiting Peggy and she wouldn't know I hadn't told her about Carolyn. Erika went off to intercept her, and did so. When I arrived a little later she was waiting outside the ward with Barbara. Inside, Peggy was climbing up the wall again.

"What are they doing with me Ken." she shrieked, "Oh Ken, they're trying to kill me." It took most of the afternoon to soothe her – but the nurses did get her out into a chair. I left after she'd had her dinner and was settling down for the night, not happily, but she was whacked.

I had a momentary shock in the morning when they told me Peggy was in X-ray: it was routine. She was really quite out of her mind when she returned. Suddenly the truth hit me: Madopar.

The nurses assured me she had had all her medication. I found her charts and looked – no slow release Madopar had been given her for three nights; moreover she hadn't had her ordinary dose that morning.

Sister, too, declared Peggy had had all her medicaments – until I thrust the charts under her nose. She had the grace to apologize and assured me she would see it all put right. I had my fingers crossed. I gave Peggy her Madopar with a little of the backlog, and she had recovered by lunch time sufficiently to eat most of her meal – despite the fact that the main dish was navarin of lamb, not one of Peggy's favourite dishes. Incredibly, she even apologised to the nurses for her morning behaviour. I went to lunch then knowing that several friends would be arriving during afternoon visiting hours, as well as the Angel Barbara as usual. They'd all been warned to silence on Carolyn.

How was I ever going to tell Peggy?

There were a number of bad sessions with Peggy over the next two days, mostly because of her refusal to take her Madopar until I arrived to give it to her.

She had some strange turns where she seemed quite lucid, speaking normally but not in relevant context: "I thought I'd see about the curtains, dear. What is this place, some sort of Institution?" She did, however, in one such phase, make her first reference to Carolyn. I had an urgent call to the lavatory.

She didn't forget, and said she didn't remember what I'd said about Carolyn. I prevaricated: "I said poor Carolyn has had her fill of hospitals." She didn't follow up.

September 1, five days after her operation, Peggy was given a blood transfusion, a six-hour drip, her haemoglobin was low. I checked with the ward sister that Peggy's liver profiles were being done. She didn't know about them. She found out, and assured me everything was in hand on them. I crossed my fingers again. A couple of days later Peggy was able to walk about ten yards with a Zimmer frame. I went home happier than usual. Erika was home early from her weekend having lost her drunk to a bottle in Guildford, and so I had dinner cooked for me.

Peggy was moved to 'Rehab.' September 4 and had a room of her own under the care of her specialist. Staff and the environment were pleasant and Peggy reacted accordingly; she was talking to a nurse and smiling when I went in. I decided I would tell her about Carolyn the next day – the funeral was the day after and I felt she must know before that. I spoke to the sister who assured me that if Peggy wanted to go to the funeral, arrangements could be made. I didn't want to subject her to that strain and hoped she wouldn't ask.

The next day I asked Lawrence to join me at the hospital. After dinner I broke the news to Peggy. Amazingly she took it quite calmly and, typical of Peggy, she was concerned more with consoling Lawrence than with herself. She had a quiet weep later. I told her about the funeral and who I thought would be there. She took an interest but had no other reaction. I had arranged with Lawrence that he didn't stay long so that I could be alone with Peggy for a while. It bothered me that she might wake up to the facts while I was not there. I thought she might react earlier without others around. She didn't.

I stayed until nine o'clock and she dozed most of the time. I went back at ten-thirty and the night staff told me she had talked about Carolyn and wept a little. She was sleeping soundly, literally, when I looked in.

Our local vicar conducted the service at the crematorium and the Rev. Peter Wood – husband of Peggy's sister, Evelyn – gave an address, an excellent one based on the 21st psalm in which he characterized Carolyn beautifully. I managed to weep without snivelling – my eyes are stinging now as I type.

There were a lot of people and they all crowded back in our house where Erika had prepared sumptuously. I ducked out after half an hour and went to see Peggy. She was miserable at first, but I watched a transformation as she adjusted to the new era. I stayed until eleven o'clock when she was sleeping peacefully, went home, watched the midnight news, did my diary, and went to bed.

A WEEK after the funeral I fetched Peggy from the hospital. It was raining hard when we got back home and Erika's drunk was sitting at a table on the front lawn. He seemed to be asleep. Peggy didn't spot him. I hardened my heart and took no notice – I had enough on my hands without wrestling with drunks. Erika was out shopping; she took him in when she arrived.

The cunning of drunks – he could have kept dry under cover on the seat outside the library window.

Peggy and I just sat around as close as possible the rest of the day. It was just wonderful to be together again. At bedtime Peggy managed the stairs very well with light support. It was a peaceful night although we had a slight problem with the waterworks – Peggy had been used to a catheter in the hospital. The District Nurse called the next day and arranged for us to get various aids.

Peggy was in amazingly good shape physically and mentally. There were occasional lapses on the mental side, but generally her conversation was fairly rational.

She was particularly good on the telephone, which seemed to concentrate her attention. Walking was still unstable but improving each time she attempted it. Her main worry was that she might wet the bed again at night, but she was reassured when the special mattress, the Kylie bed protectors and night pads arrived. However, nights were not too good thereafter, and I started getting tired again.

One early morning after a particularly sleepless night Peggy said she thought life was now over. I thought she had it about right. I saw myself spending what remained of my life attending to evacuation needs, listening to drivel, while gradually decaying. After a few minutes of self-pity, the mood passed when I thought how much worse it was for Peggy.

Daytime, walking was improving – ten days after leaving hospital she walked down the hill to the river and back. My own walking wasn't a great deal better – something had happened to one of my knees, it was painful and liable to collapse under me. I didn't think Peggy's mental condition in her off periods was worse, but it was different. She often didn't take in what I was saying. "Close the lid to the toilet . . ." led, perhaps, to her taking the tissue box apart. Also, she was sometimes lost in the house, not knowing where the toilets were, or the front door. She usually needed more than just prompting to dress properly in the morning.

It was all very variable still, and she had her periods of near normality. She was often at her worst when I was tired and intolerant, which didn't improve matters.

Peggy was going through a bad patch when Erika was taken ill. The doctor said it was a virus and she should go home and rest for a couple of weeks. Which she did, back to Surrey. The night before she left, Peggy got up to go to the lavatory twenty times. I didn't think Erika's imminent departure was connected, Peggy had been building up her score for some time. At four o'clock I risked giving her a Diazepam. In an hour she was sound asleep and didn't wake up properly until around dinner time some fourteen hours later. Then she was raving. All the following day she was confused and markedly 'Parkinsonian' – although shaking was slight and stopped after each Madopar dose. She was a little better by the evening and we went to dinner with Barbara, but Peggy was not walking well, and was still morose, shivery, and with no appetite.

The next morning Peggy's temperature was high and I asked our GP to call. Looking out of the window I saw Erika's drunk sneaking off. He had presumably spent the night in the flat with Erika. Strong stuff this sex – I seemed to remember. Erika drove off a little later for her rest in Surrey.

The doctor said Peggy had 'flu. Paracetamol reduced her temperature quite quickly and she got up to lunch. By evening her temperature was normal – remarkable – but it was up again in the morning.

Peggy's temperature yo-yo'd daily for a week and the GP then tried her on an antibiotic, Augmentin. A couple of days later when a urine sample had shown a coliform infection, he doubled the dose. No obvious effect.

Half-way up the stairs, going to bed one night, Peggy sat back on me, my knee collapsed with the extra weight and it was touch and go whether we tumbled down in a heap. We made it, but I was in a muck sweat, having almost carried Peggy to bed holding on where I could so that my leg would support me. She fell asleep immediately, but awoke two hours later for the loo. It was difficult getting her on to the commode and she did nothing when she got there.

Back in bed she was delirious, threw her arms around and gabbled. I had to hold her wrists at times to protect my face. It went on all night.

Early morning she did say distinctly for the first time that her leg was very painful and, indeed, her thigh had swollen to twice its normal size – that, presumably, was where the fluid had been going!

Our GP was surprised the double dose of Augmentin hadn't worked, although it now looked as though the infection was in the thigh prosthesis. Peggy would have to go into hospital again.

Back in Casualty, Peggy was immediately set upon by syringe-armed maidens thirsting for blood. They gave her painkillers, took temperatures, pressures, ECGs, the lot. It was a bit of a wait to see the duty surgeon, but he was worth waiting for. He was certain the femur was broken again and sent Peggy to X-ray. These he showed me. The old break was well healed and showed a good deal of new bone. The new break was at the lower end of the prosthesis, and displaced.

Mid-afternoon we were introduced to the surgeon who would take over Peggy's case, an Australian, frank and cautious. He was sure he should operate but wanted first to get Peggy's fever down. He pulled no punches on the dangers. He would probably operate the following evening. Meanwhile, Peggy's leg was put in what was called skin traction – connected to weights over pulleys but fastened to the leg with bandages, not through the bone as for long-term traction. The ward sister brought me the 'blood chit' to sign, sanctioning the operation. I said something to the effect that I didn't sign blank cheques and that I would need to know what operation was to be performed. She started to explain in child's language. I smiled and said, "First hand, Sister, please". She looked hurt and I felt sorry. I explained that we had just had one operation and Peggy was here as a result of it. True, it had been done under emergency conditions on a Sunday, but this time I needed some assurances, particularly as it was again to be done in emergency time, in the evening.

Back home I was seriously drooping; also, hungry. I invented a Brie, tongue and lettuce sandwich – since they were ingredients I found in the 'fridge – and felt a large glass of Australian Chardonnay appropriate. Human again, I rang a few people who would want to know about Peggy.

Peggy, on intravenous antibiotic, was in a good humour the following morning when the surgeon came to see us. The original intention had been to replace the prosthesis, the existing metal plate, with a longer one. They had just had a conference and decided a better plan would be to do a half-hip replacement using a ball and long shaft in the natural socket; moreover, they had decided to take the operation out of emergency time and do it the next morning in standard time, when there were more people and facilities available. I was pleased – if that's the right word to use when you're really scared stiff – pleased, that is, I had been a bit sticky over the blood chit.

When I got in the next morning, Peggy's operation had been cancelled again. They had changed their minds about the procedure – no half-hip job. They now intended to keep the good joint and put a rod, a 'nail' as it was called, from its neck deep into the fractured femur, binding all the bits. The 'machine', he said, had to come from Southampton and wouldn't arrive until the next day.

Peggy still seemed to have some sort of infection which was keeping her low – the surgeon thought it most likely to be on the site of the prosthesis; her thigh was still huge.

The day arrived. Peggy was in reasonable spirits, and alert enough to be worried, although confused on what she should be worrying about. I went with her at five-thirty in the afternoon when they took her to the theatre. Her worry, then, had condensed itself into a sore behind on which she was loudly vocal in complaint. I felt sick when they wheeled her off into the anaesthesia room.

I rang the ward at eight o'clock. Peggy was not back. I went anyway and met her coming out of the theatre on her surgical chariot. She looked all right, but asleep. In the ward the nurse said the surgeon wanted to talk to me in the morning. Peggy woke up as I kissed her good night, and I think she recognized me. I went home my mind numbed in apprehension.

In the morning I learned that they had taken off the plate and revealed infection and sewed her up again. The surgeon said Peggy would remain on intravenous antibiotics and in traction until the infection was cleared up, when he hoped they could reinstate the 'nail' plan. God! Another operation.

Four days later another change of plan. They'd decided the best bet was to take out the hip joint altogether so as not to risk infection lurking in it, and allow it to scar over, that is, leaving no hip joint – a so-called Girdlestone procedure. He said it was the safest process they could think of. I was all for safety, so I agreed. The possibility of a repeat performance with the risk of even more operations was too appalling to contemplate. He would operate that evening.

Peggy was due out of the theatre about seven-thirty but it was nearly nine o'clock when she appeared. She recognized me, and we held hands as she was wheeled down long corridors to the ward.

I saw the surgeon in the morning. He confirmed that he had removed the hip joint. He said there had been evidence of infection in the joint. There would be some flexibility when the bone tissue had grown up from the femur and the leg would be strong enough to walk on, although Peggy might need to use a frame. Younger people did quite well; the inability of older people to walk was mental not physical. Not exactly thrilling news, but much better than the alternative he'd hinted at when he had warned me of the dangers.

Over the next few days Peggy was fairly comfortable, despite her leg being in traction, this time with a large metal bolt in her calf through the bone. The fourth day after the operation she was very poorly, very pale and babbling. When I got there the nurses were with her reinforcing her dressings which she had clawed off. Around five in the evening, she complained of pains in her belly, called for a bedpan and the curtains were pulled around her. After a while, since she hadn't called, I poked my head through the curtains just in time to see her fall back. She was unconscious, eyes staring.

‘Embolism!’ streaked in blue lightning across my brain and I yelled for the nurse.

Two nurses at the end of the ward. They reacted immediately and sprinted up the ward. One ripped open the curtains and came to Peggy, the other ran on past. As the nurse felt for a pulse in the neck I saw Peggy’s eyes move. Then she gave a tiny moan and sat up. I put an arm round her shoulder to support her. I spoke to her but she looked through me with a blank stare. In seconds the other nurse was back with a large black leather case and a doctor striding alongside. Then all sorts of people arrived and stood poised for action, all eyes on the doctor, who, tense and concentrated, was connected to Peggy by his probing stethoscope. Peggy looked frightened, her eyes darting around the various faces. The nurse, holding her hand bent over and whispered something to her and she relaxed. A minute later the doctor also relaxed. He gave a sign to the others standing by and sphygmometers and syringes went to work. To me, he said he thought Peggy had just fainted. Her heart was all right and she was breathing well. “But we must find out why she fainted. We’ll look after her. Go and get a cup of tea.” He smiled and patted my hand. “Come back in half an hour and we’ll be done.”

When I got back Peggy was on oxygen, had blood being transfused with a drip, and was connected to a blood-pressure meter – it was reading very low. The nurse told me the doctor thought she probably had a general blood sepsis. She’d had three different antibiotics pending a culture to determine the organism to be targeted.

Peggy was fractious and kept on removing her oxygen mask and pulling at her tubes, but by nine o’clock her blood pressure had started to rise towards normal levels and she was sleeping.

The nurse said she would sleep all night. Why didn’t I go and get some sleep, too? I went off two hours late for dinner with Barbara, wondering whether it was safe to leave. I left telephone numbers with the nurse.

I rang the hospital early in the morning. Peggy had perked up quite a bit overnight. Barbara joined me when we went in later. The surgeon waylaid us and took us into a side room. I was quaking. Only one subject could be that serious. And that’s what it was. In his usual frank manner he told us:

“Mrs James could die within the week.”

Through buzzing thoughts I barely heard him say that her strong recovery overnight gave us hope. I was jerked back to full attention when he went on to ask me whether, if the time came, they should let her go quietly and comfortably, or subject her to heavily invasive treatment to try to save her, with no certainty of success.

I was stunned and could only say I'd make up my mind if the time came. But I really knew the answer. I could never pass a death sentence on her, Peggy, The Survivor.

Barbara and I went back to Peggy. She seemed a lot better, speaking rationally, and her blood pressure was back to normal. I fed Peggy her lunch, but she didn't eat much. She was unaware that anything untoward had happened and seemed quite contented, but tired. Even as we chatted she dozed off, and was soon sound asleep and snoring well. Barbara went off and I settled down to read.

She slept until suppertime and woke up in a happy mood, smiling and obviously very much improved. She enjoyed her supper and ate every scrap.

Drinking still gave her choking problems but she didn't do badly. After supper I rang Barbara; Peggy spoke to her for a few minutes and was delighted. I felt I mustn't be too overjoyed, but at least there was now hope.

Peggy rallied after that, but a culture had shown the presence of an anaerobic organism. I supposed this had been the behind-the-scenes ogre responsible for all Peggy's troubles since the first operation. Metronidazole was added to the cocktail of antibiotics. It worked. It was the surgeon who had done the first operation who gave me the news. A nice shy little man. I think he had been almost as worried as I had been about his infected prosthesis.

By November 3 the last three smears from the wound – which had not quite healed – had been negative. Our Australian surgeon said Peggy could come off traction in a couple of weeks and, if the wound was then intact, move to 'Rehab'.

I began to worry about organising for the great day when Peggy returned home. She wouldn't be able to climb stairs, not at first anyway, so she would have to sleep downstairs. The flat would be the best place, and Erika was vacating that in a few days – she didn't want to take on the care Peggy would need. I would have to arrange in some other way for help – even without her new disability I had been at the limit of my endurance, and sometimes beyond it.

Ian Pearce drove down from Iver in Buckinghamshire to see us and arrived in time to share the good news. Mary didn't come with him – a workday for her. Peggy took ten seconds to remember who he was and then wept tears of pleasure. Barbara came in and stayed with Peggy while Ian and I went to lunch. What would Peggy and I have done without Barbara in those desperate weeks. She had been there when I needed a confident, a shoulder or a prop, always calm, sympathetic, and helpful. For Peggy she had radiated love and kindness when most people were lunging at her with needles, knives or bedpans.

Ian had seemed anxious that I would be able to lunch with him, but I attached no significance to that since we had always enjoyed getting together. At lunch we had our usual tussle on homespun philosophy tinged with politics. Ian was a kindly man, passionately so. His politics reflected this. His leftism was no stale leftover from a teenage spree; he really wanted other people to live well even if it reduced his own standard. Me? Well, I suppose I shared his view but not his conviction, and I usually argued for argument sake. I was actually a wishy-washy middle-of-the-road man. I didn't have faith in mankind's ability to work to Ian's saintly principles. The other extreme was the natural one. Man's great strength stemmed from greed, a power behind his evolutionary survival, and greed got things done. The 'default' system, whatever social experiment was attempted, had always been one based on greed, whether frankly dictated or hidden behind the window dressing of democracy. My problem was that the middle road led nowhere and, having no foundation, was constantly eroded from either side. But we enjoyed our meal.

Then Ian broke the news. Mary had been diagnosed Parkinson's.

Devastated is so often an overstating cliché, but devastated I was. I had always thought of her as Young Mary – she was at least fifteen years younger than Peggy and me – far too young for such an affliction.

Ian had a brave face on. He said there were no marked signs yet and no medication had been prescribed. "It might be years before she's particularly troubled."

The spike was taken out of Peggy's leg 20 November 1995 and she came off traction, but it was a couple of weeks before she could be moved to 'Rehab'. Her wound continued to suppurate – the anaerobe had been defeated, but the microbiologists said that each change of antibiotic seemed to reveal another surviving pathogen. She had been out of bed on a tilting frame to stand up, and I'd been shocked to see that her left leg was now three inches shorter than the other.

The hospital had built up one shoe, but only adding an inch, the maximum they said she would be able to manage – I hadn't understood why.

A social worker of the County Council's Social Services Department came to see us to talk about help at home. She was wonderful with Peggy, so gentle and caring. Peggy warmed to her. She could only suggest we used one of the Council-approved Care Agencies. We talked about costs, which seemed enormous and, it appeared, we were not eligible for assistance. I said I thought I'd write to The Times with advice to young people: 'Enjoy your earnings while you are young. Don't save for your old age, or you won't be able to afford it'. She joked too, saying that I shouldn't worry about the cost; the sooner we ran out of money the sooner we'd get care paid for.

In 'Rehab', Peggy settled quickly. Her only worry seemed to be having to take her meals in the day room with the other patients, part of the rehabilitation process. She reacted as she had on our visits to my mother in the nursing home four years earlier when she had been so upset seeing frail old folk in quantity.

Peggy was still on antibiotics and her wound had not quite healed and it was two weeks before it was finally intact. Meanwhile, she got stronger, she could take her weight on her hipless leg, and she could walk a little with a frame and help.

The kindly social worker, fixed a 'Home Assessment' just before Christmas with a nation-wide care agency – a large one, capitalized about sixty million pounds. She and the agency's representative came to the house, and a physio, a nurse, and a social worker from the hospital brought Peggy. She was tried out in various ways – getting in and out of chairs and the bed, on and off the loo, and so on. Peggy went through it all without a complaint. She was marvellous. She was actually at home and I just wished all the other people were not there, but of course, they had to be. Peggy went back to 'Rehab' to stay until the agency could fix full night cover for us, and various pieces of equipment they regarded as essential had been acquired.

Christmas Day, and I collected Peggy from the hospital to come home for the day. My plan was detailed and a lot of it came off, even to the twenty minutes I'd allowed for Barbara to be late – which she made exactly. My cooking was by no means faultless, but I must have been proud of myself since I made detailed notes in my diary:

'Food. We had coffee and mince pies (Peg didn't like the pies). Barbara arrived, and we had Trimbach Tokay Pinot Gris – poor Peg had alcohol-free 'champagne', ugh! Snacks were: smoked salmon roundels (rolled around Phili cheese, with chives, spring onion, red and green pepper julienne); poached salmon paté with cheese straws; prawns on sticks with a cheesy dip; crinkle crisps.

Lunch was: Mushroom and watercress cream soup – made in chicken stock; gala melon with Palma ham; roast Guinea fowl with a deglaze white wine cream sauce – I forgot the cranberry sauce which I found later in the microwave – crisp-baked potato croquettes, sprouts, baby carrots, sweet corn and peas. We didn't eat a gratin dauphinois, which I'd ruined trying to make it ahead of time. Wine was 1984 Chassagne-Montrachet. A small cheese board followed, and then Christmas pudding with brandy butter.

Wine with the pud was Tokay – the Hungarian one this time – 1986 Tokaji Aszú 5 puttanos. Coffee and crackers – we wore the hats. Nobody wanted nuts or chocolates. Peggy asked our opinions on the wines – I could imagine her mental drooling, she had so appreciated fine wines

I suppose I should have gone less festive, especially on the wines, but I was concerned that Barbara had something of a Christmas dinner since she had given up the day with her family to be with us.

I drove Peggy back – we were the last back from Christmas-Day release. The day had been a good rehearsal: it had shown that I would be able to take Peggy out in the car, but that unless her mobility improved a lot, I was going to find her hard to handle around the house on my own.

The night nurse told me Peggy was short of knickers so I went home and did some washing – therapeutic.

A few days later I had a narrow squeak. As I came out of the front door at home I slid – the front paving was a sheet of ice and I careered across it like the comedy drunk on an ice rink. Somehow, I kept my feet and collided with Peggy's car, which I was using. The car was sealed in ice. To get to the garage for the other car I had to traverse the ice sheet again. Somebody had once told me that under such circumstances it was better to walk in your socks. I tried it. A cold experience, but it worked. There were over a hundred fractures attended to in Casualty at Odstock that morning.

I was in a state of suspended animation awaiting Peggy's release. I thought Peggy was too, but I was in for a surprise. She told me, crossly, she wished the woman next door with the radio wasn't so fond of pop music; she had it on all day.

I said: "Don't worry, Poomphie, you'll be home in a few days."

She looked puzzled. "I don't understand. This is home."

On December 31, Peggy's catheter fell out. They left it out and the lousy year ended.

Peggy came home on Thursday, 4 January 1996, after nearly three months away, mostly stretched on the rack. It was a wonderful honeymoon-like feeling. She seemed to like her flat and that was the first hurdle cleared. I held my breath for the second. I had moved one of the twin beds into the living room of the flat. I wheeled her past it into the bedroom. In there she said:

"Why is your bed in the other room?"

I told her it was for the girl who would be looking after her, helping her to bathe and dress.

"Where is she now?" she said, only slightly interested as she fingered the new nightdress I'd laid out on the bed.

I said she would arrive at bedtime and stay the night.

"So we'll have all day together, Ken dear, just you and me?"

"Just you and me, Poomphie." I said, as I helped her from the wheelchair to sit on the bed.

The agency 'girl' arrived promptly at ten that evening, together with a supervisory nurse who would see how things went getting Peggy to bed.

They went reasonably well, but it needed two to get Peggy on to the battery-driven contraption for lowering her into the bath. I thought it might get easier when she understood what was expected of her.

The 'girl', Clarita, was a mature Argentinian. Her English was good and softly spoken with a delightful accent. She was an experienced carer and she cared. Peggy took to her immediately.

The night was not good. Clarita said that Peggy was restless, calling out most of the night – sometimes in terror, awaking apparently from a nightmare – she also called for the commode frequently, for both real and imaginary reasons. Clarita gave up the idea of getting into bed: she stayed clothed, lying on her own bed or sitting in a chair by Peggy's, holding her hand. She thought Peggy's upset due to the change of environment, but she was actually behaving as she had in the hospital. I hoped she would be calmer as she settled into home life again.

Certainly, nobody could have been more calming than Clarita who seemed an ideal carer, but unfortunately she was only due to do Friday and Saturday nights with us every other week. Before she left on this first occasion, Peggy had declared Clarita her best friend.

Next came Sandra, then Kate and we had the three of them interlaced except for the glitches. The agency might ring and say Sandra couldn't come, they were sending someone else; or that Kate would be an hour late and would leave an hour early. One night they rang to say they were sorry but there had been ". . .a breakdown in communications", and we wouldn't be getting a carer that night. That night was a bad one. Not only did Peggy seem to have a particularly horrifying set of nightmares, but the ball valve stuck in the roof tank and water was cascading noisily from an overflow outside the window. I had to get the ladders out at midnight to see to it. This further roused Peggy since the trap door was in her bedroom ceiling. We didn't get to sleep until around six in the morning, and we were awakened at seven thirty by the agency ringing to apologize. I wasn't all that gracious.

That day wasn't too good either. I was irritable through most of it and I don't suppose Peggy really enjoyed my company, but no sooner had I moved away for some reason – to get the lunch, or to go to the loo, or just to answer the 'phone – she would start calling for me plaintively. Sometimes her call had an urgent note, a loo call, and I would rush her off. We were both tired and not functioning too well, and, as likely as not, she would turn the wrong way in the lavatory and wet everything around, including me. When Clarita turned up at ten o'clock having apparently stepped into a breech, I had been on vigil for over thirty-six hours with no real break. She saved me from a serious explosion. And, she got Peggy bathed, loo'd, medicated, and to bed, so easily.

One night, the carer just didn't turn up, but near midnight – I had already bathed Peggy and got her to bed – a stranger appeared at the door and said she was the carer. I sent her away with an apology (it wasn't her fault) saying that I couldn't risk Peggy waking up to a stranger who didn't know the ropes. I soon learned that all flexibility had to be at our end, the agency was run for its own benefit, of course, but they tended to make it blatantly obvious that their convenience came first, certainly not the clients'.

Then one of the carers complained that it was all too much for her and the agency descended on us to inspect – the local superintendent nurse did the job herself for a night. She was good and, accordingly, Peggy responded well. We passed.

All that in the first couple of weeks.

I rang Norman Colquhoun on his birthday, Norman who, so long ago, had started Peggy and me on our way. He was eighty-four. He had taken up painting seriously soon after the war – he stopped for a while in 1952 to write his well-known book, *Paint Your Own Pictures,* a Penguin. He was still painting in the nineties, despite failing eyesight. I was reminded of Renoir who continued to paint wonderfully with his brush tied to fingers rendered inoperative by arthritis. Norman also still did what he had done each year for the past fifty-odd, painted a masterpiece of a Christmas card for us, and wrote after his greeting inside, 'Nothing matters'.

Over the next couple of months, the uncertain arrangements by the agency for night care went on. There were many changes of plan and new faces which perplexed Peggy – she was often driven to tears and such remarks as "Who are all these people, Ken?" Clarita more and more stepped into the breech to help out, but she had troubles of her own – her husband was seriously ill and she couldn't always leave him. We still had nights where, unexpectedly, we were without a carer; nevertheless, I was mostly getting a good night's sleep and I was more able to face up to the day.

The days were not easy, but in Peggy's more lucid periods we enjoyed being together.

There was one interlude for me. February 6 it snowed, and I got my cross-country skis out. Barbara came and sat with Peggy while I went careering around Wiltshire hills – not quite the excitement of the Alps, but good for my morale.

Peggy's mobility had improved a lot. She could walk out into the garden using her wheeled frame and my guiding arm. She could also walk to the loo similarly; although, that wasn't a good idea since the exercise gave rise to wet skirts. She was pleased with her advance and wanted to practice a lot, but her sense of balance was not all it might have been and, unaided, she would inevitably fall. Usually this amounted to her just sinking more or less gently to the ground, and she might suffer nothing worse than a wet skirt – despite the pad she'd be wearing – or the carpet might need a wash; but it was a worry. For fear of her damaging herself, I took her around with me in her wheelchair most of the time, but that was not always possible – if I needed to go upstairs, for instance.

I gave in eventually. She stood up from the wheelchair when I went to the lavatory and fell, hurting her back. No serious damage, but it was an indication of what might happen. She had also wetted the carpet. I took her to the lavatory, and while I was getting a pad from the cupboard she again got up and messed the floor. I fetched the restraining strap that came with the wheelchair – a depressing milestone, although Peggy didn't seem bothered. One of the carers told me it was illegal to use a restraint even at home. I didn't even bother to find out whether it was true or not.

I was puzzled what to do in the longer term. I was doing neither myself nor Peggy much good as things were going. Even our pleasure at being together was, I felt, wearing a bit thin. Having done the cooking, the washing, ironing, other general chores, and the inevitable lavatorial duty-round hour by hour, I just hadn't the guts, drive and energy to do much else.

Some sort of twenty-four-hour care seemed essential if Peg was to stay at home – certainly, despite advice from all round, I wanted to keep her home as long as possible. Even Clarita's advice that I needed respite and that I should send Peggy off for daily respite care appalled me. As so many people insisted, I probably did need respite:

but what would I do with myself being respited while worrying all the time how Peg was faring. From previous experience I knew she would hate the day-care sort of atmosphere. Even during her confused periods, she recorded well what was going on around her, despite her difficulty in replay. She was well aware of the seriousness of her state, her main source of misery. She was able to talk about it in her lucid intervals and said once:

"I'd just like to be able to walk down the road. It's rotten knowing things can only get worse."

Peggy's cognition and memory were sometimes surprising. Listening together to a 'talking book' she said, just half-an-hour from lunch:

"Don't forget Ella's coming to lunch."

It had been a week since Ella, Peggy's friend since school, had said she was coming to see us. I had forgotten, and I'd done nothing about preparing lunch.

Sent off to a nursing home or day-centre, Peggy would certainly feel she was being pushed aside – ". . .you know why you've been thrown out by your family," she had said, having seen the frail old creatures in the Day Room when we visited my mother – and her misery over her own condition would increase. That, however, was not just a problem in the longer term: In a month, I was to have my second cataract operation. No problem with the operation itself – provided all went well, I'd be away from home only a few hours. I would however have to get reliable help for Peggy for about a month after that, since I was warned I would not be able to risk the strain of even taking her to the loo.

Jeremy was back from holiday in Spain – actually an advised rest period from his hectic workload following a bit of a heart problem. He said I should use the opportunity for a trial run with Peggy in a nursing home – not specifically his, but he expected to have a spare room soon if I needed it. Expected soon! That had a sinister ring. He said I should first try the nursing home a couple of hundred yards down the road from us, since it would be so convenient for me just to walk along to see Peggy.

Jeremy also told me I couldn't go on as I was, I'd have to get day help. I had come to that conclusion myself, and I was delighted when he said he would look out for a 'daily' to take on some of the housekeeping for us. He rang back with a telephone number that afternoon, and Julia joined us a few days later – and she was a good cook. She came in weekday afternoons to tidy around, sit with Peg or take her out in the wheelchair, and stayed early evenings to do dinner. She also left us meals for weekends.

March saw changes. Peggy had for some time had a tendency to keep her eyes shut for minutes at a time, while remaining quite alert. The symptom was now accentuated so that her eyes were closed for long periods, still aware of what was going on around her. If I spoke to her, she would listen and respond without opening her eyes. She appeared not to know they were closed – presumably her hallucinations peopled her world sufficiently. If I said something like "There's our two swans flying in." She would direct her face towards the river and say, perhaps, "Beautiful," without opening her eyes. Perhaps she could conjure up a vision of them. When I pressed her to open her eyes to look at something I'd put in her hands, she'd say she didn't know how to. However, the phenomenon usually occurred when Peggy was half-an-hour or so from her next Madopar dose, and faded away about half-an-hour after it.

Another symptom had become more marked – fidgetiness. She would spend many hours screwing up her skirt, her two hands constantly on the move between that and moving things randomly around her. Her place laid at table didn't last ten seconds.

Conversation, too, became more disjointed for quite long periods – phrases from nowhere and unfinished sentences – while she usually had no difficulty with the verb, she often couldn't find the noun and I found it difficult to divine the subject. She would then suddenly return to fairly normal speech but not be able to recapture the previous themes. There were still times when she didn't know who I was. One evening she kept calling "Ken!" when I was doing some sort of a job in the next room. When I went to her she said, "Hallo, Doctor," and, as far as I could tell, wanted me to take her to bed. Is that what doctors get up to?

March still, my sister Georgie rang – the last time we had met she had said that Dennis was senile. She now said that from a scan it was considered he had suffered a series of minor strokes. We were a dying generation all right.

I took Peggy on a routine visit to her specialist. He took her off antibiotics at last – sixty-three less pills a week.

Julia the part-time cook-housekeeper-carer was a treasure, and I actually got back to doing a little writing. I could also pop to the library in town, or to the shops, without making elaborate arrangements.

Peggy seemed much happier of late – she probably reflected my moods more than I'd ever suspected. One day later in the month, however, she was suddenly desperately miserable. It was Carolyn's birthday. I hadn't mentioned it nor did she, and I don't know how she could have known – if that was indeed the cause of her despondency.

The next day Peggy was back to what had become normal. However, Clarita said that Peggy was getting to be too much for her, but she would continue with us, in her turn, until my operation.

March ended with me fixing for Peggy to stay in Jeremy's Kimberly House from mid-April – nobody had died in the nursing home 'down the road'. It was one thing when accident precipitated her into hospital for long periods, but actually to decide in cold blood that she would go into a nursing home was the hardest decision I'd ever had to make – and yet there seemed no alternative. There had been times – when she had spattered her food around at meal times; when she poured her tea on the floor; when I'd got her to the loo and sat her down without leakage and she'd stood up and pissed, or worse, over her knickers, tights, skirt, shoes, floor, and my trousers; when she'd asked who I was, when she had continuously shouted for me when I was busy on chores – when I had longed for relief of this sort. But there were other times . . . and I knew I'd count the days until I could have her home again after the op.

On April 16 we took a walk with the wheelchair to Churchill Gardens, and coming back the thought hit me that this could be our last outing together. A morbid thought, but that was the mood of the moment.

Later, I used one of Peggy's handkerchiefs while I packed her bag.

CHAPTER TWENTY-ONE

I went to the New Hall Hospital for my cataract operation on a warm, showery, mid-April day of 1996. I'd taken Peggy into Kimberly House two days before. She had been apprehensive and confused at first, but settled quickly when the nurses who greeted us were so kindly and attentive. I stayed to lunch with her and explained again why she was there. She said, "I know, darling," and clung to me. She went on, "I do hope it goes well, Ken. Do come and see me as soon as you can after the operation." It wasn't often she could make such an elaborate speech.

I expected to feel guilty as I walked to freedom, but I didn't: I didn't feel free – nor, I suppose, was it the sort of freedom I wanted.

I went to see Peggy again the next morning. She had been up to her usual trick of getting out of her chair and staggering around. She had fallen, apparently without damage, but they were taking no chances and were giving her one-to-one surveillance – it appeared they were not allowed to use seat belts or any form of constraint. Their concern and the immediate response to the difficulty was impressive and I felt a lot better about her being there.

The next morning when I went in, Peggy was bedded down on a mattress on the floor in 'Reception'. They hadn't been able to keep her in her chair. They'd also called in our GP but he hadn't yet arrived. I stayed for half-an-hour or so and, with assurances of constant attention for Peggy, went off to New Hall to get my plastic eye fitted.

They were using a new system – tiny hole, liquidize the lens, suck it out with some sort of mini-Hoover, squeeze the plastic lens into place, one gnat's-whisker stitch, and a cup of tea. The last stage was the best.

I rang Kimberly when I got home. All was well – Peggy was asleep.

Barbara was on time in the morning to take me to New Hall. Bandages off and there was the world, in full Technicolor for both eyes.

I rang Peggy when I got back. The sister told me everything was all right but Peggy was asleep and they would prefer not to wake her.

The following morning, Sunday, I decided to try driving, and went over to Kimberly. No problem, with the driving anyway, but it was not so with Peggy. She was still asleep in a chair in the day room and looking ghastly. I couldn't wake her.

It turned out that the GP had recommended a sleeping pill, which they'd given her the previous evening and she hadn't woken since. An hour later I was still unable to wake her. I called for the sister. I was past anger – steely might have been descriptive.

I asked what sedative Peggy had been given. It was Melleril, an antipsychotic. I was staggered. Quite apart from Peggy's astonishing sensitivity to such drugs, it seemed to me that he couldn't have done worse than to have chosen Melleril. For one thing, it was contra-indicated for glaucoma sufferers, I thought; and for another, its action was to link on to certain receptors in the brain and block them, just where dopamine, including that produced from her Madopar, needed access. It was all so mad anyway: they couldn't use a loose belt in the wheelchair – less constraining than the seat belt of a car – but they could totally knock her out with drugs when she could scarcely be more constrained.

"No more, Sister."

"But the doctor..."

"No more! Do you realize you could kill her?" At the time, I thought I was exaggerating but I learned later that I wasn't. I went to the telephone.

Sunday, and the doctor couldn't be found. I was feeling fairly whacked and, telling the sister to ring me as soon as Peggy woke up, and repeating that she was to have no more sleeping pills of any sort, I went home to bed.

I rang in the morning and Peggy was still asleep. The sister said she was all right and that the doctor was coming in to see her. I went off to New Hall for my eye check. It was fine.

I went to see Peggy. She was still asleep.

She was still asleep in the afternoon. The sister told me the doctor had been and said they could give Peggy a much reduced dose of Melleril but only if it was really necessary for her safety. I assumed he knew what he was doing and kept quiet. It seemed to me that overnight her Madopar would be virtually inoperative if she'd had a light dose of Melleril, but if she were asleep that wouldn't matter much. When she came to, the drug would have dissipated and doubtless the Madopar would work again.

On this occasion Peggy finally woke in the evening. She was wild. An hour after her Madopar, she had calmed down. She had slept for forty-eight hours.

After that she was sometimes given a small dose of Melleril but her behaviour deteriorated and the staff found her difficult to handle. They put her mattress on the floor in her bedroom after she had been found crawling down the stairs having fallen out of bed and ripped down the curtains. The staff carers were very good and entirely conscientious but only in the daytime was constant surveillance possible.

I went in every day, and if the weather was suitable we went out together. I would take her in the wheelchair into the town, to the shops. It was May 2 when, with some trepidation, I first wheeled Peggy into a teashop in Salisbury, but we enjoyed our tea together in a little world of our own, not even realizing that in the real world outside the Tories were being trounced in the local elections. We went for picnics by the river in Churchill Gardens; or for a drive and picnic in the New Forest – what I found amazing when we drove around was Peggy's bump of location: she would direct me, saying, perhaps, "Take the next turn left, there's the baker's on the corner". She knew the names of the villages we went through and the name of the one to come. On all these forays, Peggy was contented and calm.

Barbara also visited most days, sometimes overlapping with me at the nursing home, when we would perhaps both go out with Peggy.

It was noticeable that in the mornings Peggy was often sleepy and morose and, if aroused, quite unreasoning. She flopped if an attempt was made to get her to walk, and she had to be fed her meals – presumably she was still under the influence of her light drug dose. The effect usually wore off after lunch and, in the afternoons she came to life, calmed after her Madopar, and enjoyed our outings.

The staff nurses and carers of the nursing home were wonderful, solicitous and conscientious, but there was no doubt they were having difficulty coping with Peggy's need for constant attention.

I was torn. I was pressed by most people to keep Peggy where she was even after my 'convalescence', and indeed, there was some attraction in that. Peggy would be better off being looked after without the emotional input from me, and I was certainly better with her when I was not on twenty-four-hour alert and subject to relentless urinary pressures. The uncertainty and unreliability of helpers at home also weighed heavily. With Peggy in the nursing home we had a pleasant time together most days and, with Barbara's help, and one-to-one attention from the staff when we were not there, Peggy had little of her daytime without companionship.

The flip side was that Peggy herself was desperately unhappy when I was not with her; she was difficult to manage, and there was an inherent instability in the present arrangements. Moreover, our life together now felt contrived, aimless.

Nights, too, were a worry, as was the doping. It seemed to me that Peggy's derangement in the mornings after a neuroleptic pill at night, was getting steadily worse. The doctor was outspoken: he said Peggy shouldn't go home. Jeremy, too, who had been so supportive through all this, didn't think it sensible for Peggy to return home. He thought she would be better housed at the nursing home 'down the road' from us, where she would have the same river views as from home, and I could walk down there with ease at any time.

Originally, the intention had been that Peggy would stay in the nursing home for a month. The last day came and I was still dithering. That evening at home I was playing Mozart and it got to me – it brought back our happy days together. I sat out with a glass in the sunshine, recovered, and went in to dinner. It was the last Julia would cook for me – she was leaving because she felt her little boy needed more of her attention. That was the clincher. It would be better for Peggy to stay put until I could replace Julia.

Decision made, but forces were at work to render it impotent.

The doctor saw Peggy again, and he told me the nursing home was having a lot of difficulty coping: they had asked the Old Manor Hospital for advice. I said that I still worried about the opposition of Madopar and Melleril. He said that any Parkinson's-like symptoms were the least of Peggy's worries and it would be best to stop the Madopar. Miserably, I agreed – I was smitten with self-doubt and a return of the concern that the experts had only been 'going along with me' and my contention that Peggy was suffering from Diffuse Lewy Body Disease with its affiliation to Parkinson's disease.

Peggy now came out of her drugged state in the morning in a demented state and desperately unhappy. And her unhappiness spread to the periods we were together. I tried not to jump to the conclusion that this was due to the lack of Madopar. Most likely it was the natural course of the disease.

The day came when a new pressure was turned on: the Health Authority on a routine inspection of the nursing home ruled that Peggy could not stay there, she must go into a mental hospital.

I flipped.

I demanded an interview with the people concerned, and gained a stay of execution for a proper assessment by the specialists from the Old Manor Hospital. By then, Peggy was showing positive Parkinson's-like symptoms – bent over, drooling, and difficulty in starting any action, especially walking. Mentally, she had deteriorated to the stage where I could scarcely make contact with her. I talked to our GP about Peggy's rapid change and suggested he reconsider levodopa treatment and stop the use of even the small dose of Melleril – I now didn't care whether or not he was humouring me. He reinstated the Madopar and replaced Melleril by a small dose of Diazepam.

Peggy's recovery was quick. Within a few days she was back almost to where she had been before the sleeping-pill fiasco. I had worried about her being given Diazepam again because of her extreme sensitivity to it, but as it turned out she hadn't needed any. The specialist from the Old Manor made his assessment and wrote to the Health Authority. The sentence to life-imprisonment in a mental hospital was quashed.

I was concerned that all the time I seemed to be pressing against expert advice, and I still wanted to go against the advice about not having Peggy home. I had started taking Peggy out in the wheelchair again in the afternoons and, one day, instead of stopping for our picnic tea in Churchill Gardens, on impulse, I walked on and took Peggy home to picnic in the garden. Peggy took it as a matter of course and made no fuss about returning to the nursing home, but when I kissed her goodbye to go home she said, "Why are you abandoning me, Ken?"

I met Jeremy as I went out and told him what Peggy had said.

"They all say that," he said.

I was a bit shirty: "Of course they do. They are being abandoned."

It wasn't his reply as such which stung me – Jeremy was a friend and a kindly, caring man who had helped us a great deal – it was that even he used the impersonal "they". There and then, I decided that I had to get Peggy out of the Old-Age machine.

We continued afternoon trips home, extending them after a few days to the evening for dinner before returning to the nursing home. I found Peggy a good deal more difficult to handle than I remembered. Particularly difficult were the loo visits – even if we got there in time she might start too soon, or get up before finishing, and a change of clothing would be necessary. She tried to be helpful and, for example, as I pulled up her tights with one hand while holding up her skirt and her with the other, she would be busy taking off her blouse. Subsequent laundry would include washing our shoes.

As a try out, I asked an agency to provide a carer daily to collect Peggy from the nursing home, and stay with us through dinner. It worked well, and Peggy seemed quite content to return to the nursing home to go to bed. She was happier than she had been for months and, consequently, so was I. There was one exception. On July 3, Peggy's seventy-ninth birthday, she was miserable. Antonia, the carer, was wonderful with her and, after a while, Peggy settled down and talked to her. She told Antonia, with no confusion or worrying around for words, that Carolyn had died about a year ago, and that she had been too ill even to go to the funeral. I was amazed. It was the first time as far as I was aware that Peggy had spoken of Carolyn's death to any one but me. Also, I was not aware that Peggy had any idea of the date. She also told Antonia about ". . . the poor old

Biddies at the nursing home, old ladies with bent faces." Doubtless either or both subjects could have been behind her upset. She was happy again the following day.

I arranged with the agency for the care period to extend overnight. At the nursing home Peggy usually drooped as I was about to leave for the night. I told her she would be able to come home for good in a few days. It was rewarding. I had expected her to accept what I said without fully understanding. How wrong. Her face lit up and she said:

"Good night, darling. Looking forward to seeing you again tomorrow." It had been a long time since she had spoken so happily.

Two days later the agency rang to say that they found they couldn't provide overnight care. Jean, my neighbour, also rang to say that the cleaner lady we shared would not be coming any more; she had husband problems – something about charity, or was it cleaning, began at home..

Without help, but not helpless, I rang the ever helpful social worker of the County Council's Social Services Department. She recommended another agency and we soon had a carer. Peggy came home to stay.

Freda was young and short of experience – she had looked after her granny in South Africa – but she was splendid with Peggy, who took to her. Also, she could, and did, cook.

Unfortunately, Freda was not typical of the string of backpacker carers we were subsequently subjected to. Backpackers they were, and we were a convenient stopover for free board and lodgings, and a source of finance for the next stage of their world tour. Some were conscientious and – even though they tended to pad around the house on bare feet with distorted toes accentuated with blood-red nails – did a good job. Others were content enough as long as Peggy didn't disturb them during an interesting TV show, or wake them at night. One was downright criminal.

By the end of the summer of 1996, Peggy's lucid periods when we could actually converse, had shortened considerably. Most of the time, her talk varied from the bizarre to the impenetrable. One conversation I just had to record in my diary:

"What's up, Poomphie?" She was looking me up and down:

"I've been up there twice already."

"Where?"

"The Crematorium."

"What for, dear?"

"To dispose of bodies, of course."

"Oh!"

She looked me up and down again: "I think we could leave you until tomorrow."

I said:

"Would you like some tea now?"

"Oh, yes please. You're a lovely man."

On that occasion the macabre story was clearly told but I couldn't imagine what inner thought was behind it. Sometimes, it was the other way round – output distorted but message clear. One of the carers, Vicky, was unshakeable in her patience, but I noticed Peggy always seemed to demand such patience from Vicky in particular – by this time we had graduated to live-in agency carers. At meals, when Peggy seemed disinterested in the food, Vicky would attempt to feed her, keeping up a constant stream of repetitive, persuasive talk:

"Come on now, darling, open wide now, eat this up for me, darling. Come on now, open wide . . ."

Peggy mostly kept her lips grimly closed with what I thought of as her 'awkward look'. Talking to Peggy later in one of our guessing competitions that now passed for conversation, I mentioned Vicky.

Peggy leaned forward and whispered confidentially:

"Where's Ken?" and in still lower voice, "You know, I don't really like him."

"Why's that, Poomphie?"

"She keeps on talking when I want to think."

Peggy wasn't always as discreet with her criticism. One of our earlier carers came in to see Peggy, and Vicky made coffee. The two carers then sat with Peggy but got into close conversation with each other. Peggy got more and more frustrated and eventually burst out:

"When's it all going to stop, it's got nothing to do with me," a rare, complete and totally comprehensible sentence.

They stopped.

Peggy was not the only one to express her frustration with carers. My diary detailed one occasion when I exploded. Expanding the notes, it said:

Judith, no workaholic, came with us to dinner at Barbara's. When we got back, Judith seemed to get Peggy to bed rather quickly and I realized she hadn't given her a bath. Not surprisingly, Peggy didn't settle well – only under exceptional circumstances had she previously missed her bath before bed. I didn't comment, even when at midnight Judith called for me because Peggy still hadn't settled.

I sat with Peggy and she went off to sleep after about an hour.

In the morning, Judith said she'd had a bad night with Peggy, dumped her in the living room in her dressing gown, and went back to bed. I had said to Judith that any time she lost sleep she could make it up during the day. I hadn't expected such a peremptory dumping. For one thing, Peggy had the strongest objections to sitting around in a dressing gown and had never, except when ill, had breakfast without dressing. Also, I was trapped; with Judith in bed I couldn't get into the flat to dress Peggy, so I couldn't go out with her as I had intended. I couldn't even safely leave her and go to the loo. In fact, I had just turned away to pour the coffee, when Peggy, confused and distressed, upset her wheelchair, and finished up on the floor with the chair on top of her – she was frightened, but apart from a grazed shin had escaped damage. It was nearly lunchtime when Judith emerged, had a leisurely breakfast reading the newspaper, and then took Peggy back to her bedroom to dress her.

Judith then cooked a late lunch – sardines on burnt toast. She put the plates in the dishwasher and went out for over three hours.

That evening I asked her not to bring Peggy out in the morning before dressing her.

"Why?" she said bridling.

"Because I say so." I said, mentally biting a sharper tongue.

She started to argue, "Why not, it's . . .

"Look, it's simply a question of not changing Peggy's lifestyle of half a century. It upsets her." I could have added, "– and me"

"But she had a good . . ."

"You're judging on a couple of days' experience. I've lived with Peggy a good deal longer."

She started to argue again.

Walking away, I said, "I don't want to argue about it, please just wash and dress Peggy before bringing her to breakfast."

She followed me into the library. "We have to talk about it. I can't work night and day. It's not allowed by law – especially for just £47 a day. That's forty eight hours (sic), only about a pound an hour."

"Do you know how long you've worked today?"

"All day, of course."

I detailed her activities since we had left Barbara after dinner. I went on from when she got back from her afternoon off:

"You took Peg to the loo when you got back this evening and sat with her looking at TV – a noisy programme not of any conceivable interest to Peggy, who dozed – while I cooked the dinner. You loaded the dishwasher after dinner and spent ten minutes tidying around before going back to the TV. That's forty eight hours work?"

"You don't know the strain . . ."

"Happens I do. I've had five years continuous experience of it, seven days a week. The agency pays you. What I do know is that on top of that, I pay the agency's commission, VAT, a contribution to the agency's national insurance, your travel expenses, and I pay for your food and drink, gas, electricity and water. That adds up to over £600 a week I pay for the privilege of serving you at dinner and pouring your wine.

She was shouting me down during that entire diatribe, and my voice was getting louder and louder. I forced myself to speak more calmly:

"Now, stop shouting and go away, please. All I asked was that you do not bring Peggy out in the morning before she is properly washed and dressed, and you complained about what the agency pay you." I was getting hot under the collar again and thinking myself stupid to be paying so much and putting up with this sort of nonsense. I could just not see an alternative. Any complaint to the agency was overridden by the carers' reports on the job, and the agencies seemed less concerned about losing a client – there were plenty of those – than upsetting the carers, a scarce resource. Sack one agency and you were loaded with another no better. There was another agency recommended by Clarita, the Argentinian carer Peggy had declared to be her best friend. It was even more expensive but I thought I would probably have to try it. The diary went on:

Judith was still shouting at me. "Now, just go away, please," I said loudly.

"Don't you shout at me like that."

"I'm trying to be heard above your shrieking. Now go away."

"I'll be leaving on Monday."

"You can leave now, as far as I'm concerned."

She went to bed.

I wasn't proud of myself.

Judith wasn't the last of the problem carers. They came in all shapes, mostly more or less jagged. It is fair to say that with some marked exceptions they were kindly disposed to Peggy. The difficulty for me was living in the confines of their mostly esoteric lifestyles. There was Jenny, who seemed to subsist on skimmed milk and lettuce – although the whisky bottle went down rather fast. Cheap to run but she couldn't cook an egg. There was Linda. I went to speak to her in the flat where she had taken Peg for the evening. Peg was dozing distorted over the side of her wheel chair while Linda was watching a soap on TV, sitting on the her own bed, cross-legged, eating cold baked beans out of the tin. She said:

"Could I come and have a word with you, Ken?"

In the little library I motioned her to the chair by my desk and sat in mine. She leaned forward, put her hand on my knee and said:

"Ken, what do you do about women?"

I didn't enquire more closely to discover whether this was an offer or merely part of a sociological research she was conducting. "Just dream," I said. "Would you like a cup of coffee . . ."

She sulked angrily all the next day: ' . . .no fiend in hell can match the fury of a disappointed woman . . .'

One morning, Peggy, up and dressed, was very sleepy and looked quite ill: her eyes were puffy, the left lid in particular was ballooned out and yellowish with fluid. She sat slumped in her wheel chair. By coffee time she was worse: her face was cyanosed, heart rate about 120 and her breathing shallow and rapid, temperature normal.

Peggy was improving a little when the doctor arrived. He thought Peggy might have suffered a small stroke, an embolism, heart failure – or one of several other nasties. On the whole he was of the opinion it was an advance in her dementia – which I felt was only too likely to be right. He thought the fluid retention round the eye was probably due to trauma, pressure when lying in one place in bed perhaps.

By the following morning Peggy was much improved, miraculously so. The doctor was impressed but still puzzled.

There was no recurrence, and we were back to where we were. Peggy, in the daytime, apart from her continual attempts to get out of her chair and walk, was now fairly peaceful. She seemed to view the world through a small slot and not be able to take much of it in at a time. I'd just changed our car to one less pretentious – I'd given up status symbols, and in any case they shouldn't show rust patches – and we had been out in the new one for the first time. Peggy enjoyed the ride and kept up a sort of noun-less commentary on the countryside. Sitting in the car as we arrived back I asked her how she liked the new car.

"Where is it?" she said, with obvious interest.

Early October a carer arrived, a South African, who was a backpacker, but it was soon obvious she was of a different metal than the string of them we'd had from the particular agency. By bedtime she had not only cooked an excellent dinner, but, unasked, had done a thorough spring-clean of the kitchen, all cupboards reorganized and cleaned inside and out. She was excellent with Peg too. I helped bathing Peggy although it was soon obvious my assistance was superfluous. I went off after telling the carer to sleep in if she had a bad night since Peg was usually disturbed on the first night of a new carer.

In the morning I was down early to do some writing. All was quiet in the flat. At eight o'clock I had breakfast. Still no movement in the flat and the door was shut. Ten o'clock, the same. They must have had a bad night.

Eleven o'clock I began to worry. I knocked on the door of the flat. No response. Knocked hard. Nothing. I went in. Bedclothes folded neatly on the carer's bed, but no carer. A note said, 'Sorry, I have to have my sleep'.

I went through to Peggy's bedroom. She was coiled on the floor, in a pool of urine, her nightdress over her head. She was barely conscious. She had a raging temperature.

It was two weeks before Peggy came home from hospital. Her infection, probably urinary in origin, had finally succumbed to a cocktail of antibiotics. It was a week or so before she recovered her limited mobility, but she had been sent home with a long-term catheter, which looked like making our lives a good deal simpler while relieving Peggy of one of her major worries. Looking pained, she'd say she would like to spend a penny and then smile happily when I explained she could get on with it. Unfortunately, for some reason, the device would not stay in. The District Nurse, an expert in such matters, tried variants, but without success, and we were back to pads, the loo run, and the overworked washing machine.

I had taken on a new agency that provided more mature carers, and we went through a long experimental run where the various women tried us out to see whether we suited them. It was the usual self-defeating process: as stranger after stranger violated Peggy's privacy she became more and more upset and recalcitrant. Eventually we found a team of three to rotate weekly, but it took two cycles before Peggy settled down again.

I'd had a letter from the proprietor of the agency I had sacked saying how horrified she had been that the carer had run out on us, and excusing herself on the grounds that she hadn't personally interviewed the girl. She knew, however, that all references had been checked and were exemplary . . .

I did nothing more in the matter. I'd had enough hassle already.

The year ended – my eightieth. Not a good one looking at the surface, but underneath there were mercies. Peggy had survived all Fate had thrown at her; she still knew who I was most of the time, and wanted me around. The real Peggy was still there with her quick humour below the mask of her inabilities. Earlier in the year I'd said:

"Let's go and make a cup of coffee, Poomphie. Put your glasses on."

"What, my drinking glasses?"

On another occasion, she was eating some grapes when she started to say something, her face screwed up apparently in an effort to get words out. I smiled at her and said:

"Are you complaining about something, dear?"

"Sour gripes," she said, and beamed at me.

We could still get out together for a coffee, or even a meal in a few places that knew us and were not overcrowded. My eyes were good after cataracts so I could still drive with Peggy to shop, or just to enjoy the countryside. And, perhaps the greatest contribution to a life worth living was made by the visits of Peggy's sister Barbara and our loyal friends. With more drastic hiccups we managed some continuity in the supply of carers and indeed some of them were excellent. I didn't ski on my birthday – well, you know, it's lonely out there on your own in the snow.

I typed 'End' after those lines, with a feeling that I was leaving a lot unsaid . . . Peggy called. I knelt in front of her wheelchair. Her face was creased in concentration. I held her hand:

"What's wrong Poomphie?" I didn't expect an answer. For the thousandth time I wondered what went on in her mind she couldn't express . . .

She put a hand to my face, smiled her impish smile and said softly and clearly:

"You're a lovely man. I love you so much."

EPILOGUE

"Nurse!"

It's Alf. He was on the railway, and he shouts.

"Nurse!"

"Shut up" calls Carol, peeping out from under her patchwork shawl, looking fierce – or as fierce as you can look without teeth.

"Nurse! I want to go to the toilet."

"Just coming Alf. You've just been, you know."

Jenny walks by carrying cushions. She collects cushions and when she can't hold any more she weeps. But she keeps on walking.

Myra is lying back with her mouth wide open, looking dead.

Peggy is reclining peacefully in her CQR chair, designed for comfort and difficult to get out of, hence the name, CQR, *secure!* Suddenly she looks scared as the ghostly Maud glides up as though on well-greased castors, looking fixedly through the wall. In a horror film she would be the type who went around bedrooms with a slim knife.

"Hallo Maud," I say.

Her stare remains fixed. She poofs air through pursed lips, turns and glides away.

Peggy reaches for my hand and relaxes.

I fetch a wheel chair and we go out and sit together on a park bench in the grounds. I talk a little, but I don't get answers these days. I put my arm around Peggy and she rests her head on my shoulder.

* * *

Peggy died in a nursing home, 26 August 1998, following a replacement of her remaining hip. She just stopped breathing while I was feeding her – pulmonary embolism. There were a lot of roses at her funeral.

REQUIESCAT

Strew on her roses, roses,
And never a spray of yew.
In quiet she reposes:
Ah! Would that I did too.

Her mirth the world required:
She bath'd it in smiles of glee.
But her heart was tired, tired,
And now they let her be.

Her life was turning, turning,
In mazes of heat and sound.
But for peace her soul was yearning,
And now peace laps her round.

Her cabin'd, ample Spirit,
It flutter'd and fail'd for breath.
To-night it doth inherit
The vasty Hall of Death.

Matthew Arnold